I0600949

The Quest
of
Hope

Kristin Gleeson

An Tig Beag Press

Other works by Kristin Gleeson:

CELTIC KNOT SERIES
Along the Far Shores
Raven Brought the Light
Selkie Dreams
A Treasure Beyond Worth (novelette)

RENAISSANCE SOJOURNER SERIES
A Trick of Fate (novelette)
The Imp of Eye (With Moonyeen Blakey)
The Sea of Travail

THE HIGHLAND BALLAD SERIES
The Hostage of Glenorchy
The Mists of Glenstrae

NON FICTION
Anahareo: A Wilderness Spirit

Sign up to my mailing list and get
FREE *A Treasure Beyond Worth*
www.kristingleeson.com.

ISBN: 978-0-9956281-1-3

To Moon & Eddie

CHAPTER ONE
VENICE, SUMMER, 1446
BARNABAS

I paced the length of the room, restless and sweating. The private room at the small inn was damp and musty, being close to the ship docks. The odour of rank fish hung in the air. I fought the fog that threatened to engulf my thoughts. I needed a clear head. Pausing, I took a swig of wine from the cup on the table.

Hal looked at me and gave a shake of his head. "You 'ave to give that stuff a rest, Jacko," he said in English. He called me "Jacko", short for Giacomo, my assumed name. "You ain't getting any better, you're getting worse. The opium has taken hold of you too much. Maybe you should wait on this 'til you're weaned."

I gave a snort of impatience. "I can't afford to waste time. You know that."

"But you can see yourself you ain't in a fit state to go journeying into foreign parts. Especially Africa."

"I can, and I will." I gave him a wry smile. "With your help and knowledge, of course."

"You know I've only been to Alexandria and no further. And I saw little enough of that."

I waved my hand in dismissal and looked through the window once again. There was still no sign of Captain Flores. Had he cried off? Did he find the prospect of me as his passenger so troublesome? I had searched out Flores purposely when I heard that he was to be in port. Flores who I'd last heard was lost at sea, was now seemingly recovered and sailing ships again. Flores and I had a past, linked to Mustapha al Qali, my sometime mentor. Such mentoring had now turned to hate. Flores had appeared to be al Qali's good friend when I met him first as a young lad enamoured of the sea. Now I needed to discover just how much of a friend Flores was to al Qali.

The door opened abruptly and Flores filled the entrance.

"Captain Flores," I exclaimed loudly. "Greet your old friend Giacomo."

I spoke in Italian, staring down the puzzled look on Flores's face. He had known me before I'd changed my identity under al Qali's tutelage. To Flores I was Barnabas, street urchin and imp.

"*Amico mio,*" said Flores. "You have changed so much I hardly recognise you." He moved forward and clapped me on the back with a hearty whack. "It's as though you are entirely different person, Giacomo." He enunciated the name carefully, his tone slightly teasing.

"And you, my friend, seem to have come back from the dead."

I studied him carefully. There was a slight stoop to him, despite his effort to remain erect. His faced possessed far too many lines for one of his age and there was a small scar just above his brow. It was the eyes, though, that told more of the tale. No longer twinkling, they now were guarded with just a hint of pain. Though he'd survived shipwreck, he seemed to have paid a penalty nonetheless.

I offered him a seat and poured him a cup of wine from the flagon on the table.

"I would introduce you to my friend, Hal. He is English, but we met on a ship in the Sea of Marmara. I owe him much."

I refrained from explaining more. How much I could trust Flores, and whether to trust him at all, was far from clear. Even if I had wished to relive those terrible days, at the moment there was no point in saying if not for Hal I'd be dead at the bottom of the sea. A death made certain when that bastard al Qali had bargained me away with my seer's gift to the Grand Vizier. All for a manuscript. *The* manuscript.

Flores nodded to Hal. "Any friend of Giacomo's is a friend of mine," he said in English.

"Jacko said you two met in London," said Hal. "Said you was a captain of a Portugee ship."

"That's right," said Flores. "I am a Portugee. And I met your young friend quite by chance. He came to my assistance when I was attacked by cutthroats. I owe him much for that."

"Your friend, Mustapha al Qali was there, too," I said.

Flores gave a smile that didn't reach his eyes. "*Sí*, he was. And later, you came to us for some aid in return. I regret I was unable to help, but I hope Signor al Qali was able to assist you."

I nodded, studying his face carefully. "You see the man before you. It is of al Qali's making."

Flores nodded, his eyes narrow. "I see a much different person before me, in many ways. Al Qali taught you much." Again, he gave a smile that didn't reach his eyes. "I learned some things from al Qali as well, *amico mio*," he added softly.

"You have seen him since you left England?" I asked.

Flores shook his head slightly. "But I have heard a little whisper."

I poured more wine into his cup. "A whisper?" I said in a casual tone. Beside me, Hal shuffled in his seat.

"*Si*. Our friend has travelled much since I last saw him." He gestured with his hand. "Here, there, always asking questions. Quite discreetly, you understand, but questions, nonetheless. Questions of a specific nature."

I raised my brow inquisitively. "A manuscript?"

Flores nodded slightly. "I see you know."

"*Si*, I know. He inquired at many universities about this manuscript, when I was with him."

"But you are with him no longer?"

I shook my head. "We parted ways in Hüdavendigar."

"Hüdavendigar?"

"In the land of the Ottoman Turks."

Flores studied me carefully, saying nothing. His eyes lingered on my face, taking in every detail. I tried to keep my expression bland, willed away the beads of sweat and hoped my eyes were clear enough to pass scrutiny.

"I see," he said finally. He reached across and touched my sleeve. "You have experienced much, *amico mio*."

I let the comment go. "Have you heard more than that?"

Flores pressed his lips together for a moment. He sniffed. "Yes. Africa."

I stiffened slightly. Though I knew in my heart that's where al Qali was to be found, to hear it from another source sent my blood flowing. "Any specific place?"

He shrugged. "I heard only a name."

"The name of a place?" I asked.

Flores shrugged again.

I took a deep breath. "Prester John?" I said softly.

A startled look crossed Flores's face. "You know?"

"A guess," I said.

Flores waved his hand dismissively. "Prester John. But that is a story. A tale about a Christian priest king with a realm filled with gold and jewels. That's something you tell your children at night. There is no such person or place."

"That's not the point," I said. "What he believes is the point."

"True." Flores frowned. "But what is it to you?"

"I intend to find him," I said carefully.

Flores nodded. "And?"

"There are some matters...I wish to put to him."

Flores glanced at Hal's burly figure. "Put forcefully?"

"Perhaps."

Flores sighed. "You wish to travel to Africa, to dangerous places where they would kill you for your presence alone? You are chasing shadows, my friend. Take my advice and find yourself a woman, enjoy the life you have now."

I shook my head. "You don't understand."

Flores grasped my arm again and looked into my eyes. "I understand. I understand all too well what is driving you and I say again, forget it."

"What if I said I have proof that what you think is only a tale is true? And that there are riches beyond imagining at the end of it?"

Flores looked at Hal again. "Can you trust this man?" he asked quickly in Italian.

I looked at him and laughed. "Did I not say that this man saved my life?" I responded in English.

"What proof is it that you have?" Flores said in English.

"A manuscript. One that describes in detail the place and how to get to it."

"And you know this document to be authentic?"

I nodded.

"How did you come by such a document?"

"Take my word for it. The source is impeccable. It is no counterfeit."

Flores gave a low whistle, his eyes brightening. "And al Qali has seen this document? Was this the one he was seeking?"

"I think so. But I wanted to be certain he is no longer in Venice, or indeed anywhere in Christendom."

"I think he has gone to Egypt. Perhaps to see his mother."

I smiled wryly. "Perhaps. Or he might be at the beginning of his journey south."

"South?" Flores raised his brows. "Prester John?"

I nodded.

"And where do I come in?"

I straightened. "I was hoping you would assist me. I hear Prince Henry of Portugal has an interest in Prester John."

Flores gave a roar of laughter. When he stopped, he grinned at me. "Prince Henry has many interests."

"But he has an interest in trade, in African trade routes, does he not?"

"Yes," said Flores. "I still don't understand where I come in."

I sighed. "You're a friend. We are well acquainted and we can trust each other, I think."

Flores nodded carefully.

"Also, you're Portuguese, you know your way around there, how things work."

"You want me to take you to Prince Henry. To find out more about Prester John."

"I want you to help me convince Prince Henry that this is an opportunity he cannot resist."

"You want me to help you get money from him," Flores said flatly.

I shrugged. "And men."

Flores shook his head. "You are *loco, amico mio*."

"Will you do it?"

There was a long pause while Flores stared at his hands. He gave a sigh. "*Sí*," he said. "I'll help you."

I grinned, suddenly pleased beyond words. "Good. Can you book passage for the three of us to Lisbon?"

Flores grunted. "You mean the court? Prince Henry isn't there. Didn't you know this?"

I shook my head. "What?"

"He lives in Sagres, away from court. At the navigation school. He's also the Administrator, the Grand Master, or some such, of the Knights of Christ. They have a great interest in Africa."

"The Knights of Christ?" I asked, perplexed.

"The Knights Templar. They have renamed themselves in Portugal after the Templars were banned in the last century."

I let those words settle in me. Hadn't the Templars been interested in grand expeditions in the past? Perhaps this was a good thing. Such an organisation would be more than supportive of discovering the home of a lost Christian enclave. Especially if there were riches attached to it. I tried to find comfort in those thoughts, but I couldn't help the niggling feeling that this situation might take a dangerous turn.

"Fine," I said, attempting a light tone. "We'll go to Sagres."

CHAPTER TWO
VENICE, SUMMER 1446
BARNABAS

The flame from the torch I held barely cut through the thick mist that swirled in circles around my cloak. I could hear Hal's footsteps behind me on the wet cobbles and his grunt of disgust as a wave of dank odour rose from the canal next to us. It was an apt reminder of the dirty business we'd attended to this night to obtain information.

Hal grunted again, this time louder. I looked back and three figures loomed large, a sword flashing in the torchlight. I shouted, dropped the torch and drew my own sword, cursing my lack of vigilance. Hal staggered under the attack, fighting to draw his weapon. I moved forward and swung hard, made impact and heard a clank. I'd disarmed one man at least.

Less than a breath later another man was upon me, raining blows that I fought to parry. I lunged and swung, blind in the mist. The man gave a wide sweeping undercut and sliced open the inside of my arm. I lunged again, thrusting hard and my blade plunged into something soft. I twisted it hard and withdrew it just as someone came at me from behind and threw me to the ground, knocking the wind out of me. My sword fell from my hand.

Before I could recover, the assailant was on top of me, his hands about my throat. I struggled hard, but he pressed harder. I reached wildly for my sword, searching the slick cobblestones, but it was gone. I gasped hard, struggling for air. The man's face was half-hidden under the brim of a dark hat but I aimed roughly, jabbing my fingers into his eyes. He howled in pain and released my throat. I seized the opportunity to knock his other hand away and rolled to the side.

"Jacko!" shouted Hal.

"Here," I cried weakly.

I struggled to rise and the assailant was on my back, trying to bring me down again, but Hal was at my side and he grabbed the man, threw him down and pressed his foot against the man's neck.

"The other two?" I asked in a rasping voice.

"Dead. Shall I finish the job on this one?" asked Hal softly.

"No. Let's see if we can find out who sent them."

I walked over to the torch I had carried moments before. Despite all that had passed in that brief time it still burned, the odour of the hot sulphur strong. I picked it up. Hal lifted the man from the ground, careful to keep a tight hold on him and brought him over to me. I held the torch up to his face and removed the hat that covered his head. There was a gash on the side of his cheek that bled freely but it couldn't disguise the golden cast to his skin and the dark eyes that glinted back at me.

"Who are you?" I asked in clipped tones. I spoke in Arabic. There was no doubt in my mind who'd sent this person.

He gave me an insolent look. "My name is of no consequence."

I grabbed the neckline of his tunic and twisted it. "Your clothes may be of Venice, but I think you are used to looser, flowing garments. Or perhaps no garments at all when you are in the presence of your master."

The man stiffened under my grip and pursed his mouth in a grim line. "What I wear is of no consequence either."

"Well your master, I am certain, finds something about you that is of consequence if he sent you to me. What were your orders? To kill me? You can tell him he will have to try harder than that."

"You're not letting him go?" complained Hal.

I shrugged. It was one thing to kill in defence, quite another for me to run a man through in this manner. My rage was gone. For the moment, at least. Now it was more confusion that I felt. And fear. Was Halil Pasha, the Grand Vizier and foremost minister in the Turkish Sultanate so angry that I had escaped he'd sent men to kill me? Or was the fear I might reveal the plot he'd drawn me into so great he would stop at nothing to get rid of me? Perhaps both. But I had no doubt who had sent this man. The doubts were in the decision about what to do.

I drew up and stared into the man's eyes. "If I see you near me again, be certain I won't hesitate to cut you down on the spot. Tell your master I care not about his plots and plans. I have other tasks that are far more pressing. I will be gone from here before daylight. I expect you to be gone too, back to Hüdavendigar."

I released the man and he stared for one brief moment before taking off into the dark.

"You're mad," said Hal.

"No. We will be on our way soon. Tomorrow, if we can get passage. He won't trouble to follow us." At least I hoped that would be the case.

∽

I climbed the steps to the small palazzo slowly, wiping my brow when I reached the top. The day was hot, I told myself. Even the small insects that flitted by the dank water that gathered at the steps seemed lethargic. My shoulder ached from the fall the night before and I knew there would be a bruise there soon to add to the cut on my arm. The pain was dulled by my regular dose of the drink that had become my slave master since leaving Hüdavendigar. It was nearly time for the next one, but each day I tried to forestall it, assure myself that it would take little enough to break this cursed habit. Today my body wasn't fooled. The ache in my shoulder and the sweat that gathered at my brow and along my back told me so.

I glanced up at the window overlooking the canal and thought for a moment a figure stood there peering out. I blinked. Was it Alys? I sighed. On no account would I allow myself to dwell on thoughts of her. I had my path set now and my visit here held no purpose but to wrap up business with Alessandra. Perhaps it had been Alessandra I'd seen. But surely she would be wearing the dark veil to cover the burns that scarred her face? I blinked again and the figure was gone. One of the maids, most likely, or even Joanie, Alys's maid.

Another servant answered my knock. She was familiar, but at the moment I had no notion what she was called. She recognised me and immediately let me in, ushered me upstairs to the *sala* and then went in search of her mistress. I glanced around while I waited. The drapes were partially drawn against the strong sun. The French doors were opened to catch any breeze that might be on offer. One of the chairs, elegant and spare, had been drawn over to its opening. The other pieces of furniture were just as elegant, a clear statement of Alessandra's continued prosperity. It didn't seem possible that it had been only two days since I'd been here, entertained by Alessandra and then introduced to her "lovely new protégé", Maria. I moved over to the French windows to avail of the small breath of wind that came off the canal. Once again, I admired the ambition and determination that put Alessandra here, in this well placed, though small, palazzo in Venice, where property of any sort was valuable. Few enough people knew with any certainty what Alessandra's origins were, but most assumed from her cultured appearance and language that she was from one of the many lesser noble Venetian families impoverished by exorbitant dowry costs and the volatilities of a life in trade.

"Giacomo! What a pleasure to have your company again so soon."

I turned to see Alessandra moving towards me, her posture erect, her voice calm and welcoming. She was wearing the familiar dark veil over a deep burgundy gown cut in the latest fashion. Despite the heat she wore sleeves and lace gloves. I could only guess at the scars her dress and manner hid, but I did know they were deep. I was the only one to witness the flames that had burned her skin and I had glimpsed how they had impressed themselves on her mind.

I moved to her, took her hand and kissed it lightly.

"You know only too well how powerful your charms are, Alessandra."

She cocked her head. "Or perhaps the charms of my little protégé?"

I forced a laugh and smile. "She is truly worthy of your interest Alessandra, but none can hold a candle to your charms." I winced at the use of "candle" since her current circumstances owed themselves entirely to an accident with that offending object.

Alessandra gave a trill of laughter. "You are too flattering, *amico mio*."

I gave a crooked grin. "Never."

She waved her hand in a dismissive gesture. "Enough of sweet words. Sit down. My servant will bring us refreshments."

I followed her to the chairs and took a seat after she had settled. The servant entered a moment later with a tray of wine and food. I allowed Alessandra to pour me some wine, but waved away the offer of food.

"So," she said, after I had taken a sip of my wine, "Do I owe this visit to pleasure or business? If it is to be pleasure, I am afraid I must disappoint you. Maria is unwell."

"Unwell?" The well-turned phrases and list of questions I had carefully assembled fled in the face of this news about Alys.

"I am afraid she has taken a fever," said Alessandra in a practical tone. "It appears to be serious. I have sent for the physician but her servant seems to think it is marsh fever. That would be unfortunate, if it is, for she has many engagements with her main benefactor this month."

I sat in stunned silence for a moment. "Marsh fever? Has she had it before?"

"She has certainly not had it since she came here, but I can't account for her prior life."

I thought of Alys growing up by the Thames in the heart of London's Queenhythe dock. Would she have had exposure to it there? Or was it some other deadly illness she might have contracted in her journey across France to here in the hopes of finding me? I cursed myself for the selfish scoundrel I'd become since those days in London. All the more reason to cut my ties with Alys. She could do much better than attach herself to the likes of me.

I drew myself up and tried to lay aside my concerns and act the rogue that I was. "That is unfortunate and my commiserations, Alessandra. I know you have put so much into creating the perfect courtesan that I beheld a few nights ago."

Alessandra nodded, taking her due. "She is rather good. A different type to me, but the men find her charms very appealing. There is an innocence to her, though she carries an air of sorrow that evokes a protectiveness in the clients."

I tried not to bristle at her mention of Alys's clients. The very thought of them filled me with an anger I had no right to feel.

"Ah yes," I said. "Perhaps you might consider accepting a small portion of my business earnings to see that she is cared for and to make up for any ill effects on your income as a result of the clients' disappointment."

She gave another trill of laughter. "Oh Giacomo. You are too transparent, yet I can forgive you that since you give me so much amusement with it."

I blinked and checked myself mentally, forcing a smile.

"Business. It is always business with you," she said.

I smiled in relief. For a moment I thought I had given away too much of my interest in Alys. The last thing I wanted was for Alessandra to discover my relationship with Alys and the past that went with it. Though I enjoyed Alessandra's company I was more than well aware that I couldn't count on her discretion, or that she might indeed not hesitate to make some kind of profit from it. Since her accident, Alessandra was even more a woman to be reckoned with.

"You know me well," I said. "Though you must concede that I have waited until after the pleasure I had here a few nights back, before I came in search of the state of our enterprises."

She leaned forward. "And your own adventures. Were they profitable? You spoke little last night."

I forced myself to breathe calmly. The least said about my adventures the better. They were my own personal scars and only added to what drove me forward now. "Profitable only in spirit, dear lady."

"Pity. You normally have such knack for smelling a good opportunity."

"So I take it our trading ventures have borne fruit?"

She nodded slowly. "Oh yes, *amore mio*. More than you can dream about. But we need to expand. Search out new suppliers. There is a great demand here and your contact in Bruges is anxious. Perhaps it is time we set up our own house publicly. There is no need for you or I to be named, but I have one or two people in mind who would be excellent managers for it."

"It is certainly something to consider." I was reluctant to commit to anything at this moment, with another journey in the offing and one from which I had no guarantee I would return. "Perhaps if I could see the ledgers and accounts I would have a greater understanding."

She gave a nod, rose and made her way to a small chest on the table. She drew out a chain with a key that was around her neck and unlocked the chest. Reaching inside, she lifted out a bound book and brought it over to me. I took it from her and opened it, scanning the pages quickly. It was clear that all she said was no exaggeration. I felt a momentary surge of pride at the figures I read, wondering for only a moment what my tutor, Father Thomas would make of my success. He was dead, now. Disgraced for his part in the conspiracy of witchcraft and treason that had brought down Alys's mistress, The Duchess of Gloucester, and caused the death of my own mistress, Margery Jourdemayne. But that was another lifetime.

"All you say is true. We need to make plans. I will give my signature for the proposal to request trade rights with the Doge and the Medici and anyone else you think is necessary. Make use of your connections, I know I can trust your judgement on that."

"I sense a 'but' in all this."

I gave a wry smile. "It isn't necessarily a 'but'. More of an 'and'. I intend to go to Africa--"

"Africa?" she said in a startled tone.

"Africa. There are some lucrative trade routes there. Salt, gold."

"Yes, but surely the risks are too great? We have only just begun our enterprise. This type of scheme is for someone who is more experienced, more knowledgeable about the paths and risks involved."

"You don't think me capable of grand ventures? Have I not proved myself enough?"

"You are capable, I grant you, and your schemes have been sound. But this venture is foolhardy and with little merit. You know nothing of Africa."

"Ah, but I do." I withdrew a folded parchment from within my doublet. "I have a copy of a map."

I presented the parchment to her. She took it, unfolded it carefully and, holding it to the light studied it carefully.

"Where did you get this?" she asked, her tone sharp.

I gave a shrug. "Let's just say I paid dearly for it."

"You stole it?"

I laughed. "No. Well perhaps the information, but the map is mine, made from my memory, with some gaps filled in by a few discreet inquiries."

"So, you think we should expand to Africa? But surely there is no one who would grant us the right to trade in those places."

"I have a guide."

"What?" Her tone was sceptical.

"Truly. It is all arranged. I will be leaving on the tide. I have come only to arrange for you to conduct the business in my absence and to ensure that I have sufficient funds to support this venture."

She sat in silence for a moment and then gave a peal of laughter. "Oh, I do enjoy you, Giacomo. More than you know." She raised a gloved hand and ran a finger along my lips. "More than you know."

I took her hand and clasped it to my heart. "I am always yours," I said with an impish grin.

She withdrew her hand. "*Bene.* It will be arranged. I will have the papers drawn up and the money for what you need for the journey. Do you plan to obtain your goods here for trade?"

"No, I will get what I need either in Morocco or Alexandria. And perhaps in Sagres, in Portugal."

"Sagres? Why do you go to Sagres?"

"I go to see Prince Henry of Portugal. I hope to interest him in my plans. With his support, I will have a greater chance of success for many reasons."

"I can understand that you want the backing of a prince, but why Prince Henry?"

"Have you not heard? He has a great interest in exploring unknown lands, especially Africa."

"What holds his interest in Africa?"

I gave a nonchalant shrug. "He has some notion that Prester John's kingdom exists still somewhere there. I mean to ask where."

"Prester John? Do you hope to find the fabled gems, or perhaps the magic pebbles that cure the blind?" She gave a snort. "No one believes that story. Giacomo, what are you really about in Africa?"

"Business, Alessandra, business."

"Yes, but will that business be at the cost of all profit, future and past?"

I blew her a kiss and rose. With a sweeping bow I took my leave.

CHAPTER THREE
VENICE, SUMMER 1446
ALYS

Alys tossed in her bed, damp tendrils of hair plastered to her forehead. She moaned softly and beside her Bitty whined. Alys opened her eyes and blinked, her eyes glazed and full of fever.

"Barnabas," she murmured.

"Hush," came a soft voice.

"Barnabas, you've come. I knew you would."

"Shhhhh," said the voice. "You rest."

Alys felt a damp cloth on her forehead. It was cool and soothing. A hand stroked her cheek. She was comforted.

～

Alys stared out of the window listlessly and watched the passing traffic on the canal. The day was warm, but she could smell a hint of autumn in the light breeze that occasionally stirred the curtain. She shivered a moment under the light night robe that covered her.

"Good, you have risen from your bed."

Alys spared a glance for Alessandra who stood just inside the room, her black veil and gown a dark shadow at the door. Alys resumed her gaze outside. She had few words these days and even fewer for this woman who stood behind her.

"We must have you back to yourself soon. Has Joanie given you that draught the apothecary sent?"

Alys murmured a non-committal reply. Alessandra had been pushing her to get up for days. Though the fever was gone and she no longer retched at the sight of food, Alys had little interest in doing anything. It was Joanie who'd made her rise from her bed and sat her at the window to catch the breeze. But for no one would she take that vile concoction the apothecary had made up.

"I paid good money for that draught, so I expect you to take it. The apothecary said it would improve your strength."

"You see I am up."

Alessandra gave a small grunt and took a seat on the bed next to Alys. She plucked the dog off the bed and put him on the floor. "I would prefer if you didn't let the dog up there with you."

The remark stirred something inside Alys. "Bitty isn't just a dog. He's my companion."

"I thought Joanie was your companion. At least that's what you tell me when I insist you treat her as a servant."

Alys turned to look at Alessandra. "May not a person have more than one companion?"

Alessandra frowned. "I haven't come to debate over your dog. You do in fact have a particular companion who is most anxious to see you."

Alys fought the flutter in her heart. Joanie had already told her Barnabas had come, but that had been only a few days after she'd fallen ill. Several weeks had passed and he'd not returned. Perhaps he'd sent a note?

"Who would be so anxious to see me?" she asked.

Alessandra gave an impatient snort. "Don't be obtuse, Maria. Though you have had many gallants who would seek your companionship, you know full well I could only be speaking of Cosimo Fabriano."

"Cosimo?" Alys said faintly, interest vanished. She had no wish to hear about Cosimo Fabriano. She pictured his heavy-set frame, his dark eyes and jowls and sighed.

"He has asked after your health every day."

"Can't he find someone else to amuse him? I'm still not well enough to entertain in that manner."

"He has paid handsomely for your attentions," snapped Alessandra. "He has every right to expect that you would return some interest as soon as you are able."

Alys closed her eyes slowly. "But that's just it, you see. I am not able."

"It's not up to you whether you are able, my girl. It's up to me. And I give you one week. If it weren't for the constant queries from your other admirers I would have sold you off to Signor Fabriano long ago."

Alys opened her eyes, forcing calm. "Which admirers would they be?"

"Oh, many. Even Tomaso Cortini. He seems unable to keep away, though he says he is here to see me, but I know better. And of course, Carlo. But he doesn't count because he has no money. Well, not at present, though I do hear that his latest painting has caused quite a stir. And his commission fee was increased significantly."

Alys smiled. Carlo, dear Carlo. That he'd allowed her to paint so much of that last work he was now getting recognition for suddenly gave her enormous pleasure.

The joy spread through her body and she sat more erectly.

"….And of course there is Giacomo," added Alessandra. "He heard you were ill and was quite concerned. To the point that he gave me funds to provide for your care and ensure you had sufficient time to recover. Well I've done that and more, so he cannot fault me."

"Giacomo?" Alys asked. Her mind was blank and then she smiled, remembering. Barnabas was Giacomo.

"Yes, you remember. Or perhaps you don't, since you fell ill immediately after. Giacomo Bonavillagio. He was your guest one night, *piccola mia*. I asked you at the last minute, as a favour. He is very dear friend and had been away on a most arduous journey. He seemed very pleased with you. But it's just as well he's gone away. It might have been awkward if he'd remained and had decided to seek your company on a regular basis. Cosimo isn't one to take rivals lightly." Alessandra cocked her head. "But on the other hand, it might have served us very well. Nothing like a bit of rivalry for a man to realise just how much he values something."

"Giacomo has gone away?" Alys asked.

"What? Oh, *si*," said Alessandra.

"Is he gone for long? Where did he go?" With an effort Alys made her tone nonchalant, feigning only mild interest.

Alessandra snorted. "Ah, you wouldn't believe it, the *loco*. He is off to Africa. He is a merchant and thinks he can make good trade connections there." She shrugged. "Perhaps he will succeed. And if he does I will be a very rich woman."

"Africa?" Alys couldn't keep the disbelief from her voice. What on earth was he thinking?

"I know. Crazy, eh? But perhaps very cunning. Giacomo is no simpleton and he has not steered me wrong in the past."

Alys nodded dumbly. She more than anyone knew that Barnabas was not lacking in intelligence. That wasn't the problem. That night, when she'd last seen him she'd sensed something dark in him. Something that wanted no one near him. Something that was destructive, not just to him, but to others. She had witnessed that first hand.

"So, Maria. I will tell Cosimo that you will be ready to receive him in a few days' time."

Alys nodded, distracted. Her mind sifted through the memory of her conversation with Barnabas. Had he mentioned Africa? She recalled Joanie stating that he'd gone away, but she had only thought he'd gone somewhere like Padua, or even Paris. Not Africa. She suddenly remembered throwing the leather bracelet he'd given her all those years ago into the canal. She touched the wrist where it had once rested. The anger started to rise inside her once again. All those promises, all those years ago. She gritted her teeth. What a fool she'd been to follow him all the way here to Venice. Joanie's words echoed through her mind. She would go back. Joanie was right. There was nothing here for her. She nearly had enough money to get her back to London and set herself up as a merchant's widow. She would engage a man. Invest in wool, or some such thing. She thought of her painting. Of Carlo. Would he come with her? Did she want him to? There was much to think about. Much to do.

"Will you call Joanie?" asked Alys. "I think I will dress now."

"Oh," said Alessandra. "I nearly forgot. Giacomo did send a message for you before he left. Well, not quite a message. He sent his monkey, the imp. What was his name? He said it would keep the little dog company. I thought they were not very companionable."

"No, they weren't," said Alys numbly. "And the monkey is called Tomaso."

"It matters not. I gave the monkey to Joanie to look after and told her to keep it chained in the kitchen above stairs. I won't have that animal running about my house."

Alessandra rose from the bed and with only a few more words regarding Barnabas's monkey, departed.

Alys turned to stare out the window, her mind in a whirl. Whatever did he mean by giving her Tomaso? Had he meant to mock her? She stiffened and pushed the thought from her mind. She would place that monkey into the hands of the first person who expressed an interest in him. For her part, she cared nothing for the animal.

✦

Carlo bent over Alys's hand and kissed it lightly. "Amore mia," he murmured softly. "I rejoice to see you risen from your sick bed."

"And you my dear Carlo, you have recovered well?" Alys searched his face. She could see new lines that creased the corners of his eyes, but his eyes were clear and free from pain. "How are your wounds?"

He smiled at her. "My health is perfect. Fully restored and you are to be thanked for that. You now have my life as well as my love."

His tone was light hearted, but Alys knew the words were meant with all his heart. She took up his hand to draw him away from the door of the *sala* and listening ears. He caught her to his side and encircled her, planting small kisses on her neck.

"*Amore mia*, I was sick with worry. I have missed you so," he whispered. He ran his finger along her shoulder and the rim of the neckline of her gown. She'd chosen the sapphire blue which set off her russet hair, now caught up in fashionable ringlets. The gown didn't fit her as snugly as it had before her illness, so that her breasts no longer pressed firmly against the fabric. She shrunk under his touch.

He removed his hand and lifted up his head. "I have hurt you? A thousand pardons, I wouldn't harm you for the world."

Alys took his hand and kissed the palm. "No, *cara mio*. It is only that my skin is tender after my illness." She led him to the window, where the breeze could carry their conversation and reduce it to indistinguishable murmurs.

"The painting was a success," she said in a low voice.

Carlo grinned. "But of course. With such talent and skill what else would it be?"

"*Bene*," said Alys. She smiled. "I am overjoyed to hear it. You deserve the success."

"Nonsense, my darling. It is because of you that the painting was ever completed. I only lament that you are unable to share the credit with me. But I can at least give you some of the money that was paid for it."

It would be the first time she was paid for a painting. It was more than she ever hoped for. She looked up at Carlo and gave a delighted laugh.

He tweaked a ringlet and bent down to kiss her. This time she was more prepared and she allowed it to deepen, his mouth searching and hungry. His touch was warm and inviting and for a moment she thought she might succumb, but the feeling fled. She pulled away.

"We must be careful," she told him firmly, her voice low.

"I hate this. We cannot continue in this manner. Please, let me approach Alessandra. Tell her that I will buy out your contract as soon as I have enough funds. Then we can be together. You and I, we will paint until the whole world notices us." He pulled her to him and kissed her insistently.

She drew back a moment later. "We mustn't be rash. You know Alessandra. There's no telling how she will respond to such a declaration. You must leave her to me. All in good time, when we have sufficient funds, we will begin making plans. Approaching her before we have the money leaves us open to the risk she might use the time to bargain for a higher price from Cosimo, or someone else."

Carlo frowned. "You're right of course." He took her hand and kissed it again. "Still, it is unbearable to have you so close and yet I cannot have you completely."

Alys withdrew her hand carefully. "In this house at least, we must take great care."

He grinned at her. "But in my rooms, the story may be different, eh? You will come soon?"

She nodded slowly. "A new painting. Alessandra is extremely pleased about the success of this last one, for she knows how well it reflects on her. We must plan another one."

"Yes. That was in my mind too. I have been thinking about it for weeks while I waited to see you. You will be the Madonna again. Her meeting with Elisabeth, perhaps."

"No, no," said Alys. "A different theme. Perhaps something…secular?"

Carlo shook his head. "No, the demand is for religious. I have many buyers for that type of painting."

"Could I not be someone from a Greek myth? Diana, perhaps."

In truth, she felt she couldn't model for anything of a religious nature, especially as the Virgin. She felt incapable of sitting there pretending to be something that was so far from who she now was. She'd considered this over the few days that had passed since she'd decided to dress and begin resuming her obligations. When she'd faced Cosimo Fabriano yesterday, laced into her best gown, her breasts powdered and her lips rouged, she'd decided she would never model anything as false as the Virgin Madonna. Especially when Fabriano, his sausage fingers pulling eagerly at her gown, planted wet kisses on her breasts, told her she was his little peach and he longed to taste her succulent fruit once again. She must bear it though, until she had enough money to escape, either with Carlo's help or without.

The night had been long, bereft of any music or singing to relieve Fabriano's avid attentions. He'd lain abed after he'd entered her and spent himself, his large torso planted next to her, fondling and stroking her like she was a lap dog. She'd tolerated this until, eventually, he'd fallen asleep. Waking hours later, she'd endured a few more caresses before she helped him to dress and promised to see him again the next night. With a sigh of relief when the door closed she'd rung for Joanie. This time it seemed she had washed and doused herself inside and out so often she felt it impossible she might have any skin left.

"No, not Diana. It must be the Virgin Madonna. Your face, your body, it suggests it all. You are full of expectation, confused, yet excited and frightened. Yes frightened."

She gave him a puzzled look. "Frightened. Are you saying I look frightened?"

He ran a thumb along her mouth. "Ah, you can hide nothing from me, *bambino mio*. It is there, in the back of the eyes. Never forget I am a painter. I notice things. But there's nothing to be frightened about. I'm here, by your side. I will protect you."

Alys smiled weakly, suddenly feeling hemmed in. She stepped back, her damaged leg suddenly paining her, and smoothed her dress. She wouldn't comment. What could she say? Her fears were nothing he could imagine, her confusion, well she had no time for that. Her path had to be clear, it must be. Her excitement—was that the thought of wielding the paintbrush again?

He put his finger under her chin and lifted her face to his. "You must not worry. We have the painting to create. It will be more wondrous than the previous one. You'll see."

He began to talk about the colours, the pigments they would need and the sketches he would make before he began the painting.

"I will come tomorrow and sketch you. In the early morning, when the light is good."

"I-I cannot," said Alys. "I have an appointment this evening...and it may run late."

His face darkened and he pursed his lips. "Then I will come in the afternoon. After my meeting with Signor Bembo."

Alys took a deep breath. "Oh, Carlo. I cannot. Signor Fabriano has said he will be here every evening this week to make up for lost time. I must prepare. It was all I could do to persuade Alessandra to allow me to see you now."

He looked down to where her breasts rose and fell against the gown. "Will you be wearing that gown tonight?"

She glanced down at it and shook her head. He sighed in relief. She didn't dare tell him the gown marked for this evening's meeting was even more revealing. But what did it matter when it would be removed moments after the door had shut behind them? But those remarks were best left unsaid to Carlo.

A shriek sounded in a room below. The kitchen. Tomaso? Was he loose again causing havoc among the kitchen staff?

"What was that?" asked Carlo.

"Nothing serious, I'm sure," said Alys. "Something gone amiss in the kitchen I imagine."

"Yes, well," he said. He bent down and kissed her cheek. "I will come see you first thing next week. In the morning."

She nodded. "I will send word if there is a problem."

He grunted. "In the meantime, I'll have a word with Alessandra about the painting. Perhaps with the thought of increased fame and the promise of a share of the earnings she might be more amenable to you sharing more of your time with me. And even your body?" he added in a playful tone.

She gave a little tinkle of laughter, glad that Carlo's humour was restored. She blew him a kiss and he took his leave. A moment later Joanie entered.

"Come, you must get ready," Joanie said.

"Was that Tomaso I heard?"

Joanie nodded. "'e's been stealing things off the table. I told them to tie him up in the storeroom, but they don't listen."

Alys laughed for a moment, picturing the scene. A troublemaker, causing havoc. There was no doubt whose animal he was. She must try to find someone to take him off her hands. Perhaps she would ask Cosimo tonight.

CHAPTER FOUR
VENICE, AUTUMN 1446
ALYS

Alys stroked Bitty as he sat on her lap, Alessandra's tirade of words flowing over her in a dark wave. It had been going on for at least a quarter of an hour. She noticed a fleck of paint on her palm. She smiled inwardly. Such a colour, it was. Vibrant and full of life. A promise of what was slowly unfolding on the canvas at Carlo's rooms.

"How is it you have paint on your skin?" Alessandra said sharply. "You haven't been careless with your dress, have you?"

Alys looked up and blushed under Alessandra's scrutiny. "No, no. The dress is fine. Perfect, not a tear, nor a rip nor a stain, rest assured. I only picked up one of Carlo's brushes to examine the colour. There must have been paint on the handle."

It seemed a feeble explanation and as Alessandra's eyes narrowed Alys held her breath. Would she be caught out? She couldn't bear it if Alessandra forbade her to go to Carlo's any more where she would be able to paint as well as model for him. Alessandra would never make Alys abandon modelling altogether, no, the results from modelling were too lucrative, but Alys could easily foresee that she would be made to model here at the palazzo, instead, under Alessandra's watchful eye.

"You're too pale, as I said. You have been drinking that compound I had from the apothecary, yes?"

Alys nodded, holding her gaze steady. In truth, the mixture was vile and she retched at the very thought of it.

Alessandra gave her another considering look and tsked loudly. "Well, it doesn't seem to have had much of an effect. Your clothes still hang from you like they were borrowed from your mother." She leaned over and pinched Alys's cheeks. "Will I be forced to apply more cosmetics to improve the bloom on your cheeks?"

"I am a bit off colour, 'tis all," said Alys. "It will pass."

"I have been waiting for it to pass this month and more," said Alessandra. "What does Signor Fabrianno have to say?"

Alys shrugged. "He certainly doesn't complain that my clothes hang off me."

She leaned down and nuzzled Bitty's neck. He gave a little bark. Alessandra threw her a disapproving look.

"Though he's said nothing thus far, we cannot be certain he won't in the future. He's not mentioned continuing the contract yet."

"Continuing the contract? But I thought it was all settled."

"Of course, for the time. But contracts end and others are formed. I wouldn't dream of making it a permanent arrangement just yet. You may attract other, even more prosperous admirers." She frowned. "That's only if your charms return to their full bloom."

Alys tensed, considering Alessandra's words. It's what Carlo had warned her about, had feared. "Perhaps I will be the next contender for my contract. Or perhaps Carlo."

Alessandra gave a trill of laughter. "What? You have no idea how expensive you are, I think."

"Carlo is gaining a reputation. He will soon have all of Venice at his feet."

"Ah, but *cara mia*, you forget. You nearly do have all of Venice at your feet. If they approach Carlo, it is only because of you. But you must keep up your looks."

Alys closed her eyes. She was tired of Alessandra's constant chiding. It was all too wearisome.

"What time does Signor Fabriano come this evening?"

Alys opened her eyes and sighed. "I imagine no later than eleven. He mentioned he had a banquet to attend."

"And you're not attending it with him?"

"I hardly think so since it's a state matter and his wife will be with him."

Alessandra waved aside her comment. "His wife. It's when he takes you in place of his wife then we know you have him for good."

"I think that is unlikely."

"Not true. But only the very great courtesans can boast of such an achievement."

"I thought the Venetians were too priggish for that."

Alessandra bristled. "We are not. Courtesans are the best of company, and discreet. Never let me hear you say such a thing again." She gave Alys a dark look. "I will send Julia into you to do something about your face, later. A bit of rouge and something for the lips, perhaps. For now, I want you to go to your room and rest. I will send a message to Crivelli and cancel the sitting this afternoon."

Alys's heart sank at the words. "No, that's not necessary. It's resting of a sort when I model. All I do is sit." In fact modelling was a very tiring business but it was the highlight of her days.

"Nonsense, it will be as I say." Alessandra made her way to the table where the small chest containing her writing things lay.

"If I rest today, could we not postpone the sitting until tomorrow?"

Alessandra considered a moment. "Very well," she said eventually. "It is important that the painting is completed in the time Crivelli promised. It will coincide nicely with the reconsideration of your contract with Signor Fabriano. The attention a splendid new painting of you will create can only serve to attract the very best of suitable admirers."

Alys sat quietly while Julia applied the cosmetics with expert care as Joanie looked on, frowning. Alys could almost hear the narrative running through Joanie's mind and she could only agree. She looked all of what she'd become, there was no mistake. But if this gained her the wealth to leave Alessandra, what did it matter? And it bought her time to paint. Time to sit in front of a canvas, brush in hand and lose herself in the world she created there. Even Carlo told her that her talent was special.

Julia turned from her face and started to dress her hair, weaving it into pinned braids and curls arranged along the crown of Alys's head. It took some time and the effect was quite alluring with the teasing intricacy of the fashion. The rope of pearls she'd cleverly weaved through it set off Alys's gold velvet gown to great advantage. Julia held up the pier glass for Alys to study the effect. Alys could only smile inwardly for a moment. All that work for naught. It would all come down in short while.

"Now, then my sweeting," said Joanie. "You must 'ave a little something to eat." She'd taken to calling Alys "sweeting" ever since her illness. If it was possible, Joanie had become even more protective of her.

Alys looked at the plate of cooked beef and bread. The food held very little appeal. She put her hand on her stomach, feeling it rebel at the notion of the spiced meat.

"Maybe a little bread," said Alys. "I'll be eating later with Cosimo."

It was a lie, but Joanie didn't need to know that the only contact she had with plates of food and flagons of wine that were presented during the evenings she entertained Signor Fabriano was when she served them. She couldn't bear to eat in his presence. In fact, lately she could bear little in his presence.

Joanie gave a cluck of disapproval but handed her a small chunk of bread. Alys took the chunk and tore a small piece off and placed it in her mouth. She chewed it carefully and managed to swallow, Joanie eyeing her closely. Joanie shook her head but said nothing.

She managed eventually to eat it all and felt herself settle a little. She took the cup of wine Joanie offered her and sipped it. Wine was something she managed well enough, especially if it meant a lovely haze between her and the world. She heard a commotion outside the room and sighed. She supposed it signalled Signor Fabriano's arrival. She pinched her cheeks and straightened. Joanie placed a comforting hand on her shoulder and she put her own on top for a brief time in thanks.

Alys rose from her chair and made her way to the *sala* to greet Fabriano, forcing a smile on her face. Her leg, weakened after her illness, cramped and she found herself limping again. She forced it to behave. When she entered the *sala* she saw Alessandra there with Fabriano, her dark veil draped in its usual position, but her covered hands, still slim and tapered, gesturing expressively.

"It will be the talk of Venice," she was saying. "I have it on good authority. She is like *Serenissima,* herself, a queen of the waters, desired by all."

"You have seen the painting?" asked Signor Fabriano. "It is better than the one before?"

Alessandra turned to Alys and gestured to her. "You have only to look at the original and you will see how my lovely one has only grown in beauty. Would you not even say there is something ethereal, something not of this world about her?"

Fabriano turned to study Alys, hands crossed over the paunch that even his dark flowing robe couldn't hide. As she stood there enduring his scrutiny, she gave a prayer of thanks that the candlelight was so kind and that the drawn face and listless eyes she saw when she looked in the pier glass were not so evident in such a light.

"Si, si," said Signor Fabriano. He set the cup of wine he'd been holding on the table and moved towards Alys. "Ah Maria *mia*, I am indeed fortunate you are mine." He took up her hand and planted a wet kiss on its palm.

Alessandra gave Alys an almost imperceptible nod. Taking her cue Alys cocked her head. "Oh, Cosimo, I am glad. Though I have had the offers, I desire nothing more than to belong to you....always."

Signor Fabriano turned to Alessandra. "There have been no recent offers, have there? Nothing to signify?"

"You have just testified to her beauty, signore, so of course there are constant inquiries. I do try to explain that, for now, her attentions are engaged." She shrugged. "But we can never tell what the future brings."

Signor Fabriano frowned. He turned to Alys and stroked her cheek with the back of his hand. "She is too lovely for the common person. She is a treasure and must be cherished." He pursed his fleshy mouth.

"She is a treasure, she is Serenissima, did I not just tell you?"

"She is my Serenissima," said Fabriano. His tone was firm, determined.

"Yes, of course, for the present," said Alessandra, equally firm. "And she is here now to entertain you and so I must not steal any more of your valuable time." She made her way to the door, brushing lightly against Alys and took her leave.

With the click of the door, Signor Fabriano took Alys's hand and led her to the seat by the table. He arranged the cushions behind his back and pulled her across his lap.

"Would you like something to eat first?" she asked. "There are some lovely spiced figs on the table I'm sure you would enjoy."

He ran his fingers over her cheeks, along her chin and across her breast bone, studying her as if for the first time. He lifted a curl by her neck and played with it for a moment, then cupped her chin and turned it to one side and then the other. She tried to relax under his touch, free her attention so that she was here, but not here. It was a trick she'd come to value, especially in these past months.

"Come," he said. "Let's go to your chamber."

"You would not even prefer a cup of wine first?"

"No," he said slowly. "No, we will go to your chamber."

She slid off his lap and slowly made her way to the door where he met her, a candelabra in each hand. He gave her one. She accepted it quizzically but said nothing.

Once inside her chamber he put the candelabras on the table.

"Stand there, by the table," he said.

She did as she was told and waited while he placed a chair in front of her. Carefully he turned her around and unlaced her gown. Once freed of its laces the gown dropped to her feet, leaving her dressed in a fine cream silk chemise, edged in lace, that had little practical function but set off the russet in her hair, as it was meant to.

"Take off the chemise," he said.

She loosened the ribbon that held it closed and pulled it carefully over her head. Alessandra would have a fit if it was torn in any manner. Unless of course it was by Fabriano, then she would add it to his entertainment costs.

"The stockings?" she asked when she'd finished.

He nodded, his eyes fixed on her. He was sitting so close she could feel his breath on her bare skin. She leaned over, loosed the ribbon that secured the stocking on one leg and rolled it down her leg in a suggestive manner as Alessandra had coached her. She repeated the performance with the other stocking, draping both of them along the table beside her. The task complete she straightened and stood before him, willing herself away. To be here and not here.

He sniffed. She looked over the top of his head and nearly flinched when she felt his hands once again stroking and examining her body. He cupped and weighed each breast, stroked her belly and ran his hand along the curve of her buttocks, murmuring indistinctly as he did so. He'd never acted in such a manner before and for a moment she wondered if she should do anything in response. She placed a hand on his head and stroked it tentatively. He took the hand and played with her fingers, taking each one by one and tracing his own finger along their outline.

"Yes, yes," he murmured.

"Cosimo?" she whispered.

"Shhh," he said softly.

He placed his finger on her mouth for a moment and moved back to her breasts, running his fingers along and around them. She shivered under his touch, the soft pudgy finger with its carefully trimmed nail.

He sighed. "Yes, *amore mia,* your mistress is correct. You are *Serenissima,* my own Venezia, rich with treasure, golden and ripe." He kissed her belly. "Even more than before. It's clear this life suits you. My attentions suit you."

He took her fingers and kissed them. "And I can make you riper, richer and even more lovely than ever."

"You do so much for me already, Cosimo," she said softly, uncertain if he wanted her to speak.

He nodded distractedly. "But you will be mine. I must have you."

"You do have me."

"No, you must be my *Serenissima,* mine alone. No other can be permitted to have you. Ever."

She remained silent a moment, wary of the dark tone he'd used.

He took her hand. "I will provide you with the proper setting. Something better than this." He gestured to the room. "You will have your own house, not too large, for you wouldn't need to entertain anyone but me, but with sufficient servants to see that you would want for nothing. And I would give you jewels, such jewels deserving to adorn such a treasure as you." He touched the pearls still woven through her hair. "Jewels of rare quality. Not these cheap baubles you have on now."

She licked her lips. "I'm certain that Alessandra--" she began hoarsely.

"Pah," he said. "That woman, she tries to play with me. But I know now what I desire, and I always get what I desire."

She gave a weak smile. "I know that you are a very successful man who lets little stand in his way."

He reached up and stroked her cheek. "This is very true. And I have you in my sights, and I shall not let you out of them." He pulled her down onto his lap. "But now that is settled we can move on to the pleasurable part of our connection."

He put his hand at the back of her head and pressed her close and kissed her, his large lips encasing hers, beginning his campaign on her body. Like all his plans and enterprises, he tackled them with energy as though he was waging a war that must be won at all costs. She forced her mind elsewhere again, knowing that when the morning came and he was gone there was much she had to think about and much to plan herself, for she had her own war to wage and the costs were alarmingly high.

CHAPTER FIVE
VENICE, LATE AUTUMN 1446
ALYS

Alys moved slightly, feeling the small cushion underneath her dress shift. Beads of sweat gathered on her upper lip despite the decided chill that had entered the room. The gown felt suddenly heavy on her shoulders, the velvet plush no longer rich against her skin, but dragging and oppressive.

Carlo gave her a distracted look and frowned. "Please try to hold still. I am attempting to capture your face."

"Oh Carlo, can I not do some painting myself now?"

"Not just yet, *cara mia*. I just want to get the tone perfect." He stopped a moment and gave his side a small rub.

"See," said Alys. "You need to rest. You can't fool me, your side still pains you. You're working too hard."

She rose, lifted up her skirts and withdrew the small cushion that had rested on her belly to give the illusion of pregnancy for the painting.

"Please, mistress, show some modesty!" said Joanie half-heartedly from her stool by the window. She sat there with some mending, but all pretence at sewing had been abandoned long ago.

"Oh, Joanie, it was only for a brief moment and my chemise was there," said Alys, adopting a teasing tone. "You wouldn't want me to let my baby drop to the floor?"

When she'd worked on the painting herself she'd made Joanie model for her, wearing the same gown and the cushion inserted, but, as Carlo rightly pointed out, Joanie was not of her proportions and the effect was less than ideal.

Still, when Alys moved over to the painting and surveyed it she felt she had done rather well, considering all those elements. The gown shimmered with lapis lazuli colour she'd ground and mixed with oil, and a touch of ultramarine blue hidden in the folds mixed with the burnt umber created a rich shadow. Under Carlo's coaching she'd once again taken on the oil paints, instead of the much-favoured tempera. Her russet gold hair, offset by the deep blue of the gown, emphasised the gold of the halo poised above her head. She sat on a bench, a half-finished pastoral scene behind her. She was a woman alone in her garden, contemplating the events to come. It was all her work, except for the face. And she wanted it as her own, not as Crivelli's, but as hers. But Crivelli had insisted he do the face, because he felt that she hadn't captured the expression befitting that of a woman expecting the birth of the saviour. She'd objected, insisting she had painted the joy and the wonder that Mary must have felt.

There was more than wonder and joy in the painted face that stared back at her. Though it was only starting to take shape, she could see the shadowed eyes that reflected secret joy and wonder, yes. But was the painting more convincing? She wasn't so certain. She itched to get back to it. There was more she wanted to set there, something she'd seen in the pier glass every time she'd looked at herself.

"The face is lovely," she said. "But will you let me add some of my touches, too?"

She sighed and stood back. The face was tilted slightly, but it needed something else. Was it defiance? She frowned, closed her eyes for a moment and looked again, trying to see the whole. Resignation. A Madonna who was resigned to her fate. She gave a gurgle of laughter that had an edge of hysteria.

Joanie looked up and studied her. "You're looking pale, mistress. Let me pour you a small cup of wine."

She rose and moved to a small table that held a decanter and cups, pouring one for Crivelli and one for Alys. She handed each a cup. Alys took hers and drank deeply, willing it to settle her stomach and bring back her colour. She had another appointment with Cosimo Fabriano tomorrow and wanted to be well enough to withstand it. Not that she had much to do any more. He seemed to just prefer to gaze at her the whole of the night, talking a little and eating and drinking his fill. He paid little mind to her words and so she had lapsed into silence for the most part. The nights, though, had become tedious almost beyond endurance, no matter how much she reminded herself she should be grateful for such an escape.

She still attended parties, singing and entertaining others with her wit and charm, but though they were a fewer than before, the attentions of prominent Venetians were more pressing whenever she did go out.

Crivelli came over and put his arm around her waist, facing the painting. "Yes, you were full of doubts, I know, but you didn't see what I saw." He released his arm and put his hand under her chin, turning her face towards his. He studied her dispassionately, turning her face from one side to another and then gazed into her eyes. She looked away, fearing what he'd see.

He gave a laugh. "You cannot hide from me, *bambina*. I see the troubled past that lurks in your eyes. And there's no need to conceal it. I use it; make it a part of the painting. You must learn not to fear what you see there."

She gave a weak smile and lifted her own hand to Crivelli's face, pushing back the locks that had fallen over his brow. It was a face so dear to her now, she could hardly hold back the tears that filled her eyes.

He wiped the corner of her eye with his thumb. "What's this? A tear? Am I that harsh a master that I should make you cry?"

She shook her head, not trusting her voice. "No, no," she whispered finally. "Not a harsh master at all. On the contrary, you are only too good and kind to me, and I can never thank you enough."

"You know you need not thank me," he said. "You have given back much and have helped me more than I can ever say. And look," he pointed at the painting, "you have done even more there that will only increase my reputation."

She looked over at the painting, staring, and took a deep breath. "Carlo. Would you do something for me, then?"

"Of course."

"No, no. Listen now, before you consent. I have given this some thought. Would you consider putting another name to this painting, alongside of your own?"

"Another name? But whose name would I put? I dare not put yours. You aren't my family, apprenticed in my workshop. I don't think Venetian society, conservative as they are, would approve of a woman painting without benefit of that."

"No, not my own name, but perhaps a man's name?"

"A man's name. You would put another man's name to this painting?"

"No, no. I would invent a name, make it my own. Then I could paint under that name as your apprentice."

Crivelli's brown darkened. "You would masquerade as a man when the paintings are commissioned? When they are displayed? When the person comes to collect the finished piece?"

She paled. "Not at all. Perhaps you could act for me." She hadn't thought of those elements beyond the idea that she could invent an identity and sign the painting in that manner. Would she dare to masquerade as a painter, a journeyman painter newly emerged from Crivelli's workshop? It was an idea.

"Ah, Maria, you mustn't think I don't want to help you. But you can see it is impossible. At least for now. Give me time. I might be able to think of a way to do something of what you wish." He glanced at Joanie and kissed Alys lightly on her forehead.

❧

Alys stood in her room in front of Alessandra in her dressing gown and chemise, her hair half dressed for the night to come. Alessandra put a gloved hand to her face and caressed it. She was in a good mood but it did nothing to comfort Alys and despite the warmth of the fire in the brazier, she could feel a chill down her back.

"The game is in play and the stakes are raised," said Alessandra.

"What do you mean?" asked Alys. She could hear Joanie bustling behind her.

"Only that an interest was expressed. A significant interest." There was an arch tone in Alessandra's voice.

Alys's breath caught. "A significant interest? What, in me?"

"Of course. What else could it be, after all my work, my investment."

"Someone beside Signor Fabriano?"

"Oh, yes," Alessandra said. "Someone infinitely better."

"But who? Signor Fabriano is very important."

Suddenly Alys wanted no one but Cosimo to be her patron. He was a known quantity. She could handle him, and handle the idea of him coming to her night after night. Or setting her up in a household if she couldn't compile sufficient funds to escape in time.

"Perhaps I shouldn't tell you now. Perhaps I should wait until it is more definite."

"No, please, I would prefer to know," she said, thinking quickly. "I could perhaps win him over if I knew. Attend a few parties at which he might be present."

"Yes, there is that." Alessandra thought a moment. "It is the Doge's nephew."

"The Doge's nephew?" Alys found herself gaping.

"You shouldn't underestimate your talents, my dear. Yes, the Doge's nephew has expressed an interest. He sent a note around today asking for particulars on your plans for entertaining the next several evenings."

"What did you reply?"

"Naturally I said that you were at his disposal should he wish a private entertainment, but that you were to attend a party tomorrow night at Luigi Bembo's."

Alys blinked. "And has there been further word? Am I to go to Signor Bembo's or remain here?"

"I don't know yet," said Alessandra. Her tone was light. "But I am certain you will have him here to entertain within the week."

Alys nodded, her mind racing. The Doge's nephew was a relation of Signor Bembo's. She tried to recall him from her various appearances. Was he the tall, thin man, the one who knew Nicolo Paisano's uncle?

Alessandra lay a hand on her arm and patted it. It was the closest to anything approaching affection that Alys had ever experienced from Alessandra.

"You have brought more than I ever dreamed of, *pulcino mio*," said Alessandra "I have much to thank for Carlo Crivelli's work that day he brought you here. If Giacomo's enterprise bears the fruit he promised, between the two of you, I shall be able to retire in style."

"Giacomo's enterprise?" asked Alys. A slight faintness took hold of her.

Alessandra folded her hands. "Yes," she said drawing out the word. "Africa. You remember I told you. To trade."

"Yes, I remember." She'd tried to put it from her mind and here it was again. "A dangerous venture."

"Of course there is danger, but the rewards, if one succeeds, are big."

"But the risks are far too great, surely. How many have succeeded?"

Alessandra shrugged. "Those who have are rich beyond their dreams."

Her words were firm, but Alys could hear the slight tremor in her voice. She knew Alessandra cared for Barnabas, she had heard it before in her voice and known by the words she'd spoken.

"But who is funding such an enterprise? Does Signor Bonavillagio himself have the money?"

"No, he hasn't, but he has connections and is assured that he will secure sufficient support. But enough of that. I haven't come here to talk to you about Giacomo's exploits. Though you have entertained him, it was only the once. He is none of your concern."

"Of course. I only thought you might have risked your own funds."

"Well," Alessandra began, her voice softened, "There is some of our own capital involved, but I have every confidence in Giacomo."

She ended on a firm note and with the words pronounced she turned and made her way to the door. "See that you focus on the Doge's nephew. That's where your concern is centred."

The words echoed in Alys's head. The Doge's nephew. She must discover who that was. But was it a good thing, coming to the attention of anyone connected to the Doge? Surely Alessandra must realise such a thing carried risk. Not least because the Doge's own son was recently convicted of bribery and corruption by the Council of Ten and exiled.

"Joanie, do you by chance know who the Doge's nephew is?" she asked in English.

Joanie shook her head. "I don't know for certain, sweeting, but I think she must be talking about the Dogaressa's brother's boy. Well not so much a boy. 'Nani' be his surname. I'll find out, though."

Alys put her head in her hands, suddenly bereft. What did it matter who it was? The question was, how was she to manage? What must she do? The bile rose up in her throat suddenly and she put her hand to her mouth and willed her stomach back to calm. But it wouldn't be subdued and before she knew it she was rushing for the nearest bowl, retching violently.

She felt Joanie beside her, reaching for her hair and holding it out of the way. She stared at the contents of her last meal, a disgusting mess in the bowl in front of her. Tears, a result of her retching, streamed down her face making a mockery of the carefully applied cosmetics.

"Oh, my lamb, this is the second time today," said Joanie. "You've turned over your stomach nearly every day this last fortnight. You must decide what to do."

"What do you mean?" Alys said sharply, lifting her head from the bowl.

"'ow can you pretend ignorance to me?" Joanie said in a kind voice. "The one who's stood beside you all this time. It were bound to come about."

"But I tell you I take every precaution that it doesn't."

Joanie snorted. "If it were meant to take, it takes. And don't be playing the goose with me. Aren't I the only one that sees to your rags and private things? I know they've not been wanted for two moons and more." She paused a moment. "Since Barnabas visited."

"Barnabas?" said Alys her voice still sharp. "Barnabas has nothing to do with this situation. If there is a situation."

Joanie gave another snort. "Oh there is a situation, no doubt about it. And you can't gull me. I know that you had no visitors at all when you was sick. And that your artist fella hasn't bedded you, neither. And you can't be telling me that you met someone at one of your parties."

"If I am with child it will be Signor Fabriano's, of course."

Joanie rang a peal of laughter. "That's what you might tell Alessandra, if you can make her believe it, and the signore, himself, but don't gammon me."

Alys's eyes suddenly filled with tears. She dashed them away and straightened. "The child is Signor Fabriano's. And I am sure he will be delighted to know that he will soon have a son."

"Lord, I hope so, if that's the game you're playing." said Joanie, tsking.

CHAPTER SIX
LAGOS, EARLY AUTUMN, 1446
BARNABAS

The wind whipped across my face, stinging my cheeks. The sun shone strongly on my back, warming the chill that had set in me from the time we'd landed at Lagos a few hours before. All around me I could hear the shouts of men loading and unloading kegs from various ships onto the clinker boats at their sides.

The journey had been rough enough and I'd almost been glad when Flores insisted we put into Lagos until the coming storm had passed. Landing at Sagres, something he'd not ever been done before, nor anyone else on his ship, was best done in daylight and in calm weather. Thrust out as it was into the rough seas, its rocky coast was nothing like the waters that surrounded the harbour of Lagos, according to Flores.

Beside me Hal shifted uncomfortably. We had been waiting on the dockside for a good hour while Flores unearthed some local transportation to get us to Sagres. Flores's men, meanwhile, shouted and joked with each other on the ship a few yards away.

"Look," said Hal softly in English. "'e's coming now."

I turned and caught sight of a group of men making their way down the slipway to the quay where we stood, Flores at their head. He waved a hand in greeting at the sight of us. I made an effort to clear my head. The draught of my drug mixture I'd taken not long since was still in the first rush.

The men with Flores were dressed in dark attire, well enough made, but bearing no luxury in the cloth or style. Their beards were well trimmed, but the overall effect was dour and severe.

"May I introduce you to Senhor Pedro Juan Gonsales and Senhor Jao Garcia Alvares," said Flores. "They are accompanied by their respective household men, come to welcome you formally."

Hal and I bowed while Flores made the introductions, speaking in rapid Portuguese. Gonsales replied equally rapidly. I listened, catching only a few words. When Gonsales had finished, Flores turned to me.

"He bids you welcome and asks that you accept his hospitality," Flores said in Italian. "I told them briefly that we were seeking audience with Prince Henry but he would like to hear more of the details. He asks that you come to his home where he may offer you rest and refreshment and where we can talk more comfortably."

I could feel Hal looking at me and sensed his dislike of the situation. He'd grown very cautious since Venice. Or before that. Since the night of the attack. But there was naught of that to fear in Lagos, surely.

"We would be delighted to accept his hospitality," I said, for what else could I say? Faced with such a delegation who clearly could call men to their aid, we would hardly be able to make our way to Sagres without their consent.

Flores nodded and turned to the men, giving what I presumed were the proper words of acceptance. His face was unreadable and though he'd been friendly enough on the voyage, speaking little of al Qali except once in passing, I still wasn't certain he was committed to this venture. I only hoped with Prince Henry's backing Flores would be more open in his manner.

We arrived at Gonsales's home after a short walk to the edge of the town. People peered from their shops and from their carts and astride their mules as we passed them by. I was surprised to see blackamoors among them, dressing as any Portuguese servants would, carrying burdens or walking behind their masters, their eyes downcast. We made a queer procession, I knew, with the local men soberly dressed, Flores only a little less sober in his leather jerkin and boots with silver buckles, while my own garb of blue silk velvet, drab by Venetian standards, stood out like a veritable peacock.

Gonsales's house was well appointed, given the state of the others we'd passed, with two storeys to its credit, its whitewashed plaster dazzling us all in the morning sun. We entered and were led to what I guessed was the sala, its large arched windows opened to catch the breeze off the sea. The floor was tiled plainly and the furniture severe. Gonsales gestured me to a chair of dark wood, the only piece that had any bit of carved ornamentation. A cushion was placed carefully at its back. I took the proffered seat and Gonsales and Alvares found seats on the spare chairs and Flores and Hal on a long bench.

Once refreshments had been ordered and brought by a sallow faced girl, Gonsales turned to Flores and spoke at length in Portuguese. I waited patiently until Flores translated.

"He would like to know exactly what you want with Prince Henry. He says that Prince Henry is a saintly man, not given to contemplation of mundane matters. He is a man who thinks of heavenly things and as someone who has taken particular care of the good people of Lagos, Gonsales has taken it upon himself to ensure that Prince Henry should be allowed to carry on his good works without being troubled by minor considerations."

"Is that all he said?" I asked with a touch of humour.

Flores gave a small shrug. "I paraphrased. You get the idea. But don't take these men for fools. I assure you they are not."

"I haven't," I said, adopting a sober tone. "You may tell Senhor Gonsales that we do not seek Prince Henry on any small matter, and because it's no small matter I'm not prepared to discuss it."

Flores raised a brow, but said nothing, turning to Gonsales and Alvares and speaking Portuguese. Alvares gave me a dark look and shot a phrase at Flores. Flores replied, his tone even and calm. Gonsales looked puzzled for a moment and then gave me an appraising look. He spoke a few brief sentences, his tone more submissive.

Flores looked at me and I detected a small twinkle in his eyes. I waited.

"The senhors rightly asked who you are that you can presume to know what need concern Prince Henry."

"And what did you say?" I asked, wondering if I would like what Flores had offered as an explanation.

"Why that you were a personal acquaintance of the Duke of Burgundy and had met his lady wife, niece to Prince Henry."

I opened my mouth to protest and shut it, glancing at the two senhors, looking on patiently now. How the devil had Flores known about his meeting with the Duke of Burgundy? Had Hal told him?

"Of course. A slight exaggeration, but nonetheless the truth at its core. How foolish of me not to have pointed out that connection sooner," I said.

Gonsales spoke up again, talking at length while Flores listened patiently. I picked up only a few words here and there, my ears pricking up at the words "Guinea" and "ships." I would be very much interested in any mention of the Prince's involvement in Africa, especially if it were recent.

"He says the Prince has long been interested in Africa. He has a great desire to save the people there from the unholy clutches of the Arabs, and have their souls instead for the one true God. The Mamelukes are closing in on the blackamoors now, and for many, many years other Arab peoples have tried to make them as themselves—infidels. But the heathen themselves are canny folk, led astray by their heathenish beliefs. Prince Henry has sent out many ships to the land of Guinea and beyond, to discover these very lands, make them known to all Christians, so that these people's souls can eventually come to God. It has been at great cost; many men have lost their lives. One such person was their own townsman, Gonsalo de Cintra, killed with many others by these people with poison arrows. Only last year they begged Prince Henry to send ships to avenge his death and he sent a veritable armada of thirty ships and extracted a just payment. That alone demonstrates how much involvement they have in the affairs of Prince Henry, so they say any service they can perform they will happily do so."

I took in this long explanation and sifted it with the fragments I had known about the Prince. That he'd had protracted contact with Africa had been glaringly apparent the moment I'd seen the blackamoors in Lagos. Taken, no doubt, by the Prince's men on these voyages of discovery. Given my own recent experiences, I could feel some sympathy with these people who'd shot the poison arrows and briefly mourn the no doubt exacting revenge that was taken. How many lives lost on both sides? How many blackamoors taken as slaves?

"I thank Senhor Gonsales for his helpful accounts of Prince Henry's valued work. It is not quite of that nature that we wish to discuss with the esteemed Prince, however."

A brief exchange between Flores and Gonsales followed, ending with another shrug from Flores.

"He says that there can be no other topic that would interest Prince Henry. He concerns himself only with voyages to Africa and one other interest."

"And that would be?" I asked.

Flores gave a wry smile. "Why Prester John of course."

"Of course," I said evenly. "Well you may tell them that my business falls into the latter category."

"Yes, that's wise. I think they would discover it soon enough."

I gave him a puzzled look.

"I fear it has somehow become known among my men. An overheard conversation, perhaps?" He made a small sweeping gesture.

"Perhaps," I said. "Well, no matter. Please let the senhors know." I would consider this matter of "overheard conversations" later, something, to the best of my knowledge I'd taken care to avoid.

Flores recounted my words in Portuguese and two sceptical faces turned towards me before Gonsales spoke. When he'd finished Flores turned to me, showing a rueful expression.

"He says he wishes you well, but is doubtful of your success, both with the Prince in supporting any business about Prester John, and your ability to find him. He asks if you knew that Fra Tommaso da Firenze returned from searching for Prester John only recently after being held prisoner by the Turks?"

I blinked. This was indeed news for me. But it was the mention of Turks that had me speechless and unable to answer. Was I on the wrong track all this time? Was al Qali still somewhere in the Ottoman sultanate?

A cool breeze came off the sea and lifted the light cloth that hung across a chair in the corner behind Prince Henry. Earlier he'd wiped his hands on it, bathing them carefully first in the bowl on the small table beside him. He was meticulous in that way, I'd noticed, in the few hours I'd been in his company since we'd arrived the day before.

Hal stood quietly beside me, but I could feel the tension in him. We'd had nothing to eat that morning, being summoned just after first light to appear with Flores before His Highness. I hadn't had time even to take my draught and fought the raw gnawing in my stomach. I'd briefed Flores the best I could, but hoped that I could also present my case in Latin, as Flores assured me the Prince would be well versed in the language.

Others milled around us, members of the Prince's household, a mixed group of learned men and adventurers bent on expanding their knowledge of the world or their purse, dressed as soberly as the Prince. I was thankful that my own doublet of a more flamboyant red silk was hidden for the most part by the leather jerkin, and my hose, though white, was plain enough. Though we were in a large fortress the room was airy, the windows uncovered and the tiled floors bare for the most part, except for a small carpet at the Prince's feet, I was surprised to note, in the Turkish style. In summer such a design and décor would be welcome, but the autumn morning was chilly.

The Prince showed no hint of discomfort from the coolness, in his dark doublet and dark hat draped in in an equally dark cloth. He frowned over the document in his hands. In front of me I heard a man mutter something in Italian.

I politely touched his arm and bowed. "Forgive me, signore," I said in Italian. "I couldn't help but hear you speak in my native tongue. Allow me to introduce myself. I am Giacomo Bonavillagio, lately of Venice."

The man gave him a haughty stare. "A Venetian. Milan is my home."

I bowed again, aware that Venice had long been at war with Milan. "Ah, but I said only that I was lately come from Venice. I am no Venetian."

The man's face softened a little and he gave a small bow. "Ah, yes, signore. I am Polo Bellini."

"A pleasure, signore. Have you been long here in Sagres?"

Bellini gave a small shrug. "The best part of six months."

I raised a brow. "You are part of the navigation school?"

"No, no, though I have to confess I have talked at length with those who are here about the new discoveries and examined the charts, learning much."

"Ah, you have examined the charts?" I asked politely. "You plan a voyage yourself?"

Bellini nodded. "With God's grace and the Prince's help. I hope to go to the land of Guinea. There are rich pickings there, I'm told."

I could only imagine what rich pickings he made, but smiled nonetheless. "Rich pickings?"

"Slaves. You may gather them up on the shores, I've heard. There is a growing market for them."

"You haven't done this yourself, though, in any previous voyage?"

Bellini shook his head. "No, but I hope to get some experienced crew. I have sailed to the Canaries and other places along the coast of Spain."

"And the Prince will grant you a ship and crew?"

"It is my hope. He is mad for the blackamoors. He wants to save them from conversion by the Mameluks and other of the infidel who might have them in the Prince's stead. Bring them to Christ."

"And to slavery," I muttered quietly.

"Oh you mistake it, signore. It's sanctioned by the very Order of Christ themselves led by Prince Henry, who is Governor and Master. The Moors have done it for years but I assure you that the slaves we take are treated kindly. There is nothing cruel about it. They come to know God and with it the ways of civilisation. To dress properly, to live well. Their masters treat them as one of their household. Some learn a trade. And to be sure, they sometimes attain their own freedom when it's clear they can behave well and support themselves."

"I am indeed assured by your words," I said, trying to keep the sour note from my voice. However much comfort I'd lived in, or how well it appeared I was treated, there was nothing in my experience as a captive that would ever convince me that what he and his like were doing was for the best.

"And you, signore, are you here to petition the Prince for support to go to Guinea, or are you hoping to spend time at the navigation school?"

I gave a pleasant smile. "Oh neither, signore. I am here for the purpose of enlisting the Prince's support on account of one of his other interests. Prester John."

Bellini raised his brows in alarm. "Prester John, you say? Have you not heard about Fra Tommaso da Firenze?"

"I have heard something of it." My eyes blurred for a moment and my stomach seized up under a sharp knife-edge pain. I must get the draught soon.

"But surely hearing about it you would abandon your plans."

"But he was held by the Turks, wasn't he?" asked Hal in Italian, giving me a questioning look. He'd warned me the day before that my need for the opiate draught had become too great to satisfy.

Hal's Italian was competent enough, but not so much that it stopped Bellini from giving him a disdainful frown. I made a brief introduction and Bellini gave Hal a curt nod before speaking pointedly to me.

"Si, it is true that Fra Firenze tried on three separate occasions to find Prester John, at great risk, but each time he only suffered hardship and captivity. He was forced to conclude after this last time that Prester John no longer exists, if he ever did at all. I mean, signore, only consider. Prester John wrote his letter centuries ago. He would hardly exist himself now. And though his kingdom might still be somewhere, it's unlikely to be the glorious place he'd described in the 12th century. Fra Firenze may only be a Florentine, but you cannot dispute the results."

"I don't dispute the results," I said calmly, putting a hand on my stomach. I had begun to sweat. "But what was it that made the good father believe Prester John's kingdom was in the land of the Turks?"

Bellini shrugged. "Something in the letter from Prester John? I know not, for I haven't seen the letter, nor the one the Pope sent to Prester John with his emissary, Master Phillip."

"Master Phillip?" I asked. "Was he a Frenchman?" I thought of the manuscript I had tucked away which told of an encounter with someone connected with Prester John written by one Guilluame le Franc.

"No. I don't believe so. A Venetian, I think," he said and smirked. "But they do say that Master Phillip sent letters back to the Pope during his journey to Prester John's kingdom."

"But he never reached Prester John's kingdom, did he?" asked Hal, his tone careful.

"I would think not," said Bellini coolly. "Or if he had, he never communicated it. Ask Prince Henry. He will know of course."

I nodded feeling a little excitement stir. Perhaps this Master Phillip was the person mentioned. I looked over at the Prince. He was involved in a terse conversation with a young man and tapping sharply at the document in his hand.

"Do you know what it is that's giving the Prince cause for concern at this moment?" I asked.

Bellini's face darkened. "Oh. From what I understand from my earlier questions to one of his household,

Senhor Antam Gonsalvez, it concerns Nuño Tristam. He is dear to the Prince, having been brought up in his household. Tristam sailed recently to explore beyond Cape Verde. According to Senhor Gonsalvez, Tristam and others were brutally killed by the natives somewhere beyond the Cape. You will see it's a terrible thing, signore and afflicts the Prince sorely. He will certainly not be in the humour to support my cause after such a tragedy."

I gave him a reassuring pat. "Perhaps, Signor Bellini, it will make him only the more determined."

Bellini gave a weak smile. "I only hope you're right. I have invested much just in my journey here. I would hate for all my plans to be dashed."

I nodded, wondering how this piece of news would affect my request. "Signore, you mentioned you were acquainted with Senhor Gonsalvez? Would you mind favouring us with an introduction?"

Bellini studied me for a moment and gave a wry smile. "Yes. Of course."

Beside me, Hal gave me a slight, disapproving nudge. It was clear he didn't think me fit to continue any interview. I ignored him.

"Signor Giacomo, I believe Captain Flores would like a word," said Hal.

"I have no doubt he does," I said. "But it will keep for the moment." I took out a cloth and wiped my brow. "I believe something I ate has disagreed with me, Signor Bellini. But not so much that I must forego your kind introduction."

CHAPTER SEVEN
SAGRES, EARLY AUTUMN 1446
BARNABAS

Antam Gonsalvez glanced through the document I'd handed him, nodding as he read. I'd spoken in Latin to him after Bellini had made the introduction and was relieved to find he conversed easily in the language.

I was sweating more. Under my jerkin, I knew my doublet was nearly drenched and my hair was damp across my brow. I had lost weight in the last weeks, but it felt as though I'd lost half a stone since I'd arrived here. I was glad now for the cooling breeze that came in from the sea and tried to disregard the periodic quizzing looks from Gonsalvez. Hal stood silently next to me, but his disapproval rang loud and clear. He'd collected Flores earlier and Flores now stood on my other side, ready to translate should the need arise.

Eventually Gonsalvez looked up, re-rolled the manuscript and handed it back to me.

I took it and handed it over to Hal, unwilling to handle the document for long or slip it inside my damp jerkin.

"Very interesting," said Gonsalvez.

"Interesting enough to bring to the Prince's attention?" I asked. A sharp pain filled my head and I blinked.

"Yes, perhaps."

"And could I presume upon your good graces to put it to the Prince to consider an audience for myself and my companions?"

Flores added a few words in Portuguese and I hoped it would lend strength to my pleas. Gonsalvez studied me carefully, then Hal and finally, Flores before he gave a curt nod.

"I will see what I can do, senhor. But it will not be today. Today is set aside now for mourning Nuño Tristam, a martyr to the cause of Christ."

"One more question, Senhor, if you would be so good," I said. "Would you have perchance heard of a man, a blackamoor of sorts, called Mustapha al Qali?"

"A blackamoor infidel? How is that?"

"He was born in Cairo, but I think his people come from parts further south. He is a scholar of sorts. Interested in manuscripts such as this."

Gonsalvez considered for a few moments, then shook his head. "No, I don't think so." He frowned. "Wait. Yes. Perhaps. There was a man who wrote to Prince Henry some time ago looking for some information. That might have been his name."

"How long ago?"

"I'm not certain. Several months ago, perhaps?"

"Would you know where he wrote from?" I was nearly faint with the pain, but I needed to hear the answer.

"It might have been Cairo. I can't recall exactly. The Prince might be able to remember. If he grants you an audience you can ask him."

❧

The Prince eyed me up and down, his daunting stare severe. He wore the same sober, undecorated brown doublet and hose as yesterday and this time I felt my own attire was well matched since I'd taken to heart the previous day's observations and worn only plain black. In fact, today I felt refreshed and more able to meet the severity of his gaze after a healthy draught of my opiate some hours earlier and a light meal a short while ago. Hal seemed more at ease, as did Flores. Antam Gonsalvez, stiff and formal, made the introductions in French, a tongue with which the Prince was very familiar, as it turned out.

"I offer my condolences on the very sad news," I said after bowing deeply when Gonsalvez had finished.

The Prince gave a curt nod from his chair. His face, bare of all but a dark moustache, was careworn, but his dark eyes held a compassion and sincerity that gave me cause to hope.

"I thank you for your words, Senhor Bonavillagio," he said. "My dear friend has died a martyr's death and is now in heaven."

The Prince crossed himself, as did Gonsalvez. I followed suit, the old gestures rising up automatically from years before. Beside me, Hal and Flores did likewise.

The Prince did not mince his words. "Dom Antam says that you have a manuscript I might find interesting. That it has nothing to do with Guinea, but with Prester John."

"That is so, your highness. At least it is my hope you will find something of interest in this manuscript."

The Prince narrowed his eyes. "You have heard of Fra Tommaso's tale?"

"Only lately," I said. I kept my face passive, trying to read the Prince's own view of the tale. I caught only a flicker behind the eyes, now turned grave.

"And what does this manuscript say? Who is its author?"

"It was written by one Guillaume le Franc. It tells of his journeys during and after the crusades. In it, he speaks of an encounter with someone who has been to the land of Prester John."

The Prince nodded. "And you have this manuscript with you?"

"I do, your highness. But it's written in the language of the Turks. Probably translated into that language some many hundreds of years ago."

The Prince raised a brow. "The language of the Turks you say? Yet you can read it? How is that, senhor?"

"I can read and write the Turkish language, lord, along with many other languages."

"Ah," said the Prince with a nod. "And so this document talks of Prester John in the land of the Turks. Yet Fra Tomaso has just returned and is heard to state clearly that there exists no kingdom nor any ruler called Prester John."

"Forgive me, lord, but I don't mean to imply that Prester John's kingdom is in the land of the Turks. I believe it is somewhere else. In Africa."

"Indeed?" said the Prince, his eyes darkening. "And exactly where in Africa do you believe it is? It's a large place, yet my own explorers have traversed the western coast past our newly named Cape Verde and there is no sign of this sainted kingdom."

I gave a wry smile, understanding the test. I wouldn't play my hand in entirely. "Of course there is no need to think that Prester John is in that area of Africa. There are no tales, nor written evidence to support that. But my manuscript would show that Prester John is elsewhere and now I hear there are other manuscripts that provide evidence."

"Other manuscripts?" asked the Prince carefully.

"The Pope wrote to Prester John. And the emissary wrote letters of his journey."

The Prince gave an amused smile. "You have seen these letters?"

I shook my head and gave him a rueful look. "No, I only heard of them recently. But they seem to reinforce my own conclusions based on the reading of the manuscript I speak to you about. Prester John's kingdom is in Africa."

"You have the manuscript with you?"

I reached carefully inside my doublet, withdrew the rolled manuscript wrapped in its oiled cloth and handed it to the Prince. He removed the cloth and unfurled the codex, revealing the bound edges. I'd done my best to protect the manuscript since I'd removed it from the Grand Vizier's library, but it definitely had suffered in my hands since then. There was a small water stain from my escape and other soil marks on the first few pages. Yet despite that the Turkish script was distinct. The Prince glanced over it, turning the pages carefully until eventually, he handed it back.

"Well there is no doubt you have in your possession a manuscript. But sadly I cannot vouch for the contents," said the Prince. He studied me carefully. "What is it that interests you in Prester John so much? Do you seek riches?"

I paused, collecting my thoughts. I had been prepared for this question and had thought to charm and bluff my way into the Prince's good graces and secure his support in that manner. But faced with him and his serious demeanour, I'd found the usual charms I'd employed seemed inappropriate. I would try for something else. Something close to the truth. Hal was visibly tense beside me, clearly nervous of what might transpire. Flores, though seemingly a passive bystander, watched us both carefully, I knew, missing nothing.

"I had a teacher, your grace. And it was he who had a deep interest in Prester John and his kingdom. He was an unusual man, secretive, yet full of knowledge that he imparted to me. He taught me languages and culture of other lands. Took me on his travels, seeking manuscripts and the knowledge they contained. When last we journeyed together we went among the Ottomans in the land of the Turks. And there he disappeared. And now I seek him, knowing only that he desired above all to find Prester John's kingdom. I think that if I can find the kingdom I will find this man."

"And it is through this man that you are able to understand the meaning of this codex?" asked the Prince.

I nodded. He nodded and stroked his moustache. "And what is the name of this man?"

"Mustapha al Qali."

The Prince registered surprise. "A Moor? No, wait. I seem to recall someone of that name."

A flicker of hope stirred in me. "Perhaps he inquired about Prester John in a letter to your grace?"

The Prince considered for a few moments. "Yes, perhaps. Indeed I believe so. It was some months back. I'm afraid I could offer him no more information than what he already knew. It was of course before Fra

Tommaso had returned." He gave me a wry smile. "But then as you and I believe, Prester John is to be found in Africa. And of course your esteemed friend believes that as well."

It wasn't until the Prince expressed his own preference for the location of Prester John's kingdom and confirmed al Qali's belief that I realised how much tension I'd felt at the thought that I could be so terribly wrong.

"Was there any indication where al Qali sent the letter from?" I asked carefully.

The Prince shook his head. "I don't recall. But I will have someone check. And where is it in Africa that you think Prester John's kingdom to be?"

"Somewhere near a great desert. I believe if you follow one of the salt trade routes you will come to the kingdom."

"But which salt route? There is the one that leaves from Oran, near my own port of Ceuta. Or do you mean the one further east?"

"Oran I believe. But I was hoping that the letter from Senhor al Qali would help confirm that choice."

The Prince looked at me sceptically. "I'm afraid I must contradict you myself, young man. Prester John's kingdom must assuredly be further east. In the land of the Ethiopes."

I took a deep breath, trying to take in this statement. "Would it be impertinent to ask how your grace has come to that conclusion?"

"Not at all. You mentioned Master Phillip's letters. Well I have seen copies of fragments of those letters that describe part of his journey. And there is little doubt that he spent time in Cairo and from there journeyed south."

Cairo. It made sense with al Qali's background that the kingdom might be south of there. There was a salt route there as well, though not as well travelled as the one from Oran.

"I can't doubt your reasoning, your grace. I am in your debt for enlightening me on this matter."

The Prince gave a satisfied nod. "In the meantime, can I assume you require my support in your enterprise?"

I bowed low. "If your grace wills it. With such support, I would endeavour to find Prester John's kingdom. But I know such enterprises don't fund themselves, so I would offer my knowledge and experience as a merchant and establish a trade caravan to assist me in the initial stages of the journey."

The Prince raised his brows. "But such an approach is fraught with danger. What goods would you trade? What route would you take that can guarantee a market as well as your safety?"

"I would attempt to take with me spices, salt and any other items that might be deemed worthy. There I would attempt to travel on the salt route, joining a caravan, or forming my own."

"It is a noble idea, but I have some reservations about your safety. The land doesn't treat kindly to those from Christendom."

I gave him a direct look. "I understand your concerns, but may I remind your grace that I have learned many languages, including Arabic, and I am well versed in their ways, mannerisms and dress?"

The Prince narrowed his eyes. "But once you have passed out of the land where the Mameluks now dominate, such knowledge will be of no advantage. And to employ those mannerisms and dress may bring you only grief."

I nodded gravely. "I understand the risks, your grace. More than you know."

The Prince waved his hand. "That being the case, I can only give you my blessing as well as my support. I will have the matter arranged and send word to you when all is ready. In the meantime, you are welcome here to converse and study as befits the scholar you clearly appear to be."

~

I paced up and down the small room that served as a chamber for me as well as Hal. The sweat poured down my face and a raw pain gripped my stomach. I reached for the bowl that rested on the table and retched for the third time that morning.

"You 'ave to take some," said Hal in English quietly. "Ye're in no shape to go near the Prince."

I shook my head and wiped the sweat from my brow. "I must break myself of this before the journey."

"It's no good, you can't cut it off like this. You 'ave to wean yourself. Slowly, like a bairn from 'is mother's teat."

I bit my lip. The thought of the opiate draught was irresistible, dragging at my mind, my lips. I fought it hard until another severe cramp took hold of me, nearly blinding me with its force. In the fortnight since I'd arrived at Sagres, I'd tried countless times to cut myself off from the draught, instructing Hal to discard it and then railing at him when he wouldn't give it to me, and in the end forcing him to relent. I would try his suggestion, one that he'd made before and I had discarded as the weak-willed approach to the iron grip the opiate had on me.

"Make up the draught, if you will, Hal. Tomorrow I will do as you suggest."

Hal nodded and without a word took a key to one of the small chests and withdrew the ingredients, mixing it carefully with a cup of wine. I took it eagerly from his hand and gulped down the mixture until the cup was empty. I placed it on the table and waited for the wonderful rush, the euphoria that often greeted me. I pushed aside the troubling thoughts and breathed a sigh of relief when the cramps eased.

A knock sounded. Hal made his way to the door and opened it. A messenger held a folded parchment, the royal ribbon and seal clearly evident. He bowed and gave it to Hal, and without a word, retreated. Hal closed the door and handed me the missive. I stared at it, noting the Prince's script spelling out my name. Or rather the name of the adventurer merchant, one Giacomo Bonavillagio. The man who would have his revenge on Mustapha al Qali. The innocent, Barnabas of Eye by Westminster, ward of Canon Thomas Southwell, was gone, buried in the dark recesses of his mind.

Carefully I opened the document and read the words I'd been waiting for. The words that would allow me to take ship first to Cueta and then on to Cairo and acquire goods for trade along the way——and travel forth from there to the land of Prester John.

CHAPTER EIGHT
CAIRO, EGYPT, LATE AUTUMN 1446
BARNABAS

Around me I could hear the call of alms-beseechers, storytellers and tradesman shouting their desires, services and wares to the crowds of people who pushed their way through the stalls of the various markets. People shouted back, bargaining or demanding. The stalls were filled with everything from exotic fruits to marquetry of the finest quality, silks and inkstands. Tall towers rose above in the distance, the perch from whence the religious men issued their call to prayers in the many mosques that filled Cairo. There was colour everywhere in the goods and the dress. Vibrant purples, golds and greens of various cloths, fruits and vegetables and other goods piled into stalls and on blankets. Despite the beauty of the colour, the stench of the camels, mules and horses threatened to overpower the aromatic scents of spices and perfumes on sale.

I couldn't help but appreciate the splendour and variety Cairo presented, but was at the same time all too conscious of the darker side of the markets, streets and buildings. A side that had men strapped to donkeys, awaiting auction at the market. I noted that many of them were Christians. It was a cautionary sight and one that I would heed well. I was glad I had adopted Arab garb upon my arrival and seen fit to insist the others do the same. There were only the three of us; more would be too risky, I felt. Hal had been amenable to the change in clothes, but Flores was none too happy.

I spied a group of men, darker skinned than others walking around, gathered just outside the market, fitting out their camels and mules for travel. Tuaregs, or "Mulatthamin", I'd heard them called. "The veiled ones". They were men of the desert. The men who dominated the trade between Cairo and into the heart of Africa. I eyed my mule doubtfully. It had been hired the day before with the intention it would carry me south out of Cairo. The mules Flores and Hal rode seemed no better. I could only hope our companion, one Ezekiel who professed to be a Christian, knew what he was about, but I had my doubts. Though Antam Gonsalvez had engaged his services a few days earlier, before Gonsalvez had embarked on his return journey to Sagres, I found it difficult to trust the man who claimed to know the way through the desert to the land of the Ethiopes. His own mule was no less mangy and unruly than ours, and his hooded dark eyes failed to make contact. He spoke only a halting Arabic and even less Greek. He was a Coptic Christian and his main language was Nubian. He also spoke Amaharic, one of the languages of the Ethiopes. Both languages I knew nothing about, but was determined to master to some degree before many days.

Still, he made his way forward, towards the group of Tuareg traders. I realised now that these must be the men

Ezekiel had promised he would secure us leave to travel with across the desert. They were tall and slim, wearing swirling white robes and turbans of indigo with trailing lengths draped across mouths, noses and around their necks, so that only their eyes showed.

I held back, signalling the others to do the same. Sweating under the glare of the late morning sun, I observed the exchange between Ezekiel and the Tuaregs. It was animated and none too friendly. Periodically, Ezekiel bowed politely and gestured to their animals and the burdens they carried. After some time, Ezekiel returned to us.

"A thousand apologies, lord," he said in Arabic. "They say they require more money because the risk is so great."

"Why is the risk too great?" I asked suspiciously. Was this man planning to ask for a larger fee for them, only to pocket the extra money for himself?

"They say that though you dress as men of this place, they know you for foreigners, as will anyone who gets close to you."

"And by what particular manner do we give ourselves away?"

Ezekiel's eyes flickered to the ground. "They say it is by your smell they can tell."

I suppressed a momentary urge to laugh. "And were we to bathe I presume the price would remain the same?"

Ezekiel shifted uncomfortably. "I'm not sure it's a matter of bathing, lord," he muttered.

I sighed. "Exactly how much more do they demand?"

"They say they will need to inspect your trade goods and retain half of your profits should you travel with them."

It was an outrageous demand, but I was at their mercy. They knew it and I knew it. "They may inspect our goods, which I am confident they will find more than satisfactory, but I will only agree to one-third of the profit."

Ezekiel bowed and trotted off to them, his loose-limbed stride giving him a kind of horse like gait. He spent some time conferring with them, while one or two Tuareg cast dark looks at us. Eventually Ezekiel took his leave of them and came over to us.

"They will concede to your request if you will give them half the profit of three different goods that you have. The rest you may retain two-thirds profit, as you wished."

I gave a tight smile. Bargaining was an art form and passion among the Arabs, I knew, but I wasn't certain it was the same for these people and I didn't feel I could trust Ezekiel enough to ask him. In fact, not so long ago, I would have revelled in the negotiation, driven by the sheer pleasure of the interaction. I had in Bruges and certainly again in Venice. But now, the cramping stomach pain and throbbing headache that had seized me all too often in these past weeks threatened to overtake me. My attempts to cut back on my opiate draught were proving far more difficult than even I had imagined. And lately I had given in far too early, ignoring Hal's frowns and mumbled warnings. I stared at Ezekiel, my thoughts dwelling on the sweetness of a good strong draught of the opiate. Suddenly I had no patience with these Tuareg.

"Agreed," I said, finally. "We will bring the goods tomorrow and they may make their selection then."

Ezekiel bowed and trotted back across, but this time I followed him. I wanted this bargaining over. He spoke what I hope were the appropriate words haltingly to the tallest man, whose unusual golden eyes watched me all the while. After Ezekiel had finished this same man answered him, his voice deep and confident. Ezekiel sighed perceptibly and nodding, turned to me.

"They will come with us now and inspect the goods at your quarters to make their selection."

It was a test, I understood that. I wasn't a fool to be told once they arrived at my quarters that none of my goods would be sufficient enough for trade and they wouldn't allow us to accompany them as they traversed across the desert to the Ethiope lands. And then later, by stealth at night, they would return and steal our goods.

I shook my head. "No," I said firmly and gave the tall man a direct look. "We will bring the goods here first thing tomorrow."

The tall man regarded me curiously, his eyes betraying nothing. After a moment he nodded his head. He spoke rapidly to Ezekiel, waved me away and turned to his companions. They all laughed. A moment later they were back at their work, loading and securing chests, sacks and other items to the animals, my presence forgotten.

"Well?" I said to Ezekiel.

"He says he will meet you here tomorrow with your goods."

I raised a brow to him. "And? What was the remark that made them laugh?"

"I-I don't know, lord. I didn't catch it."

I gave him a doubtful look, but wasted no more time on it. There were more important things that needed attention.

⚬⚬⚬

"I don't like it," said Flores in Italian. He threw his head cloth on the table and scratched his beard. Our quarters consisted of two rooms, in a cramped alley in a less aromatic section of Cairo, bare of furniture except for a few items and the sacks, chests and amphora containing our trade goods. "We'll be at the mercy of those men. We can't even see their faces."

"Ezekiel insists they are trustworthy," I said calmly.

"Are you certain we can trust Ezekiel?" said Hal.

I gave a humourless smile. "Now that's a good question."

"You're mad!" said Flores. "We are going blind into danger we know little about, and have even less ability to defend ourselves against. I don't even have my sword. Do you think our daggers are any match for thieves and marauders on this journey? And if these men, these Tuareg, decide to turn on us and steal our goods there's little we can do to stop them."

I forced a smile. "And that's why I intend to have half the payment for escorting us remain here, to be given to them only when they return us safely to Cairo."

Flores gave a disgusted noise. "Pah, as if that would make little difference to thieves."

"Oh, I think it is sufficient enough to make a difference. Prince Henry supplied enough ducats for more than trade goods."

Flores gave me a curious look but made no reply.

"I still don't know that you can trust Ezekiel. Have you made the same arrangement with him?" asked Hal.

"Ezekiel is a Christian, Hal."

Flores snorted. "As if that made a difference."

"Ezekiel is a devoted Christian," I said in a prim voice. "And I might have mentioned that I have a connection to a person who possesses a most holy manuscript written by a most holy man of Nubia, and if he is able to assist us, I will be able to secure from that person that very manuscript."

"You didn't Jacko," said Hal, laughing. "And he believed you?"

"Oh but he did."

"He will be in for a sore disappointment," said Flores.

"On the contrary, he'll be amply rewarded," I said.

"But there is no manuscript, is there?" asked Hal.

I smiled enigmatically. "You forget where I spent a good number of months."

Hal's eyes widened. "You would never get a manuscript from Halil Pasha's library, Jacko. Flores is right. You're mad."

I sighed and shook my head. "It's the knowledge of the manuscript's existence that is important here. Nothing more. Later, if everything comes to fruition, who knows what I might be able to arrange? In the meantime, we must prepare the goods for the Tuareg's inspection."

Flores frowned. "And give them half the profit of the best goods. That will hardly make it worth my while. The gold, and profit from the salt and the pepper. That's the only reason I'm here, as you well know. It matters not to me whether you find al Qali."

I was finished with the conversation. I wanted only to slip away and prepare my draught, out of sight of Hal. "Don't worry, Flores. I will see that you get a more than an ample share of the gold and profit from the salt and pepper."

I pointed to the sacks of pepper which made up a significant portion of the goods. Pepper was highly valued and I had no doubt that the Tuareg would appropriate all of it if I let them.

"Put some of the pepper sacks aside in the back room. I have an idea."

"What?" said Hal.

"I'll tell you when I'm certain it will work. In the meantime I must go out. I shan't be long."

Hal nodded, already lifting some the sacks of pepper. Flores shook his head and grumbled to himself in Portuguese. I pulled my white robe around me and made my way out of the door.

～

The man's hands were grubby, the nails chipped and grime encrusted. The small stoppered amphora he passed to me contained the opiate syrup. It seemed inadequate for the projected trip, but it was all I could secure given the circumstances. I had combed the small streets looking for someone who could supply me with the opiate, asking questions as discreetly as I could and this is where I'd ended up, conscious that the sun was sinking towards sunset. The transaction completed, I was gone from the man, the amphora hidden safely in the sack slung across my shoulder.

When enough streets had been put between me and the dark narrow shop where I'd purchased the syrup, I found an archway and ducked in. There I withdrew the amphora, removed the stopper and held the amphora to my mouth, my hand shaking. I took a small sip. It slid down my throat and I nearly cried as it made its silky path into my body. I sank down to a squat, waiting for the blissful relief. I closed my eyes, feeling my limbs relax, my gut slowly release.

A while later I became aware of a familiar sound. A sound that set my teeth on edge and recalled me to a time and place that held little else but pain. And a person that had brought me to this pass, to this lowering addiction. Halil Pasha, the sultan's right-hand man. Yet I couldn't help but respond to this sound, this call to prayer that for five times a day every day for months on end, I was forced to obey. Compelled to make my ablutions and kneel in prayer to the god of the Ottaman Turks.

I forced myself to stand up, to block my ears. It wasn't Halil Pasha that was to blame. It was Mustapha al Qali. He who had sold me to Halil Pasha, to be used and abused in manner no man should bear. And for that, al Qali would pay.

〰

The goods were strapped securely to the mules. As I had expected, the Tuareg had selected the pepper for their higher percentage cut and already the mules carrying those sacks were included in the so-called protection of their caravan. I turned to my mule, ready to mount. Ezekiel tugged on my arm.

"Lord, their leader asks that you travel at the back, so that you won't be as visible to those who approach us from the front."

I smiled grimly. "And what of those who approach us from the side? Or for that matter, the rear?"

Ezekiel shrugged. "I know not. I know only what they asked me to tell you."

I nodded. There was not much else to say. I had no experience of travelling in a caravan across the desert and only knew what my common sense and instinct told me. I eyed the leader, trying to discern his intent, but as usual there little to be read from his eyes.

Beside me, Flores only grunted. He walked over to his mule, mounted and gave it a good slap to move it forward. It stood there stubbornly. My mule was of opposite temperament at the moment and moved restlessly and I was hard pressed to keep it still long enough to mount. Hal moved over and steadied my mule and finally I was able to climb up on its back.

I turned to Ezekiel who was sitting tentatively on his mule. "What is the name of the Tuareg leader, do you know?"

"Yes, lord. He calls himself Mousa ag Amastan."

I nodded. I slapped my mule. "Now Mousa," I addressed the mule in English. "You will learn to behave yourself."

Hal snorted and coughed, growing red trying to control his laughter. I grinned over at him. "Better mount up, Hal. We don't want to be left behind."

A few moments later we were all astride our respective animals, the Tuaregs on their camels and their laden mules trailing behind them. I led our own small party, Hal beside me the mules trailing behind me while Flores brought up the rear, his eyes already scanning the distance, looking for threats.

CHAPTER NINE
VENICE, CHRISTMAS SEASON, 1446
ALYS

Alys climbed the steps, stumbling slightly in the dim torchlight. It was her limp, she knew. A hand clutched her arm, steadying her. She turned and smiled at the charming face beside her. His expression was all concern, but his eyes held a hint of something else. Wariness?

"Thank you, Antonio," said Alys.

His heavy perfume was so strong it overpowered the odour that wafted from the canal below. He was tall, dark and slender, his long fingers adorned with rings, his hair curling at his shoulders. All these elements might convey a sense of foppishness, but that would be to mistake the man. Antonio was no one's fool. Beneath the air of elegance and ornamentation was a hint of menace.

Alys took a deep breath, trying to fill her lungs with air so the urge to gag would recede. The two of them were on their way to an exclusive house party hosted by one of Antonio's friends in honour of the Christmas season.

Though everyone was well acquainted, they had all been required to wear masks and dress in a manner that would disguise them to some degree. It had been the mask and the dimness that had caused her difficulty with the steps, she told herself, and not that she was already a little breathless from the climb.

The chill air suddenly penetrated the thick cloak she wore over the top of her gown. The gown had been Antonio's choice, made and paid for at his behest and to Alessandra's grudging approval and praise at his eye for design. It had only shocked and horrified Alys, she who had thought she could no longer be shocked, for it revealed more than it concealed.

She was Venus, her hair tumbling in loose curls from her head along her shoulders and down her back, a tiny rope of pearls woven throughout. If only her hair concealed more than her shoulders and back and would drape all across her body so that the gown, nothing more than some few yards of transparent silk of the palest cream held together with some interestingly placed gold clasps and trailing ribbons, would be fully concealed. She had insisted on a shawl, but Antonio would have none of it. The cloak, however, wasn't to be refused in this winter cold.

Antonio bent over and kissed her neck. "You will be the most beautiful woman there tonight, I don't doubt." He tugged on her arm. "But come, *bella mia*, they must see you first, to make it so."

She took a deep breath and continued her climb, Antonio firmly guiding her with his hand. Once inside the large *sala* in which they were to be entertained, she nearly gagged once more at the oppressive heat and the smells of heavy perfumes mixing with more earthy body odours.

There seemed no excuse to keep her cloak on in such warmth, but she would try as long as she could.

Though there were many braziers placed around the room to create the high temperatures, there were only a few clusters of candelabras to provide light, which cast everyone in a half glow. She was grateful for the half-light, if only that it made her dress, or lack of it, less noticeable. At least she hoped so. But she was no novice, and knew the dimness was to facilitate a night of sensual bodily pleasures.

She glanced around to see if she recognised anyone. They were all giving a nodding pretence to the masquerade, duly wearing face coverings, but there was little to mistake the identities of the men and women at this gathering. The women, like her, were courtesans, chosen from the best and most expensive, accustomed to only the finest and wealthiest of patrons, the men who accompanied them. Alessandra would be pleased. She had made it to the highest of ranks, it seemed. Mostly due to Antonio Nani, the Doge's nephew.

"I'll take your cloak now, *cara mia*," said Antonio, tugging the clasp at her throat.

For a moment she thought to resist, but gave in. It would do no good to make a scene, she knew better than that. There was a dark glint in Antonio's handsome eyes and she had no inclination to test him. No, she must bide her time until her slow accumulation of money was sufficient. But she would need to be careful. That much was clear.

In the month since Alessandra had accepted his patronage, Alys had seen Antonio frequently, sometimes three times a week, balancing out the days when Cosimo came to her. He'd taken her to many house parties, where she would sing and recite poetry, or even play a hand or two at cards. But that was mostly in the beginning. Lately, the parties he had taken her to were more exclusive, with little twists, as he called them, to spice up the evening.

These twists had taken the form of playing cards for favours, usually forfeited amid laughter as one lost a ribbon or shoe, or something more. Another twist was blindfolding each partner and have them guess who it was by their touch. Fortunately, she was adept enough that she had bared little more than her foot and the blindfold game had been played only once, with little indignity on her part. She'd been the one to seek out someone and had guessed them easily from their perfume.

Tonight, there was something in the air and an extra edge to the laughter, as if everyone was expecting more than what was currently in evidence. The costumes were daring enough. Several women wore short tunics and had anything ranging from ivy or flowers to leaves and twigs trailing in their loosened hair. Wood nymphs perhaps? Several of the men wore tunics suggesting mythic gods, with laurels adorning their heads. She heard one man declaring himself as Bacchus and she gave an inward smile as she regarded his ample frame, over which a capacious robe was draped.

She turned and regarded Antonio who had removed his cloak to reveal his own costume. A gold edged tunic stretched across his muscular frame and fell to just above his knees. Like her, he wore no hose, and his feet were encased in short leather boots. The effect might have been comical on someone else, but not on Antonio.

"Behold," he said. "I am Mars, to your Venus."

"No one could doubt it," said Alys. She forced a bright smile.

He put his arm around her and led her forward. The laughter and chattering enveloped her and soon men and their companions were drawing both of them into their circle. Eventually, she forgot for a time how bare she felt in the heat of the room and the dress of all the other guests, who, it seemed, portrayed one Roman deity or another. It was as if they had all been assigned their roles, for there was no overlapping.

At one point a lute was pressed into her hands and she sat and played a piece or two for them, grateful that while all eyes were focused on her, she had her hair and her lute to cover her. There was much praise for her skill and she offered to play more, if only to keep the comfort of the lute in front of her.

It was when the night seemed to be at its close that Antonio clapped his hands and called for attention. "This has indeed been an evening for the gods."

There were noises of agreement until Antonio held up his hand. "And where would our gods be without their lovely goddesses?"

He smiled at Alys and she returned it, grateful that the evening was coming to an end. He reached for her hand and led her forward to a little platform on which a large plate had been placed. He urged her up on it and turned to face the group, his hand stretched toward Alys.

"I offer you, Venus, the goddess of love. She looks benignly down upon you all and asks that you make offerings to her, so that she will bestow upon you a night filled with sensual pleasure."

Alys looked at Antonio blankly amid cries of "brava" and "bellissima". Antonio pulled a ring from his finger and placed it on the plate.

"My own offering," he said loudly. "I wish for the most pleasurable night possible."

"My offering is here!" said Felipo, one of Antonio's close friends.

He moved forward with purpose, his stocky legs encased in strapped sandals. He pulled a gold earring from his ear and placed it on the plate, grinning broadly at Antonio, then stepped back and took up the hand of his companion, a dark-haired beauty Alys vaguely recalled was named Constanza. Her deep cleavage was barely contained in the bodice of her gown of sheer green silk, the rouged nipples showing clearly through the fabric.

One by one the gathered men, some twelve in all it seemed, presented gifts on the plate before Alys, while she grew more and more tense, wondering what the real purpose of this show was. When all had completed their offerings Antonio moved forward, a large silver chased cup in his hand. He offered it to Alys.

"Drink of this cup, my goddess Venus, and then share it with your gathered worshippers so that all may be assured of the promised pleasure for the night."

Alys looked at Antonio quizzically, but she could read nothing there. He pressed the cup insistently to her and she took it, raised it to her lips, sipping cautiously. The wine it contained was sweet and heavy. It slipped down her throat to her stomach, calming it. A glow began to spread outwards, travelling into her limbs and her head, relaxing her all at once. She smiled at Antonio.

He led her down from the small dais, and took her to each person one by one to offer the cup to them to drink. At the back of her mind she thought for a moment that what she was doing was near to blasphemy, but the idea fled.

When everyone had drunk from the large cup, Antonio took it from her and set it aside. He put his arm around her, caressing her shoulder. She could feel the heat of his touch, setting her alight. As if sensing it, he leaned down, lifted her hair and kissed her neck, slowly, sensuously.

Another man, was it Felipo? came up to her and kissed the other side of her neck, lifted her hand and putting her finger into his mouth. She tried to pull away, but Antonio shushed her. "It is the night for love," he whispered in her ear.

Antonio gripped her arm and led her to one of the large cushioned couches that lined the room, Felipo following. Dully, she was aware of other couples in twos and threes finding places around the room. Antonio laid her back on the couch, his body pressed against hers, Felipo lay beside them. Her head began to spin. The wine and her delicate stomach rebelled in one violent instant and she thrust herself upward, pushing Antonio away and retched.

The retching lasted for a very short while, but it was enough to leave her breathless and sweating.

"My apologies, dear Antonio," said Alys. "I fear that the heat and everything quite overcame me."

"Something has made you unwell," he said darkly.

"I am so sorry," Alys said.

Antonio moved away from her, sitting upright. Felipo stood, swaying uncertainly. Antonio waved him away and he moved off towards another couch.

Alys ran a hand across her sweating brow. "Perhaps it's best if I leave. I can go alone, so that you may find someone else here with which to take your pleasure. I'm certain anyone here would be anxious to accommodate you. I should hate for your night to be spoiled."

Antonio frowned. "Nonsense. You will have an escort."

It wasn't long before she was bundled away in her cloak, accompanied by one of the household servants. It wasn't a good omen of the humour of her recent patron, but Alys could only hope that it would all be forgotten in the days to come. She sat in the gondola on her journey home, the dawn light breaking in the distance, and breathed deeply, trying to clear her mind. The wine had been unusually strong and she could still feel the heat of desire that had aroused so quickly in her. A desire that made the thought of consummating her relationship with Antonio even appealing. Such desire had escaped her in the past weeks since she'd met him. Her body couldn't respond to his touch. And privately she could only be glad. She found the whole idea of being his paramour, or anyone else's for that matter, increasingly repugnant. She was grateful too, that in such a frame of mind, Cosimo still had not insisted on anything else but stroking her and kissing her on the days he called.

No, it was clear that Antonio's idea of 'little twists' were increasingly not to her liking. Tonight had been one step further and particularly unappealing in the abstract, though Alessandra, she suspected, would have laughed at her prudishness. A threesome, amid many other threesomes, she would have said, could only add spice to the coupling. Alys tasted the faint traces of bile that still lingered in her mouth. Prudish she might be, but at least her body saved her from going against her own will. She stroked her stomach, aware of increase in the size of her belly and the growing fullness of her breasts. Somehow she must find a way out of this and protect herself and the child. If not for herself then for the memory of Barnabas. The old Barnabas, the one she had loved and who had loved her.

∾

Alys woke suddenly to someone shaking her shoulder. She focused slowly, a hand gripping her arm, dragging her out of bed.

"Get up!" shouted Alessandra.

"What? What is it?" Alys said, her brain fogged with sleep and the drink of the night before.

Alessandra dragged her to the window and drew back the heavy curtains, Bitty yapping loudly at her heels at the disturbance. "Stand there, in the light."

Alys shushed the dog and did as she was told, aware that she still had her costume on from the night before. She vaguely remembered telling Joanie to leave it, she was too tired to do anything more than crawl into bed.

"Take off that gown," Alessandra said firmly.

Alys removed it, aware of the cool air around her. She crossed her arms against her chest, shivering.

"Take your arms down. You know you can hide nothing from me."

Alys released her arms, aware of Alessandra's intense scrutiny. Alessandra pinched Alys's nipples and Alys gave a tiny yelp. Bitty started to yap again, alarmed at his mistress's distress. She shushed him.

"Tender and sore. As I thought. The colour, too." Alessandra raised her eyes to Alys and slapped her hard across the face. "What have I taught you? And you dare to keep it secret?"

Alys stared at her, trying to keep her face expressionless. She leaned down and lifted the dog into her arms, calming him with a few strokes.

"I knew it. You thought yesterday to keep it from me when you placed your cloak so quickly on your shoulders, but I saw you standing there in the candlelight in that filmy tunic, plain as day. 'It couldn't be', I said to myself.

'She knows better than to allow herself to fall pregnant. And she would have told me'."

Alessandra slapped Alys again and Alys flinched at the impact. "Now, answer me now, how far gone are you?"

Alys took a deep breath. "Just over three months, I think," she whispered.

Alessandra snorted. "Three months? I don't believe it. Four maybe, curse you."

Alys shrugged. "Four then."

Alessandra slapped her again, this time harder. Alys's cheek stung.

"You stupid girl. You should have told me sooner. It is too dangerous to get rid of it now, don't you realise that?" Alessandra stamped her foot. "You dare to throw away all that I've given you and destroy my plans? I should throw you out on the street like the silly slut you are."

"I don't see what you are so upset about. Signor Fabriano is pleased to know that he is to be a father."

Alessandra, her hand raised for another slap, lowered her arm. "What do you mean? Are you saying that you've told Fabriano already? Before you consulted with me?"

"I am sorry, Alessandra. I thought dear Cosimo would be so pleased, as he has indicated to me in the past that he would be nothing but joyous if I should be so fortunate as to bear him a child."

"Really," said Alessandra, her tone disbelieving. "And you are sure it is his child?"

"Of course, I'm sure. It could be no one else's," Alys said in a firm tone.

"Well it certainly isn't Antonio Nani's child, more's the pity." said Alessandra her voice tight. She turned from Alys and began to pace a little. "You have gone against my will. But I won't let this get the better of me." She stopped and turned to Alys. "This may be put to right, but this doesn't excuse the fact that you haven't consulted me first, and most especially, that you are pregnant."

Alessandra left the room and Alys remained standing clutching her belly. She felt a slight flutter there and she stilled, trying to fathom its meaning. Another flutter. Was it a sign from the babe about what she must do? Carlo or Cosimo? But hadn't she sealed her fate already, by her delay in deciding? She must talk to Cosimo soon. Before Alessandra had a chance to have a word with him.

CHAPTER TEN
VENICE, WINTER 1446/1447
ALYS

Alys knelt on the bench, and bent her head for a brief prayer. That completed, she glanced around carefully. The veil that covered her head obscured her identity from others, but it also restricted her sight.

"Is there any sign of him?" Alys whispered to Joanie in English.

"No, not yet." Joanie shifted position to get a better view of the pews to the left of her.

The church of St Simeon Profeta was a fair-sized stone building just off the Grand Canal and Rio Marin. It was far enough away from Alessandra's that she shouldn't be recognised. There were only a few other people in this parish church, mostly black clad and heavily veiled wives of merchants, who had no private chapel at home, their duenna or servant accompanying them. In one or two cases, daughters of indeterminate age were present as well. There was only one man evident at the moment, a small thin fellow who seemed to practise a trade, judging by his plain dress.

Was she right to send him here? She thought it sufficiently apart from knowledgeable and prying eyes. Everyone must know that they consorted in some manner, but she didn't think he would want any blatant display of their relationship, to throw it the face of the whole world.

Alys sighed and sat back in her pew, resigning herself to a wait. She glanced up at the painting that hung in the chancel, over the altar. It was an image of Mary sitting on a throne, holding Jesus, his torso massive compared to the size of his tiny head and even tinier arms. Mary was no better, though instead of a massive torso she had a massive head and thin hands that seemed incapable of bearing the weight of Jesus' heavy body. Gold leaf surrounded the image setting off Mary, her throne and the men who stood below her in adoration, virtual dwarves to the two images above them.

She stared at the image, frowning at the style and noting how different it was to the one that Carlo had guided her towards. His observational skill was reflected in his accurate depiction of the human body and one in which he took some pride. Such technical ability she'd understood now was something to value. She felt a strong pang of tenderness towards him and blinked back the sudden tears that filled her eyes.

"He's here," Joanie whispered.

Alys turned her head slightly and saw Cosimo take a seat in a pew across the aisle opposite her, after a crossing himself and bowing briefly. He made no acknowledgement of her presence, only lowering his head as if in prayer. After a few moments she rose and went to the small lady chapel off to the left, Joanie following. She pulled back the heavy curtain that shut it off from the rest of the church and entered. Joanie remained outside, a model of discretion to her lady's private prayers and prostrations. Inside, Alys knelt in front of the altar dedicated to St Simeon and waited. It wasn't long before the curtain was drawn back and Cosimo entered.

Alys rose, lifted her veil and went to him, holding out her hand. "Thank you so much for coming here and meeting me like this," she said in a voice barely above a whisper. She gave him a tentative peck on the cheek.

Cosimo gave her a puzzled frown. "What is it that causes you to request I attend you in such a place, in such a manner, *cara mia*? Can you not speak at Alessandra's? Is Alessandra threatening you? Has some disaster befallen her or her finances that you find yourself cast adrift?"

She took his hand and stroked it. "No, no, *amore mia*, it is nothing like that. Well not quite. It is possible that once Alessandra knows what I am to tell you she might feel that she would be best rid of me, that her business will suffer and she will be ruined."

She looked up at him searching him for evidence that what she was about to tell him would be well received.

"And what is it you have to tell me?" he asked, his voice containing a dangerous edge.

She flinched slightly. It was the first time she'd ever heard him use such a menacing tone. She knew his reputation was ruthless, but his manner toward her in the past had been such that she'd never given the ruthlessness much countenance. Now she wasn't so certain.

"I would bring you what I think is good news," she said tentatively. She took his hand to her mouth and kissed it lightly, looking up into his eyes. "I am to have your child."

He stared at her, his face uncomprehending. "You are having my child? What? How?"

She forced a small tinkle of laughter. "There is no question how you conceived a child with me, is there? In fact, I think it is you who taught me."

He sputtered a little. "But...." His voice trailed off and a large smile spread across his face. He straightened and puffed out his chest, then drew her into his arms. "Yes of course. This is news indeed. It—I just hadn't thought to get a child on you. Not with my children already grown." He kissed her brow and held her away from him. "You are well? There is no trouble with the babe?"

She patted his arm. "I am well, never fear. And the babe is fine." She pulled aside her cloak and rested his hand on the small swell of her stomach. "A boy, I'm certain."

He rested his hand there for what seemed an interminable amount of time, before pulling it away and frowning.

"You're belly seems very small. I hope he will not be a feeble child. That wouldn't do."

"A slow start, Cosimo, but sure and he will grow strong as time progresses. I feel him now moving and strengthening his limbs."

Fabriano's brow cleared and he placed his hands once again on her stomach. He paused and she willed the child to move under his touch. Moments passed without a stir from her womb.

Fabriano looked at her and grinned. "Ah *si, si*, I can feel the babe."

Alys gave him a bemused smile and nodded. "He responds to you already, *amore mio*."

"But of course," he said. He gave her a considered look. "So, Alessandra doesn't know of the child's existence yet?"

"I haven't told her." Alys lied. "But it won't be long before she knows." Alys pressed the fabric of her gown against the swelling and pushed out her stomach as much as possible. "She can hardly mistake the change in my shape."

Cosimo nodded. "And you think she'll take the news badly?"

"I have no notion, but there is good chance that she will take it badly. For how can I continue to entertain others in my present state? Her income will drop and that won't please her."

"Yes, but I am your patron. I have a contract. She has income from that."

Alys looked up at him sadly. "I know, but she will think it insufficient as the sole source of her support."

Cosimo gave a disgusted sound. "Pah. The woman's avarice knows no bounds."

"I know, Cosimo." Alys sighed. "But what can I do? I am in no position to make demands of her."

"There is no need, *cara mia*. I will talk to her." He kissed her on the lips. "Now go, and rest easy, now. You mustn't worry yourself. It's not good for the child."

She smiled at him and nodded. She replaced the veil over her face and made her way out of the lady chapel. Joanie glanced at her and pursed her lips, but said nothing as she followed Alys out of the church.

Once on the square she spoke to her in a low voice in English. "I 'ope you know what you're doing."

"I have no choice, Joanie. You know that."

"You must let Barnabas know. 'e should know."

Alys rounded on her and spoke in a tight voice. "And just how am I to do that, may I ask?"

"There's bound to be someone who can get word to 'im. Didn't Alessandra say where 'e was going?"

"Africa, don't you recall? Should I send a message to one Giacomo Bonavillagio in Africa? Or just Barnabas, lately of Eye by Westminster?"

"What about going back to London? That signore will never agree to our leaving with the babe if he thinks it's 'is."

"I'll just have to face that when it comes time. In the meantime there are other battles to fight."

～

"Where have you been?" Alessandra demanded when she entered the *sala* on her return.

Alys removed the veil and threw it on the table. "Nowhere remarkable. To church."

"To church? Do you feel a need to confess your sins?" Alessandra asked in a sardonic tone.

"Not especially. But I find it calming in my present state."

Alessandra snorted. "You need calm?"

Alys shrugged and looked at Alessandra. There was no reading of her face under the heavy veil, but there was something present in her voice she hadn't detected before. An edge.

"Were you looking for me for a particular reason?" Alys asked quietly.

"Are you still feeling ill?"

"Ill? No, I'm much better now, thank you."

"I've just had word from Signor Nani. He mentioned you were ill and hoped you recover soon, for he wouldn't like to have you in his company if that should be the case."

"I assure you, it wasn't anything but the drink I was given. There was something in it, I'm certain."

"You can't fool me. It's the babe. This is the cause of all the trouble. You should have told me earlier so that I could have disposed of it. There is no place for a child in a courtesan's household. My mother said it to me, time and time again. And did I not say it to you, so often I can't count the number?"

There was a hint of hysteria in her voice that took Alys aback. She'd never seen Alessandra lose control before and it seemed she was on the verge of it now.

"But surely others have travelled this path before me?" said Alys.

"Are you disputing my mother's counsel? What do you know of it!" Alessandra snapped. "Others may have travelled it but it doesn't mean that it is the best path."

"But as I told you, Cosimo is happy about the news. He will ensure that you aren't discommoded by the turn of events."

"You know that, do you? Have you such confidence in your lover? Let me tell you that I know from experience, you cannot trust what they say, these Cosimos of the world. They may make promises when they fondle your breasts and your swelling stomach, but when it comes to the actual steps they will fail to make good their words."

Alys stood staring at her, taken aback by the harsh tone and words. What experience was Alessandra drawing on? The consequences of her scarred body?

"I'm sorry, Alessandra," Alys said in a soothing tone. "I know I should have consulted you first but Signor Fabriano's attentiveness and words left me assured that he would greet the news gladly. And he did. He's promised to speak to you about a new arrangement."

"No. I have a different plan. You will go to the country, to a convent that I know. There you will have the child and no one will know. After that you'll return, resume your place as if nothing had happened except an extended period of illness that will make you even more interesting."

"But the child? And Signor Fabriano. What of him?"

Alessandra shrugged. "I will tell him that you lost the child and have gone to the convent to recover your health. The contract will still hold, I'll see to that."

Alys shook her head in disbelief. "But the child? You would deny him the child?"

"He will be none the wiser. And the child will be out of the way."

A kernel of fear rose in Alys. "Out of the way? What do you mean?"

"A home will be found for it. Something suitable."

Alys opened her mouth to protest and then shut it. She tried to calm herself and collect her thoughts.

"Please just wait until you talk to Signor Fabriano. You can judge his sincerity and ensure it with a contract. If nothing else, he'll honour a contract."

A few moments passed before Alessandra spoke. "I will wait to hear what terms he offers."

She turned abruptly and left the room, slamming the door behind her. Alys remained unmoving, alarmed at the conversation that had just passed between them. Something serious was troubling Alessandra, there was no doubt. Though the hysteria had gone from her voice, the tight edge was still present. She only hoped now that Alessandra would see reason and Cosimo would offer an arrangement that would outweigh the other plan.

∾

Alys watched the door expectantly and fidgeted with her hands. Over at the easel Carlo made disapproving noises.

"Keep still, carissima. How many times must I tell you?"

He rose and came over to her. "And now you have changed the drape of the cloth."

Before she could protest he placed his hands on the gown she wore and rearranged it, his hands pausing and resting on her stomach. When she had donned the gown for the sitting, it had seemed to her that her stomach had swelled to nearly twice its size, though she knew it hadn't. It was only her apprehension at Carlo's discovery of her condition. She knew it would be inevitable, but she still had hoped it wouldn't be until after the arrangement with Cosimo was completed. Her hopes of settling the arrangement immediately had been dashed when Cosimo had sent word the day after her discussion with Alessandra that he must leave the city for a fortnight or more.

Alessandra had greeted this news with a snort of derision, but Alys had kept up her protestations of Cosimo's loyalty. Now, when more than three weeks had passed, she awaited Cosimo's return with increasing anxiety. She'd even asked Alessandra if the sittings for the painting could be moved to her sala. Alessandra had agreed readily, unwilling to have Alys out of her sight for too long. The arrangement meant Alys could only assume the role of a model and had to forego all aspects of actual painting. Carlo was heartily displeased with the new situation, but his protests had been overruled by Alessandra with a few curt words about his indebtedness to her for his success.

Now, he pressed his hand on her belly, his eyes holding hers, inquiring. He frowned.

"Who?" he asked in a low voice.

"Signor Fabriano," she said in a whisper, tears at the back of her throat. "I'm sorry, Carlo."

He straightened his face clouded with anger. "So, did his contract include planting a child in you?"

Alys shook her head miserably and reached for his hand. "Don't be this way, Carlo. It cannot be helped and that's all there is to it."

He drew back from her. "So, you are truly the Madonna with child." He gave a bitter laugh. "Well I can now paint with a veracity I hadn't imagined."

He leaned over and draped the cloth around her to emphasize her belly and placed her hand over it. He stood back and looked at her in an objective manner, moving forward to adjust a fold.

"Please, Carlo, there's no reason to behave in this manner."

He looked up at her dispassionately. "How else am I to behave? Clearly I am nothing more than a painter for whom you model. And I must express gratitude at the lengths you have gone to provide me with an accurate subject matter." He bowed. "I thank you madonna, your efforts won't be in vain. You'll make me famous."

The welling tears spilled over and Alys raised her hand to brush them away. She could only hope in time that he would come around and they could take up where they'd left off in their relationship. But exactly what was it? Was he her lover? Her friend? Her mentor? A combination of all three? She didn't really know and for now, it didn't matter.

CHAPTER ELEVEN
THE DESERT, LATE WINTER 1447
BARNABAS

I tried to keep myself lulled by the swaying of the camel, but in truth it was making me feel increasingly ill. Since we'd left Aswan some weeks past it had seemed as if my whole world was on fire. Above me the sun baked away at the sand beneath me, causing a searing heat that threatened to erupt my body into flame. Hal hadn't escaped the consequences of the extreme heat either. His skin was ablaze with a severe heat rash from which he could find little relief during the day. The night provided the other extreme. We huddled around our fires against the cold wind, eating dried fruit and thick stew, until we were forced to retreat to our beds in the tent Ezekiel had acquired for us in Cairo.

Our sufferings met with amused or indifferent looks from our escorts, who seemed to take delight in warning us about the giant red spiders in the sand, or the crocodrylii, as Ezekiel called them, present in the water of the Nile. A small part of me smiled still at such scaremongering, but another part of me kept a cautionary distance.

They also warned us about the many bandits on the prowl for any potential rich pickings. That, I could see, wasn't a jest. The Tuareg scanned the horizon constantly, ever on alert, their hands ready to grab their knives, swords and arrows.

The journey had been endless, one day merging into the next, only occasionally broken by the rest stops where others also gathered. We changed mules a few times, until finally, at Aswan, we purchased camels from some Nubian merchants. By then I had a smattering of the language, but less than I would have hoped for. My intellectual powers seemed to have all but deserted me. Still, I managed the trade with Ezekiel's help, but couldn't help but think I was the worse for the bargain struck.

A swirl of dust blew into my eyes and I raised an edge of the cloth to wipe them. I'd adopted the Tuareg practice of enveloping my head in a cloth to create a turban and covering that protected my nose and mouth from the constant grit of the desert. I strained my eyes to see ahead and could make out nothing but a haze of heat rising from the bare sand and scrub. Sweat poured down my back in deep rivulets. In front of me, the long string of camels seemed to rise from the ground and float through the air. I shook my head to clear my eyes. One of the men rose from his camel, his dark turban transforming into a giant spider that clawed the air. I halted, uncertain about what I was seeing. A moment later the spider receded and the turban resumed its normal proportions. Was it the leader, Amastan, whose turban had become the giant spider before me?

I struggled with the question. It was the second time this had happened and I tried to puzzle it out in my fogged mind. After the first time, I had convinced myself it had been an unwanted side effect of the opiate syrup or the desert heat itself. I knew that the syrup of poppies would cause hallucinations to visit me sooner or later, and I'd been hoping I could fend them off until after I'd confronted al Qali and wreaked my revenge. When I saw the spider first rise up from Amastan in the middle of a blazing sun I just thought that fate had denied me this one piece of luck.

But now, a second time, I wasn't so certain. Would a man hallucinate in the exact same manner? I closed my eyes, fought the nausea and tried to recall what I knew. I sighed after nothing new came to my mind and urged my camel forward. It turned a malevolent eye towards me and for a moment I thought it would spit.

"Hal," I called, my voice thrown to the wind.

Hal turned and slowed his camel the best he could manage. A few moments later I caught up.

"You look like death," said Hal. He scanned my eyes which I was certain were bloodshot from the constant grit.

"I feel as though I'm beyond death. How are you faring?"

Hal grimaced. "My legs and crotch feel like they're on fire."

"My head is no better."

Hal grunted. His cloth slipped from his nose for a moment and I could see the peeling red skin there. His fair skin suffered more than mine, I knew. "Are your eyes sore as well?" I scanned them carefully. They were brown in colour and though there was some sign of tiredness and discomfort they didn't look half as sore as mine felt.

Hal shrugged. "They water sometimes."

"When you look through the haze, do you sometimes see strange images?"

Hal laughed. "Fruit-bearing trees and gardens surrounding a palace filled with plump, willing women? Only in my dreams."

Hal's remark made me smile. I could trust this good friend to help pull me back from the deep darkness that was threatening me now.

"How's Flores?" I asked. "He's not spoken a word to me in the last few days."

Hal cast a glance up ahead. "Sulking, if you ask me. Though 'e seems to be bearing up under the heat, I think 'e's annoyed that you've given more of the pepper away."

I snorted. "Who told him that? Ezekiel?" I frowned at the man who was guide, interpreter and hospitaler, setting up camp, cooking meals and packing our belongings the next day.

"I fear Ezekiel's worth is sometimes questionable," I said.

"I don't trust 'im," said Hal. "We've no way of knowing exactly what 'e's been saying to the dark fellas. We can only 'ope it's what you tell 'im."

"I know, and to some degree it's my fault. I haven't picked up as much of his language or the Tuareg's language as I'd hoped."

Hal glanced at me, his eyes narrowed. "You 'aving trouble concentrating?"

"It's the heat," I said in careful voice. "And the dust. It seems to have got into my mind as well as my mouth."

"Are you sure that's all it is? You said earlier about seeing things. Are you?"

I hesitated. "What do you know about the progress of the use of poppy syrup? You mentioned once that you've seen its effects."

Hal turned in his saddle to face me. "You are seeing things. Do they come on you unawares? Are you 'aving trouble sleeping? And you're sick, am I right? Sick in your gut?"

"Hal, calm yourself. All of those things could be ascribed to the effects of this awful heat."

"Then why do you ask if you know the answer already?" said Hal sharply. "You must have a care, Jacko. That syrup can do you no good."

I remained silent for a moment, preferring to let Hal's comments drift out onto the sand.

"Hal," I said after a while. "It's true that I have seen a terrifying image twice in the past few days. And it's also true that it could be a mixture of the effects of the drug, the heat and the fact that the Tuaregs have used every opportunity to show us we know nothing about the dangers of desert crossing. But what I do think, but can't be certain of, is that this image might have nothing to do with any of that. It might be something else entirely."

Something in me was reluctant to put exact words to what I knew deep down. What I had resisted since the very first appearance of the large spider rearing towards me.

"What is it, then, if it ain't the drugs?" asked Hal.

"I-I think it might be a warning."

"A warning? What are you on about? What kind of warning?"

I remained silent a moment, trying to speak the words.

Hal sucked in his breath. "You mean you've had a seeing? But I thought you needed the showstone to do that?"

"Not always," I said quietly. "Sometimes I would have them come to me. When I was young, sometimes Limping Sam came to me and showed me things."

"Did 'e come then? Did 'e show you something?"

"No, no he didn't come."

"Then what? Who's showing you what's to come?"

"I'm not sure. It was just our Tuareg friend. Twice now he's taken the shape of a large spider, rearing up towards me."

Hal looked at me and then broke into a laugh. "Really? Is that all? Well if I were looking to put a finger on where our greatest danger was it would be 'im."

I tried to find reassurance in Hal's quick humour and disregard for the image I'd seen. Perhaps he was right. Perhaps I was just giving my imagination free rein for my suspicions. Still, it did no harm to be extra vigilant.

⌒

It seemed like hours later that we halted to make camp. I'd eaten nothing all day except some dried fruit and taken periodic swigs from my drinking gourd. I'd said nothing more to Hal on the subject of my vision, but had instead allowed the easy manner and air between us give me comfort on the trek.

It was only when Flores sat down at the fire, after taking a plate of thick, heavily seasoned soup from Ezekiel, that a slight charge arose in the air.

"How many more days are we to endure this?" asked Flores in Italian.

He unwrapped the cloth from around his head and tossed it aside. Grime ringed his neck and brow. Water was kept for the primary and most necessary purpose of keeping everyone alive, not the luxuries of washing away dirt. It was a situation that Flores was not unaccustomed to, but at sea he was the captain and the journey's dangers well known. Here, Flores was at the mercy of not only those trials that nature threw at him, but also men that he knew next to nothing about. He eyed the Tuaregs now, a deep frown across his face.

I shrugged. "My guess, from what the Tuaregs say, is that we have another fifteen days, perhaps, before we come into the territory of the Ethiopes."

Flores grunted. "Is that what Ezekiel says, or what you think you understood the Tuaregs to say?"

"You think they differ?"

"I think you understand less than you think."

I sighed. "Flores, you know that there is little changing the number of days in the journey, whatever they are."

Flores ate in silence for a moment. "But you're certain there will be gold and other rewards at the end of it?"

"Gold in return for pepper," I said.

Flores grunted. "And what of this revenge you seek?"

"What of it?"

"Will that pose any obstacle to the safe removal of the gold?"

"I shouldn't think so. We'll make the trade before we ever reach al Qali."

Flores gave a small laugh. "How can you be so certain? Do you know exactly where he is?"

"No."

"Then how do you propose to find him?"

I noticed Hal shift uncomfortably from his perch on the ground. I gave Flores a direct look. "I don't. I'll let him find me."

Flores stared at me. "And you're certain that will draw him out?"

I nodded. "Oh, I'm sure of it."

"And what will you do when he does?" Flores cocked his head. "Exactly what did he do to you? You have never fully explained. I heard long ago that he can be ruthless in pursuing his desires, but he and I never had a quarrel and he tended me well when after that stabbing. You knew it would happen, didn't you? Had a vision and you came to my aid." He took a deep swig from the flask by his side. "I have much reason to be indebted to you, I do know that. And my debt of gratitude is why I'm here now. But there are limits."

"You saw that he was going to be stabbed?" asked Hal. "When was this? Was it like the one you told me about?"

I shrugged. "It was some years ago, Hal. I was a young lad. I came to his aid, like he said. Nothing more than that."

I recalled the incident and the feeling that had surrounded me at that point. I was living in a different time, a different life. Then, I was Barnabas, ready to duck and weave from any trouble that might head my way. But was that feeling I would get whenever a vision would come on the same as what I felt earlier and a few days previously? I paused, trying to assess it clearly, but gave up. Things were changed now and I was so altered that I couldn't be certain. Would it be any good to try to conjure up an old spirit, or cast my eyes on a pool of water to see if I could read what was to come?

I shook the feeling away. I had fought for so long now to rid myself of any traces of the sight because of all the evil and poison that I associated with it now. Perhaps in all that effort I was no longer able to tell what was true sight, or what were just some conjured delusions born of a terrible addiction. I shook my head and sighed.

I rose and made my way to the tent, ducking to enter and felt Hal touch my shoulder. I stood up and turned to him.

"That image, you say it was a spider…?" asked Hal.

"Yes. Why?"

"It was real, wasn't it? I mean you saw it. It wasn't anything to do with the poppy syrup."

"What makes you say that now? You were telling me earlier that it was just my instinct showing me what we all know, so why are you changing your opinion now?"

"Your face. When you said it just now, I don't know. Just something about 'ow you said it and your eyes. Like they were looking distant. Like you were somewhere else. It was the same when you told me about the spider. I didn't remark on it before, but I know different now. When you told me you could see things, I wasn't certain you meant it. But I know now, it's true."

"Thanks, I think," I said. "But I'm not certain myself."

"Well, just the same. I think we should be careful. In fact I might just have a watch myself tonight. I'll have Flores share the watch with me."

"Divide it among the three of us. I'll take the turn in the middle," I said. "Just get me when you're ready for a break." I patted him on the shoulder and ducked inside the tent.

∽

The stone walls closed in, pressing on my back and in front of me, my arms trapped at my sides. My chest struggled to expand against the increasing weight of the stones and suddenly I found it impossible to breath. I gulped the air and willed it into my body. I blinked away the sweat that poured into my eyes and into my open mouth. Someone shouted and others added their voices so it was one cacophony babbling away.

I awoke suddenly and sat up and looked around me, the darkness still pressing in. Shouts rang out everywhere. "Flores!" I called above the din. Was he still asleep in all this noise? I stumbled to my feet and fought for the tent flap, my dagger in hand. Outside, the stars lit the sky, transforming the dark and showed men running through the camp, scrambling the animals. The scene blurred and I blinked, trying to clear my vision. I searched desperately for any sign of Hal or Flores, but my desire was no match for the clouds of dust and my throbbing head. Bile rose to my throat and I clutched my stomach, leaned over and retched.

Hands grabbed me from behind and a sack was shoved over my head. I was dragged, stumbling and thrown over the back of camel, the breath knocked from me, and then secured there. Triumphant ululating added to the shouts and the camel I was slung across rose and moved away quickly, tossing me up and down, despite the bindings. What remained of my stomach tried to retch its way out of me, but with little breath and the bouncing, it couldn't be done. Mercifully, a few moments later I passed out.

When I came to, the camel had stopped and I was removed from the its back and thrown to the ground. Before I could catch my breath, I was hauled to my feet and dragged into a tent. There, the sack was unceremoniously removed and the person withdrew before I could see my captor.

I stretched my hands and my feet tentatively and tried to focus on my surroundings. The early morning light was strong and bright, but it did little to relieve the worn mat and faded blanket that lay folded beside it. I stood there for a few moments contemplating it and then went to the tent flap and looked outside. A man stood in front of the tent, dressed in the clothes of a desert man. I couldn't tell if he wore the tell-tale indigo coloured *tagelmust* headcovering.

I let the tent flap fall closed and took a seat on the mat. I rubbed my hand across my face and scratched the beard that had grown to fullness in the many days of our journey. In the scramble the night before my head covering had been left where I'd thrown it, beside my sleeping mat. But its loss I couldn't mourn as much as the small amphora that had been tucked away in my belongings. Though there were only a few drops of the precious syrup left, those few drops were calling out to me which such strength, it was all I could do to think of something else. Such as the identity of my captor.

Was it the Tuareg, Mousa ag Amastan that held me now? And for what reason? Surely he didn't need me to steal the pepper I knew he suspected had been stored in my other packs. If it was he, then it gave truth to the visions of the spider I'd seen. But if it wasn't Amastan who held me captive, it could only mean one thing. As I had planned, al Qali had sought me out. Only he had done it much sooner than I'd expected and I wasn't prepared.

CHAPTER TWELVE
THE DESERT, LATE WINTER 1447
BARNABAS

I was shaken roughly from my troubled sleep, sweating and shivering at once. I opened my eyes and could see figures moving around me, white ghosts drifting back and forth. I closed my eyes again, the light and the white ghosts too much.

Hands shook me roughly again and someone spoke sharply. I struggled to open my eyes. A wave of shivering swept over me and I clutched my robe tighter. A figure crouched before me. It was a man, his head swathed in a white cloth, his dark eyes peering at me. He spoke again and I shook my head in incomprehension.

I tried to gather the few phrases of the Tuareg language I knew and spoke. "Who are you? What do you want with me?"

The man looked up at the three other figures gathered around him. They spoke softly to him and he nodded.

"You are ill," he said in halting Greek.

I looked at him in surprise amid my shivering. "My friends? What of my friends?" I asked.

"I know nothing of your friends. I know only that you are ill."

He reached over and pulled back my left eyelid and then my right. He shook his head. "How long?" he asked.

I stared at him a moment, noting that though I shivered and goosebumps had formed on my skin, I was still sweating. I knew I was in a bad state and wasn't certain exactly what this man had deduced from his cursory examination of me.

"How long?" the man repeated.

"How long w-what?" I said, my teeth chattering.

"The poppy. You take it. How long."

I frowned. Would the truth be best? I fought again to clear the fog from my brain, but the stomach cramps seized me suddenly and I rose and bent over double, clutching my middle.

"Too long, I think," said the man.

I nodded and started to open my cracked lips to speak, but I could only croak. He pushed me back on the bed and rose. He spoke to the men again. One of them replied in turn, his tone sharp and insistent. My Greek speaker gave a small sigh and knelt beside me once again.

"You have a holy text. You must give it to the men."

I gave him a puzzled look. "A holy text?"

The man pursed his lips. "We have knowledge that you have a holy text. It belongs to our people. You must give it to the men, or it will not go well for you."

My mouth started to form the words of denial, but then I stopped. Could they mean the manuscript that told of Prester John? Surely not.

"You are from the kingdom of Prester John?" I asked.

The man frowned. "Prester John? Why do you speak of Prester John?"

"He is the priest king I seek, or rather I seek his kingdom. The manuscript I have concerns him."

The man considered my words, his face puzzled. A few moments later he rose again and consulted with the other men. A short discussion took place, the Greek speaker nodded and then crouched beside me once more.

"This priest king, he is Christian?"

I nodded. "His kingdom is south of here. But I have only heard of it, I have not been there."

"And you have a text about him. You do not have a holy book belonging to us?"

"Whose holy book? What people are you?"

A sudden thought seized me and my anxiety increased. I added a few words of Arabic to see if it was by some chance Pasha Halil's tentacles reaching this remote place to retrieve his missing manuscripts.

The man narrowed his eyes. Behind him the men gathered closer. "We are Copts."

"Copts?" I repeated blankly. A momentary relief washed over me to think that Pasha Halil wasn't involved in this.

"You do not have a Copt holy book?"

The puzzle started to come together. I realised the text he meant was the one I had bribed Ezekiel with. The text, whose existence I had grabbed from the far reaches of my mind, thinking it a clever way in which to guarantee our safe passage through the desert. I nearly laughed at the foolhardiness, at my own overweening confidence I could outwit the Ezekiels of this continent.

"Ah," I said. "That text."

"Well?" said the man. "These men want answers."

"And you do not?" I gave a wry smile.

He snorted. "I am here to tend you and interpret."

"You speak Greek. You are a priest?"

"It matters not what I am. You must answer the question."

I sighed. "I hardly have the text with me. As I think I explained. I know where it can be found."

The man studied me carefully, trying to discern if I spoke the truth. A few moments later he rose again and relayed what I said. There was much shuffling and arguing. Finally, one of them, presumably their leader, spoke in a sharp and commanding voice. The others subsided and the Greek speaker nodded. He turned and knelt beside me.

"Where is the holy text? Who has it?"

I frowned. I knew this would be their next question and my answer was prepared.

"The person I know who can obtain it is in Venice."

"Venice?" The Greek speaker mouthed the word slowly.

"Yes, across the sea, north of Alexandria."

"And this man does not have it, but can obtain it? How? Where is it?"

"He knows who possesses it. He trades with him often and will undertake to purchase this text."

"And how do you know this text is in this man's possession?"

"Because I have seen it."

"But yet you do not offer to trade it yourself?"

"No, I'm afraid I am no longer on good terms with this person."

The man nodded. "I see. Yet your friend is on good terms still."

"He is."

"And would he be willing to do such a thing for you?"

"For a tidy profit, he would of course."

"But where is the holy text kept?"

I paused. I had blended truth with lie and I wasn't certain to keep to the truth or give the more acceptable lie. I chose the truth.

"It's at the palace of the Grand Vizier. In the land of the Turks."

The man stared at me, clearly surprised. His eyes narrowed and then he nodded. He gathered his robes as if he needed their protection and rose once again, for what I hoped was the last time. He explained what had passed between us and the men cast dark glances at me as he did so. The leader gave a grunt and spoke a few words. The Greek speaker nodded and turned to me.

"He says you must do as they say. You will write to this man and have him go to Alexandria. I have told them that in the meantime I must tend to your sickness. When you are recovered, you will be taken there to meet this man and direct him to make the trade with the money you had with you."

"You have the money?"

"They have what is necessary."

"And afterwards?"

"We seek only our holy text. That is all. We do not wish to harm you. But make no mistake. If they find you are lying, they will not hesitate to kill you or your friend."

"My friend? You have my friend here as well? May I see him?"

The man glanced over at the others and back at me. He turned and followed the others out of the tent. I laid back down, shivering again so hard that I could hardly stay on the mat, yet still my mind whirled. Did he mean Hal? Or Flores? And what had happened to the other one?

I moaned loudly, the pain overtaking me. It came suddenly each time, gripped me so fiercely I all but lost consciousness. If only I could. It would be a pleasure to slip away from all the pain and tremors that racked my body. But when I lost consciousness it wasn't long before visions came—terrible and horrifying, smothering me to such an extent I could only gasp for breath rather than cry out.

Between the bouts my Greek speaker, whose name I learned was Paulos, ministered to me, murmuring words of comfort, sponging my face and feeding me a thin broth containing something potent that relaxed my spasms. I began to look on Paulos with great kindness. His Greek had improved with use and I used that improvement to attempt to get more information from him about Hal and Flores, but he refused to be drawn.

"You must think of nothing but recovering your true self, young one."

His words rang through my mind and lingered there in the days to come. Long ago I had lost my true self. The self that was Barnabas. It had been buried under fears for my safety and attempts to achieve great scholarship. But even that was corrupted into something more malevolent when a whim to garner riches turned into a pursuit for revenge. Was it truly al Qali who had brought me to this state? Whenever I reached that thought I pushed it from my mind and turned to other things, until the next spasm of pain seized me and I called for a bowl to retch in or pleaded for respite from this terrible course Paulos had set me on.

"Please, wouldn't it just be easier to give me some of the poppy syrup?" I asked on what was my tenth day or perhaps my twentieth day of captivity. I'd lost count and interest. "If you have none I'm certain it would be easily obtained."

Paulos knelt beside me and offered me a sip of broth. "You will thank me for leading you back from that path. You would not thank me for leading you further along it."

"I wouldn't. I give my word. Just a small sip. That's all I need," I begged, hating the whine in my voice.

"It is the hardest part now. You will see. Things will improve soon, I promise you."

He urged the small bowl of broth on me once again. This time I took a sip, hoping that it would settle my stomach as it usually did. It took some while this time and I looked at Paulos inquiringly. He merely smiled and shook his head.

"You must rest, now, young one. Dream of that pretty young girl about which you speak so often."

"Girl?" I asked. "I speak about a girl? When?"

Paulos shrugged. "When you are in fever. You speak of Alys. You have love for her, I think."

I frowned. "Have I said anything else?"

"Only things that do not matter. But Alys, she matters."

I said nothing and turned my head away.

"It is for Alys you must do this," Paulos said softly.

"It is impossible," I said and pressed my lips together.

"Impossible, how? Does this Alys not love you?"

"Once," I said. "But now—she can only hate me."

"But surely not. A woman's love does not disappear without good cause."

"There is good cause, I assure you," I said.

I shut my eyes, refusing to allow the tears to gather. I hated the extreme emotions that constantly threatened to overrun me at the slightest provocation. I felt a hand on my shoulder and opened them, looking into the dark, expressive face now filled with compassion and understanding. From the early days of his ministrations he'd omitted his head covering on his visits, revealing coarse black curls that clung tightly to his head and a beard threaded with white.

"Hatred takes great energy and strength. And so often that emotion can come from love. Love taking the wrong path."

"That might be true. But it is I who turned that love to hate by my actions."

"Is what you have done so awful that it doesn't deserve forgiveness?"

My first impulse was to tell it was beyond forgiveness, but I paused. I thought of al Qali and how he had made me as much of a whore as I'd made Alys. "I don't know. But if it was asked of me, I would find it difficult."

"Have you asked her forgiveness?"

"There is no place to ask for forgiveness. It's best that I remove myself completely from her life."

"But you do this woman wrong by not allowing her the opportunity to make that choice. You may be surprised."

"No," I said and looked away. "There's no point. I must do what I set out to do. Alys has no place in that pursuit."

"And is this pursuit worthy of a man who in his heart asks only forgiveness of this woman he says he loves?"

I regarded him carefully. "Are you certain that all I speak about in my bouts of delirium is Alys?"

"I didn't say that," said Paulos calmly. "I said you spoke about things that mattered little."

∾

I opened my eyes to the sound of distant music. I could detect rhythmic playing of strings and a kind of drum. Intrigued, I sat up and pulled some cushions behind me for support. In the days, or was it weeks, perhaps more than a month, since I'd arrived, some efforts had been made to provide me with a small amount of comfort. My bed was a pallet, covered with blankets against the cold nights, and colourful cushions were scattered around for sitting on or reclining against.

I'd seen nothing beyond this tent since my arrival. Paulos was the only person who tended to me, so my world had drawn close around me. Now, hearing the music I wondered for the first time in a while, what lay beyond the flaps of the tent. And who. Was Hal hearing the very music that now roused my interest? Or was it Flores?

Tentatively, I rose from my pallet and stood quietly a moment, trying to get my balance. It had been some time since I'd risen from the bed and my legs felt weak with the effort. Carefully I made my way to the tent door and drew it aside. The sun shone brightly and I shut my eyes for a moment against its strength. When I opened them again, I saw an array of tents of varying shapes and sizes billowing in the desert breeze. Several stunted trees clustered to the left where goats were tied or pegged. Men dressed in long, colourful robes or tunics passed, heading towards the music. I leaned out and saw a group of men sitting on the ground. Three of them played a gourd shaped instrument with long necks of wood while two others beat on small drums sat in front of them.

I stood at the entrance, listening, unaware of the time that passed, until I felt a tap on my shoulder. I turned and saw Paulos. I grinned.

"You are feeling better?"

"For now," I said.

With a firm hand on my shoulder he guided me back inside the tent to my pallet and gestured for me to lay back down on it.

"You must take it slowly. Your body and spirit have much to recover from."

"Thank you, I know. But will you tell me now about my friend? Is he in good health?

"He is in good health, you may be assured. He suffered no injury."

"May I see him?"

"That isn't for me to say. It is early days to tax yourself with such matters, though it speaks well of you that you are concerned."

"May I at least know which of my friends you have here?"

"Of course. It is the man with the fair hair."

"Fair hair? You are sure?"

Paulos nodded. I smiled and squeezed his hand. It could only be Hal. He was here somewhere and I was determined I would find him. And together we would find our way out of this mess.

CHAPTER THIRTEEN
NUBIA, SPRING 1447
BARNABAS

I glanced around me, marvelling at the Christian fixtures that seemed so exotic in the landscape that surrounded us. The altar, constructed of wood, was worn and scarred by years of use. A threadbare cloth covered half of it and a wooden cross, each end divided into three equal points, stood on top of the cloth. The cross was newly painted and seemed almost garish in the faded simplicity of the altar and the rundown stone and mud building that housed it. Except for the murals that covered every inch of the interior. Angels smiled down at me along with other figures from the Bible. Each of them was gloriously and expensively painted with rich blues, reds, greens and halos of gold so bright that they dazzled the eye in the light of the lamps. The air was thick with the scent of burning incense.

I tried to take it all in, refraining from an unexpected urge to kneel and offer prayers that hadn't crossed my lips for some time. I turned to Paulos.

"It's impressive," I said quietly.

He bowed, acknowledging the truth of my statement. "It is all for God's glory, nothing more."

We were alone, just the two of us. I'd left the tent for the first time under his guiding hand only a few moments before and he'd escorted me here. In the two days since I'd peered through the tent opening, Paulos had deflected all my questions about Hal, telling me only that I had proceeded to the next stage of my recovery.

Now I stood beside him in the church, wondering why he'd brought me here. "You would like me to pray?" I said lightly. "Or you are asking to hear my confession. I fear there's little left to confess. I'm sure I said it all in my delirium."

Paulos smiled. "Your jest shows that you are ready for this task."

"Task?" My tone was cautious.

He pointed to the small table and chair at the back of the church where a small lamp was lit. "Sit there."

I did as I was told but kept my eyes on him. He made his way to the back of the altar and, taking a key from a niche in the wall, opened a small door in the wall. Inside was a cupboard, lined with shelves upon which lay rolled and bound manuscripts. He reached to the bottom and withdrew some paper, a reed pen and a small pot of what I presumed was ink, then made his way to me and set the items down on the table.

"Are those some of your holy texts in there?"

He nodded and smiled again. "Ah the interest of a scholar is piqued, I see. Yes. The books of our prophets, the books of Jesus, and other holy texts."

"The Bible?"

"Like the Bible of you Christians who follow Rome. But ours is not complete. In these many, many centuries of being overrun by the Arabs, and others, we have lost some of these holy texts."

"And it's one of these holy texts that you want me to help you acquire?"

"To reclaim what is ours," said Paulos. "So, if you would be so good as to write to your friend and tell him to come to Alexandria so that you can give him the funds and instruction to purchase this text for us, it would be appreciated. As would your fair-headed friend, I'm sure."

I gave him a dubious look. "Appreciation" was an embroidered turn of phrase for what I knew was an order. There was no mistaking the underlying threat to Hal, and no matter how much I was indebted to Paulos, and how much we'd shared of scholarship and philosophy, I couldn't ever forget who he was and where his true loyalties were placed.

I pulled the paper towards me, though for a moment I couldn't help but raise it to the light to inspect it. The paper, though somewhat worn, was made of linen, not goat parchment as I'd been expecting. What kind of people was I among who seemed so poor and nomadic yet at the same time showed evidence of great learning and sophistication?

I pulled myself away from such speculation and tried to gather my thoughts. Just who would I write to, posing them as my friend and fellow trader who wouldn't balk at travelling into the territory of the Ottoman Turks? Or at least the pretence of it, for I couldn't imagine I would ever get anyone to pry any of the manuscripts from Halil Pasha's clutches, not at any price. I could only hope that once in Alexandria I could figure out a way to escape that wouldn't endanger Hal.

I lifted my pen and dipped it into the inkpot. And with a slow, sure hand I began to write my letter. I decided to address it in Latin, ostensibly to Alessandra, hoping that its contents would more or less remain obscure to my captors. After great deliberation that put nearly too much upon hope, chance and the delusion that Alys, if not caring for me any more, might at least enjoy the inference and pun, I worded the missive in veiled allusions I knew Alessandra would struggle with. Though she might be vain enough to refuse to consult Alys, I hoped that Alessandra's curiosity would get the better of her. And Alys, upon reading it, would decide to persuade Alessandra to act upon it. A lot of 'ifs'.

When I'd finished, I waved the letter to dry the ink, folded it up and handed it to Paulos. "I hope that will satisfy you and the others." I said, holding onto the manuscript as he grasped it.

"I will take this to the Kephale now. He'll ensure its delivery," said Paulos. "He will of course ask your friend to translate it."

I gave him a deprecating smile. "I'm afraid my friend doesn't read that language."

"Ah, but I will look it over myself, then. I have some Latin, and though it's been many years, I am certain I can read enough to satisfy the Kephale that you are honouring your word."

"But how do I know that my friend is really here? However truthful I have been, you might not have been equally so."

"Rest assured your friend is here," said Paulos. He gave a firm tug to the letter and I released it. "I will take you to him now."

I rose from the chair and followed him eagerly. Paulos made his way to the altar first, bowed three times and then crossed himself carefully. I hesitated and then did the same, unable to resist the compelling force of his action and the surroundings. We left the church and he headed past a few more mud buildings and tents to a tiny mud hut. A small wooden gate barred the entrance and a heavily knotted rope tied it shut. I knelt beside the entrance and peered through the wooden slatted opening. Darkness greeted me.

"Hal," I called softly.

"Jacko?" came a croaky voice.

I made out a form crouched in a corner. "Hal, what have they done to you?" I said in English.

Hal stirred, stood up clumsily and made his way to the entrance. "Is it really you, Jacko?"

I nodded. "Yes. Yes. And you my dear friend, are you well?"

"I am now. I thought you were dead, Jacko. They wouldn't tell me anything. I've been sitting here these months just watching and waiting, 'oping I might see a sign of you or Flores."

"Flores isn't here," I said. "At least that's what I've been told. I don't know where he is."

Hal reached out for my hand and I gave it a squeeze. "We'll be out of here soon enough, don't you worry."

"I know you'll see it right. I know you will." He peered at me closely. "You look like 'ell."

"Well you're not any beauty yourself," I said. I cast a glance at the sweat stained shirt and a ragged robe that covered a frame that no longer contained the hard-packed muscles it had before.

"How are you faring? You know…the syrup?" Hal's eyes completed the sentence.

I gave an awkward laugh. "If you think I look hell, it's only because I have been there twice over."

Hal pulled me closer so that my face was near to his. I let him examine me closely.

"Is it gone?" he asked finally. "Are you quit of that evilness?"

I shrugged. "Hal, I don't know if I can ever be quit of it. I just thank God and the good priest that I am able to pass a day without craving it beyond all else."

"Well, that's a start," said Hal, grinning suddenly. "And with that behind you, things can only get better for us."

❧

I begged Paulos to take me to the church on the excuse that I wanted to pray before God to help me refrain from any future use of the poppy syrup, in the hope that I might see Hal on the journey. Though Paulos was sceptical of my sudden religious inclinations, he still agreed to escort me there daily. Only occasionally was I allowed to visit Hal and only then for a few moments. Still, it kept our spirits up and Hal looked marginally improved each time.

On one such visit to the church, about ten days after the first one, I asked Paulos about the manuscripts that were piled on the shelves. Seeing my curiosity was real, he withdrew one of them and carried it over to the small table along with the oil lamp from the altar so I might examine it.

It was bound in a plain leather cover over wooden boards, the leather faded from passage of time. But embedded in the leather was an array of small emeralds, each the size of my fingernail and worth a fortune. I stared at them for a moment and then, collecting myself, opened the manuscript and read the Greek words under the ancient Ge'ez language that formed the title page.

"The Book of Enoch?" I said. "I'm not familiar with that work."

"It's part of the holy book. It tells of the history of the world and how it will end."

"An apocryphal text, like Revelations?"

"Yes," he said. "Very sacred."

"I can see that by the very gems on the cover. They must have been had at a great price."

He shrugged, his eyes giving away nothing. "It is a holy text. Where else would you place precious stones?"

I nodded and let the matter of the emeralds drop. It was clear there was nothing more to be had from Paulos about their origin. Carefully, I turned the pages and read parts of the text. I became completely absorbed in it, because it spoke not only of the end of the world but the arrangements of the stars in the heavens, the seasons, nature and all manner of observations about the weather. Eventually I looked up at Paulos in wonder.

"This is a marvellous text," I said and truly meant it. "The text that you wish me to obtain, how do you know it's the one you're missing?"

Paulos gave me an amused look. "We would desire any text that is a part of our holy book."

I nodded. It explained their lack of curiosity about which text I knew was in Halil Pasha's library. I turned back to read on but Paulos smiled at me gently and shook his head. "No, young one, another time. We must leave now."

On the journey back I asked Paulos to allow me to stop and see Hal.

"I'm afraid your friend is no longer with us."

I stopped and stared at him, alarmed. "What's happened to him? Was he suddenly taken ill? Or was it—." I stopped, unable to complete the sentence. They couldn't have killed him. It made no sense. They would have done it from the first if they desired it him dead.

Paulos laid a hand on my arm. "No, he is not dead. He has gone with your message. The Kephale arranged for an escort. He left two days ago."

I hadn't expected that. They had used Hal to ensure my cooperation, but now he was gone and so it appeared my cooperation was no longer important. The letter was sent.

"Your friend will be safe, you've no cause to worry. He will await your friend in Alexandria along with the escort and then ensure the instructions are given and the funds presented once the manuscript is delivered."

"That could take some time," I said.

"It will take as long as it takes."

A shout rang out and I turned my head to see men running towards the camels. Behind me was Paulos, his brow creased in worry.

"What is it?" I asked. "What's happening?"

"I don't know," said Paulos. "Some men have appeared in the distance."

"Are they enemies?"

Paulos gave me a direct look. "We offer them the hospitality of the desert, of course, but we keep a wary eye, nonetheless."

I nodded, distracted by thoughts of Hal. I tried not to put too much hope in this turn of events. If Hal could escape his escort, he might, by some luck, find his way to secure money from Alessandra to arrange for assistance to come and rescue me. He would have to kill the escort, though, or they would return here as soon as they'd discovered Hal had gone and I would then count the hours before I was dead. There were many ifs riding on this hope, but it was all I had.

❦

I could hear the music and other sounds of revelry deep into the night. To some extent it kept me awake, but I wasn't certain it had anything to do with the restlessness that overtook me. The words of the text I had read that day kept running through my mind, as did the number and size of the emeralds. My mind was piqued by both puzzles and it flitted back and forth between the two. How had such a text come to be here? The text I'd seen mentioned in the list of manuscripts contained in Halil Pasha's library was described as the Book of Jubilee. Its title had intrigued me briefly as did the two-word description, "Little Genesis". I had no idea if that was one of the texts from their holy book, but it seemed possible. The armies of Saladin had laid waste to much of the area I was in now, and many a Coptic text could have fallen into Saracen hands.

The emeralds, of course, were another puzzle. It was difficult to say how old those emeralds were and when they had been placed in the cover. But could they somehow have come from the often-mentioned riches of Prester John's kingdom? Was it close by? The priest had said nothing definite about Prester John and what he had said was bordering on dismissal. But that could just as easily be a ruse and Prester John could have been a Copt and his kingdom in this region.

I decided in the end to combine a thorough examination of the text with some close questioning of Paulos, and if possible the leader, the man he called "Kephale". With that settled in my mind I drifted off to sleep, the music and laughter still loud.

Some hours later, someone clapped a hand over my mouth. When I opened my eyes, I had only a brief moment to see a dark figure looming over me before I was blindfolded, gagged and my hands bound in front of me. I was shoved firmly out of the tent and then dragged to a camel. This time I was allowed some of my dignity, and instead of being thrown over its back, I was mounted carefully on the camel with another rider at my back. Quietly, we moved quickly and silently on into the night. I clasped the steep saddle horn in front of me to keep my balance against the camel's gait, which eventually quickened. I could hear the other camels snorting occasionally, so that I knew there wasn't just the lone rider behind me, but it was difficult to tell their exact number. Once again I had no head covering and the cool air stung my ears. The days had grown warmer, but the nights were still cold and the thinness of my robes soon became apparent so that I was grateful for the heat of the person behind me.

We went on for what seemed like hours and eventually the camel came to a halt and I was removed from its back, stumbling as I did so. I was led across some sand and told to sit, noting that they spoke to me in Arabic. Was I too quick to dismiss my fears about Halil Pasha? Had the intention in my letter already come to his notice and this was his answer? I brushed that thought aside as impossible, but knew it only underlined the very real fear I still had of that man.

I tried to breathe calmly and when they removed my gag I only spat a few times and asked them for a drink. They placed it in my hands and refused my request to remove my blindfold, so I ate and drank with the help of one of them.

"Where are you taking me?" I asked.

"You will see in time," a voice replied.

"Hal? I said loudly. I hoped that if he was here he would hear me and answer. A slap across the face was the answer.

"You will remain silent while you eat."

I resumed my eating, my mind working furiously. My experience among the Turks had taught me that my captors wouldn't hesitate to act quickly and brutally, if necessary, should I attempt any kind of foolhardy escape, or even try to remove my blindfold without their permission. I might have been promised alive to whoever sought me, but that didn't mean I had to have all my limbs or both eyes.

We rested a while longer and then pressed on, covering more territory, this time in sweltering heat. My naked head baked in the sun and I sweated behind my blindfold. My gag had been replaced and my throat became parched beyond all belief, until finally, choking and pointing, I convinced my fellow passenger that I needed a drink. He briefly removed my gag and shoved a goatskin flask in my hand. I drank deeply until he grabbed it from me and shoved the gag back in my mouth.

Finally, the camels slowed and stopped and voices shouted around me. I listened intently, trying to make out anything that would tell me who my captor was. And it was then that I heard a familiar voice.

"Welcome, young Giacomo. I hope your journey was not too unpleasant," said Mustapha al Qali.

I sat unmoving, just waiting to see what he would do and thanked God that my mouth was gagged, because all the rage that rose up and filled me would have spilled from my mouth in every single damning phrase and word of Arabic, Latin, Greek, Italian, French and all the other languages this man had taught me.

CHAPTER FOURTEEN
VENICE, EARLY SUMMER 1447
ALYS

Alys frowned down at her swollen belly and wished she could force out the offending object by the sheer force of her temper. In the past week, she felt she had acquired every sort of ache and pain it was possible for anyone to have in one body. It didn't help that Alessandra kept saying she must do something about her puffy face and the hollows under her eyes. Can one have a puffy face and hollows under his eyes, she'd said once in an acerbic tone, but all that had got her was a quick slap. At least Alessandra hadn't mentioned retiring to a convent any more. She seemed to have discarded that idea.

In the past months she'd tried to still her tongue, knowing that as much as Fabriano protested his desire to make Alys his permanent mistress with her own household, he had yet to do so, and so Alessandra must be kept in a sweet humour at all costs. The state of affairs hadn't helped Alys's temper either. She'd done all she could to encourage Fabriano to conclude a contract swiftly, but he'd remained elusive as a butterfly, a comparison that when she'd thought of it, only made her smile sourly.

Alys realised Signor Fabriano hadn't achieved his success on social position and family connections alone. The man was clever, for all his declarations about her winning charms. No amount of placing his hand on her ever-increasing belly or other allusions to his forthcoming child managed to halt his references to the various obstacles his lawyers were discussing and make him put his name on the parchment. He was hedging his bets. Deep down she knew he wanted to be certain the child was a suitable sex and, of course, resembled him in some convincing degree.

She sighed and rubbed her back. The room suddenly seemed stuffy and hot and she moved over to the window to open it wider and catch the breeze off the canal. Bitty scrambled after her. At least one male hadn't abandoned her.

"For goodness sake, don't open it wider. The bad 'umours will 'arm the babe," said Joanie in English. She was sitting in a chair, letting out one of Alys's less expensive gowns yet again.

"I don't care," said Alys petulantly. "Let it be so, if it means I get it out of me any quicker."

"Ah, you don't mean it," said Joanie.

"I do mean it. I'm sick to death of it already and will be heartily glad when it is out of my body. Then it can trouble you or the wet nurse, rather than me."

"You'll change your mind, you'll see. Once that little 'un comes out and gives its first cry your heart will melt. You'll be begging Signor Fabriano to send the wet nurse away, not pleading for him to hire one."

"I doubt that," Alys said.

Alys spoke the truth. She'd deliberately distanced herself from this child that grew inside her. Why would she want the burden of caring for it since Fabriano would no doubt take it away to be raised discreetly with a family in a fashion that befitted a by-blow of an important Venetian citizen? And if Fabriano refused to have any part of the child, she could be sure that Alessandra would dispose of the child to a family equally far away, but much less privileged.

Alys walked around the room, trying to find some comfort in the movement. A dull ache spread across her back and down along the front of her belly, throwing periodic twinges of pain.

"Shall I rub your back for you, sweeting?" asked Joanie.

She dropped her sewing on the chair and came over to Alys who leaned gratefully on the table while Joanie kneaded vigorously along her back. It gave her some ease until a twinge became a large cramping pain. She stood up suddenly and clutched her belly.

Joanie reached around and felt her stomach. "Is it time?"

"How could it be? It's too early, surely."

"Babes are known to come in their own time."

Alys clutched Joanie's hand. "I'm afraid, Joanie," she whispered.

Joanie clucked at her. "Now, it's going to be fine, don't you worry. You'll deliver a healthy babe, you'll see."

"But what if it's fair, Joanie? What if it has that impish grin on its face?" Alys whispered.

"Then you must grin back at the little one and say how much the child favours your mother," said Joanie.

Alys sighed, feeling reassured for the moment, until another pain seized her.

∿

Alys heard a squalling sound in the distance and closed her eyes tightly against it. Take it away, she thought and let me be. She stirred restlessly and hands restrained her. She felt the sweat trickle down her forehead and along her back. A cool cloth was placed on her brow and she opened her eyes. A figure loomed over her.

"Joanie?" she croaked.

"Shhh, sweeting."

"Is it over, now?"

"Not quite. We must get the afterbirth out of you." Joanie lifted her head and held a cup to her lips. "Drink this, now."

Alys took only a sip before she let her head fall back.

Joanie drew her head closer. "You must drink it, sweeting if you're to be well."

Alys did her best, but only managed a third of the brew. "I'm too tired," she said and turned her head away.

Joanie lowered her head back onto the bed and took the cup away. Alys closed her eyes once again and let the blessing of unconsciousness overtake her.

She awoke sometime later, feverish and desperately thirsty. The room was lit only by a single candle. Joanie sat in a small chair beside her.

"A drink, Joanie. I need a drink," she whispered and attempted to sit up.

"You lay back and rest, now. I'll give you a sip of cool ale."

Joanie rose and returned a moment later, a cup of weak ale in her hand. She raised Alys's head and held the cup to her lips. After several sips, Alys fell back against her arm, too exhausted to manage more.

"You've a fine and 'ealthy bairn, you'll be glad to know," said Joanie in a reassuring tone. "She's just waiting to get a peek at her mother. Shall I bring 'er to you?"

"No," said Alys. "I just want to rest."

She closed her eyes against the thoughts, the sounds and anything else that would interfere with the blessed oblivion she'd found moments before. It didn't take long, only this time dreams assailed her. She fought them hard, ran from the figure that sought to grasp her and hold her so tightly she could hardly breathe. She recognised the sandy hair, the eyes and broad grin. She called out to him to leave her be.

"Shhhhh," came the reply. "You're safe now."

Arms went around her. She resisted and told him to leave. He whispered in her ear, "Help me." The words echoed over and over. She fought against him, against his pleas. She wanted nothing more from him.

Light streamed in on Alys's face and penetrated her closed eyes. Carefully, she opened them and looked around. Joanie sat beside the bed, her face filled with concern. Her expression cleared when she saw Alys was awake and she smiled.

"How do you feel?" she asked.

"Aching and sore," said Alys hoarsely.

Joanie patted her hand. "You will do, of course. But your fever is gone and your colour has improved."

"How long have I been this way?"

"Several days. Nearly a week. It was uncertain at one point whether you'd make it."

Alys smiled listlessly. "It wouldn't have mattered."

Joanie frowned. "'ow can you say that? With me, who loves you like a sister. The small bairn needs you even more."

Alys frowned. "It is easily said because you will look after the babe. I'm not needed."

"You cannot say so. Let me fetch her so that you will see for yourself that she needs you."

"I'd prefer it if you fetched Bitty. Or wait. Tomaso. I have a fancy to see the monkey."

"But the bairn doesn't even have a name. Just take a little peek. You'll see. You won't be able to resist."

"If she wants to see her dog, then let her see him," said Alessandra sharply as she entered the room. "He is more attractive and far less trouble. The monkey, however, is another story. The sooner the kitchen staff poison that stupid animal the better."

Joanie frowned and shook her head. She gave Alys one last glance before withdrawing.

"You are awake, finally, I see." said Alessandra.

"Only now. But I'm feeling very weak."

"According to your servant you had childbirth fever. A serious condition, as she so carefully explained to me. Still, you're on the mend now, so we can only hope that all the losses incurred these past two months will have been worth it."

Alys looked away. She'd been unable to manage even the occasional parties and entertainments in her most obvious condition. For who would think of lovemaking when she was so unappealing and large? At least that's what Alessandra had kept saying over the weeks. She'd not seen anything of Signor Nani since the night she was sick in front of him and was certain he would have no interest now.

"Has Signor Fabriano been informed about the child?" she asked.

Alessandra waved her hand. "Oh I leave the news of that great joy to you, *cara mia*," she said in a searing tone. "I'm certain he will be more than charmed when he hears you have seen fit to present him with a mere girl. Let us see now, how much are dowries costing for a woman of good breeding? But then again, he will have no obligation to this female, will he? So therefore she will cost him nothing."

"You think he won't want her," Alys said flatly.

"Isn't that what I just said? But of course, I leave it to you to persuade him otherwise."

"He might be charmed by her all on her own," said Alys. What did she care? It was just that she felt quarrelsome with Alessandra who always felt she knew better.

"What's the child to be called? Have you picked out a name? I can hardly keep referring to her as 'she' or 'the child'," can I?"

"Why trouble to name her if, as you say, no one will want her," said Alys in a harsh tone. "Her name is Eleanor."

"Eleanor? No, no. It can hardly be that. That is all too English. Eleonora, perhaps, or Leonora."

"No, she's called Eleanor." Alys kept her tone firm.

Alessandra shrugged. "Well, what do I care, anyway." She turned to go. "You will have your chance to put your case to Signor Fabriano. He has agreed to call tomorrow."

Without a word further she left, closing the door behind her. Alys laid back against the pillows and bit her lip. Why had she antagonised Alessandra? It only served Alys ill in the end. And for some reason the name Alys had stated had clearly annoyed Alessandra. The name had come to her out of the blue, as if the Duchess herself was speaking in her ear. How Barnabas would hate it. To call his child after her beloved mistress and the cause of Barnabas's flight from England. How fitting.

~~~

Joanie laced up the back of her gown, frowning. "It's no use, the gown is too tight."

"You mean I am too fat," said Alys dismally. "Can you let it out? It's new, I've had no chance to wear it."

Joanie examined the gown's seams and sighed. "Perhaps, but only across the bust. The rest of you is far too thin for having just born a child."

"Then bind my breasts tighter," said Alys in a firm voice.

"I can't. You're in enough pain as it is." Joanie patted her arm. "You mustn't worry. The milk will leave soon enough."

Alys felt tears come to her eyes. It was all too much. Not only did she not want to see the child, she wanted all reminders of it removed from her body. Especially if she was to face Fabriano with any sort of allure. Her plan was only half formed in her mind, but she must at least attempt it.

She was barely laced in a different gown, her hair arranged and her face and lips delicately rouged when the summons came. She drew in a breath and gathered her courage, pasting a smile of welcome on her face and made her way to the *sala*. She could hear Alessandra's banter and Fabriano's clipped answers before she opened the door.

They turned to her when she entered and she gave Fabriano her most dazzling smile. "Cosimo, I am so glad to see you. I have missed you so."

Fabriano's eyes lit for a moment and she drew courage and hope from that. He took her hand and bent over it to kiss it. When he rose he was frowning.

"You're pale, *cara mia*, too pale."

"As she has said, she has been pining for you," Alessandra said. She came beside Alys and put her arm around her. "She needs nourishment of the particular kind only you can give, signore."

Alys tried to remain still under the discomfort of Alessandra's touch. After a moment she moved forward, took Fabriano's hand and led him to the cushioned bench near the window. She settled him there and poured wine from the flagon on the table into a goblet of Murano glass.

She handed it to him. "Come, share a glass of wine and a plate of figs."

He took the glass from her and she began to fill a small silver plate with figs from the bowl next to it. She noted Alessandra had ensured that much care was taken in providing just the kinds of things to tempt Fabriano. It was clear how much Alessandra counted on her to make this a success, despite all her derisive words.

Behind Alys, Alessandra took her leave, murmuring encouraging words and praise of both Alys and Fabriano, as well as assuring Fabriano he would delight in the evening as he'd always had done.

Alys took her own glass of wine and the plate of figs, sat beside Fabriano and offered the fruit to him. He took the plate and placed it on the bench beside him. He sniffed the glass, shook it and then sniffed again. This wasn't unusual for him, he liked to pride himself on understanding the nature and benefits of wine, but this time the smile was missing. This time he didn't look at her as he shook and sniffed.

He took a sip and gave a little frown of distaste. "This wine is too hot for this season. Alessandra should know that."

"Shall I get you a different wine? Or something else?"

He waved his hand. "No, no. I shall eat the figs without." He picked up the plate and picked at one gingerly.

Alys watched him nervously. She moved closer to him and placed a hand on his arm. "Cosimo, I am glad you've come. I missed your company. Come, you must tell me how you fare and any news that you have."

He cocked his head thoughtfully. "There is much talk of the war with Milan. It's gone on too long and causes great disturbances with trade."

"I've heard as much. But I'm certain you understand the nuances of trade and you can weather this storm with no ill effects."

He gave Alys a flat smile and nodded. There was silence for a few moments.

"Shall I play some music for you?" She half rose to get her lute but he grabbed her hand and stopped her.

"No, sit down a moment."

Alys sat. He opened his mouth to say something but Alys spoke before he could. "The child, Cosimo. It was safely delivered and, as you know it was a girl. I won't trouble you with its name, or the fact that it exists at all. Unless you have an interest, the child is to go immediately to a suitable place far from here. It will be as if the child never happened and we can go on." She looked at him, widening her eyes and made a great effort to fill them with admiration. "We can go on," she continued, "not as we were, as such, but towards something more. Something better. I could be yours, Cosimo. All yours. If you could give me the funds to set up a household, I could arrange it all."

He gave her a sceptical look. "What of your contract with Alessandra?"

Alys shrugged. "I could leave."

"You would have me set you up and buy out your contract? But she wouldn't settle when I asked her before."

"I'm sure she would now." Alys kept the plea from her voice. "But we could do this without her consent, without paying her. With your protection, it wouldn't be a problem."

Fabriano gave a short bark of a laugh. "The tables are turned now, I see. She would fend off her tarnished goods on me."

Alys took up his hand and kissed it. He withdrew it and placed her own hand back on her lap.

"I'm sorry, *cara mia*, I must take my leave. I fear that we have run our course. Since I saw you last there has been another lovely young morsel that has come to my attention." His face softened for the first time and he looked toward the window. "She is one so pure and sweet, it's as if she is from heaven itself."

He gave her a brief smile and rose. "So I must take my leave of you for the last time, madonna." He gave a little chuckle and shook his head at his own wit. "Madonna, yes."

Alys watched him as he bowed slightly and without further word left the room.

CHAPTER FIFTEEN
VENICE, SUMMER 1447
ALYS

Shouts rang out from some distant piazza, the sound muffled by the buildings that crowded the waterway. Alys barely noticed as she dragged her hand through the water, the gondola gliding along the canal in the direction of San Marco. She loved to go there in the afternoon, a bit of time when she might enjoy the soaring heights of the dome or the wonders of the art that hung there. That had been before, when her thoughts had been consumed by her painting, when she wasn't entertaining.

Now she must quit the gondola before San Marco. Now she must disembark at the steps of a lesser place. But this was the place that in the past had also drawn her up the steps with great eagerness and even further to the rooms of Carlo Crivelli. This time however, all was different. This time she must persuade and cajole Carlo that she must sit for him and create yet another wonderful painting that would restore Alessandra's fortunes and her reputation. She sighed at the thought. She had no energy for any of it.

The gondolier spoke to her. Beside her, Joanie gave a nudge to her ribs. "Come sweeting. Let's get this done."

Alys nodded and with the gondolier's help, she disembarked and made her way up to the stairs, Joanie close behind. The two of them picked their way along the narrow, cobbled street that led to Crivelli's rooms, careful even in their wooden pattens, slowed by Alys's gait. Her limp seemed to have worsened again since she'd given birth, whether from an actual physical problem or plain despair, she didn't know. Though it was summer now, the slime on the cobbles was still treacherous in a street that saw little sun. Joanie's hand was firmly on her arm as she led Alys up the steps of Crivelli's building.

"Take heart, sweeting," Joanie whispered. "Crivelli could never resist painting you. Nor could he manage now without your assistance."

Joanie's words echoed in her mind a few moments later when Crivelli reluctantly admitted the two of them. The room was strewn with clothes, plates filled with half eaten bread and chunks of cheese, cups half drunk, pots of pigment with some of their contents spilled, brushes and crumpled bits of paper. The smell of sour wine and sweat overhung it all.

"You've been busy," said Alys in a neutral tone.

Crivelli gave a bitter laugh. "Busy at nothing."

Alys moved forward and went towards a blank board that lay propped against one wall. She turned it around and saw a dark, mottled painting of a procession. She bent down to study it. The colours were flat, the proportions and perspective off.

"Put it back. There's nothing to see there."

Alys looked up at him. "This is yours? It's not your usual subject matter."

"You mean it's not a painting of you," he said harshly.

"Not that. I mean you have much to deal with in this scene, which I presume is the procession of the Magi."

"Your words condemn the quality of the painting exactly. You presume. You're not certain."

"It's not a finished painting, Carlo. All paintings go through stages where you would rather throw them in the fire than complete them."

Crivelli gave a small snort but remained silent. Sensing that his manner had relented somewhat, Alys rose and moved towards him.

"Give it some time, Carlo. Let it mature in your mind as well as on the board. It can all be righted. A stroke here, a dab there and soon it transforms into what it's supposed to be."

Alys ventured to squeeze his arm and saw he took some comfort in her words. She sighed inwardly and looked down at the painting. It was awful and would need much work if anything was to be made of it.

Eventually, she coaxed him to his easel and placed the half-worked painting on it. Joanie meanwhile, worked quietly to clear up the mess around them. Alys studied the painting while she spoke phrases of encouragement, picking out successful brushstrokes while he nodded and tried to be convinced. She reached for a palette, still wet with daubs of paint and picked up a mixing knife. She worked a few of the colours, but after a moment she shook her head and put the palette down.

"I'll mix afresh. We must have something bright now, to highlight the dark."

Crivelli watched as she went over to his worktable and mixed up the new colours, grinding the pigment first and then mixing it with the oil. She used the time to consider what might be done to salvage the work and was surprised to find a kernel of joy and contentment sat within her at the thought of it. She went on mixing, and when she was satisfied she put her results on a clean palette. Crivelli remained unmoving by the easel but his eyes had a flicker of hope in them.

It took some patient work, but after an hour she found herself hopeful too. Something was emerging. The Magi ceased to look like apple trees gone awry and the horses like pigs picking their way along a muddy road. The men now had crowns on their heads and capes draped over the flanks of majestic horses. She'd decided to have mules following behind, with chests strapped to their sides. It was passable, but it was as cumbersome as the board it was depicted on, in her mind.

"Yes, yes," said Crivelli. "I can see it now." He took the brush from her and laid a few daubs on it. He stood back and stared at it silently, then shook his head. "No. I was mistaken. For a few moments there you gave me hope." He looked up at her, his large eyes no longer dull and listless. "But I thank you for your effort." He stared at her for some moments and she held his gaze.

"Come now, signore," said Joanie. "Sit down and have a sip of wine and a bit of food."

Alys looked up from the painting and around the room. Joanie had restored a semblance of order in the place and on the small table in the corner had set a plate of fresh bread, olives and a flagon of ale.

"Where did you conjure that from?" asked Alys, smiling.

"I slipped out and bought it in the market at the piazza."

Alys was astonished. "You did? When was that? I didn't hear you go."

Joanie gave a small laugh. "You notice nothing when you're painting."

She pulled Alys over to the table and Crivelli followed. They sat on the small stools beside it. Crivelli picked up a cup of ale and drank deeply. Alys watched as he devoured a hunk of bread and cheese.

"You haven't been eating," she said.

He shook his head. "No."

She frowned at him. "You can't paint well if you don't eat."

He shrugged. "I am better now. You've no need to worry."

"I hope so. It would hardly do for Venice's most prominent painter to die from lack of food."

He laughed. "Hardly that, yet. But I will be. You'll see. Forget that painting. I'll start anew. You were right that it wasn't a subject to paint. It doesn't suit my style."

She smiled weakly. It seemed to her that it was more that he had lost his way and had regressed in his skill, and less the fault of the subject matter.

He reached across for her hand and squeezed it. There was no spark, nothing sensual behind it. He was only an artist appraising his work. "I know what I must paint. And I was blind not to see it."

Alys gave him a reassuring squeeze back. "I'm glad you've found inspiration again. What is it you plan to paint?"

"You, of course. The Madonna and child. Who better than you and your child for the model?"

"My child?" Alys asked dumbly. "But you can't mean that."

"Of course I do. You can bring the child here to the studio. Your servant will see to its needs when necessary."

Alys glanced over at Joanie who gave her a considering look. "It would be good for you to get out. And you can help, of course. Signor Crivelli always needs your help." Joanie smiled in a deprecating manner to Crivelli.

"*Si*, of course. You'll sit in a blue robe with the child naked in your lap, his pure innocence evident for all to see."

"The child is a girl," said Alys. "Eleanor."

"What?" said Crivelli, and paused to take in her words. "No matter, we will drape a cloth along her groin. She will be the baby Jesus."

"Carlo," said Alys. "You seem to forget that my time is not my own. Alessandra might have something to say to this. I believe she has other plans for the child."

"No, no. She will change her mind once I tell her of my plan. With this painting and the last one, our fortune will be made. You mark my words."

"You haven't sold the other one yet?" asked Alys.

He waved his hand in dismissal. "Ah, no. I have done nothing about it, as yet. But now, with the promise of the other one, I have no doubt I will secure a buyer who will purchase them both, at a price of a small fortune."

Alys dragged herself up the stairs to her room, tired and limping after her hours at Crivelli's rooms. Joanie was ahead of her, climbing the stairs to the floor above, to the kitchen, to fetch Alys some broth. Crivelli had eaten most of the food at his place, but Alys had been glad to give him her share at the time. Now she wondered at her graciousness, given his plan to paint her. She could only hope that Alessandra would send the child away soon, rather than permit Crivelli to paint her with the baby.

Crivelli could find a different subject matter. She realised she was willing enough to pose, if it allowed her to paint again. She had loved having the brush in her hand once again, the way the colour came alive on the board and how shapes and figures emerged under her eye.

She heard a soft murmuring as she made her way across to her room and paused. It was coming from the other end of the corridor, towards Alessandra's rooms. Curious, she walked quietly to the room and paused outside the door. It was ajar and she could hear soft cooing now. She peered in cautiously and saw Alessandra leaning over her bed, her back to Alys. Lying on the bed was the baby, gurgling softly under Alessandra's gaze. Alessandra bent her head and kissed the baby's belly and head and laughed. The baby reached up and pulled at Alessandra's hair, loosening a strand so that it fell on the baby's body, tickling her. The baby gurgled again. It was then that Alys realised Alessandra was bare-headed and her veil lay discarded on the bed beside the child. From this angle Alys couldn't see anything but the back of Alessandra's head, but she could see the scars on the bare hands that now lifted up the baby to her shoulder. She turned her face towards the baby and kissed her head. A scarred cheek and mouth, distorted by the ruined skin, showed itself to Alys.

Tears came to Alys's eyes and she drew away blindly, retracing her steps to her door. There she entered, closed the door swiftly behind her and leaned against it. She clasped her hand to her mouth as if to stop the tears that filled her eyes. Blinking hard, she willed herself to calm. She would put these last moments out of her mind and not think of them again, but not because she would deny any sense of compassion towards Alessandra. The tears weren't for Alessandra, the tears were for the sight of

Alessandra holding the baby like any mother would. It was her child. Not Alessandra's.

❧

The weight was warm and heavy on her lap, heavier than Bitty when he sat there. Much heavier. She opened her eyes reluctantly and gazed out of the window, noting each rooftop of each building opposite them that lined the canal. A distant bell sounded from one of the nearby churches, another met its ring, sounding the mass, or a death. Possibly a death, she thought, since there would be no mass at this time.

"Look down, Maria, and spread your hands, palms outward by the child's head and foot," said Crivelli. "You're full of wonder and adoration at what God has presented you with."

She gazed down at the child on her lap with an adoring expression and tried not to see what lay across the deep rich blue of her gown. She tried not to see the perfect little limbs on which were perfect little fingers with perfect little nails. And most of all she tried not to see the large eyes that gazed up at her and the pert little nose and sweet mouth. A mouth that reminded her too much of its origins.

"You look as if you're about to weep," said Crivelli crossly. "You should be joyful, adoring."

Since the start of the painting he'd offered nothing but instruction for her poses and consultation about the progress of his painting. Their painting. She'd chosen some of the colours and made the brushstrokes for the background and her gown. But the intimacy, the sensuous pleasure they had taken in creating something together was gone.

"I am foreshadowing what is to come," she said. "A mother to lose her child."

"But he will be a man, then. You have a sweet babe to rejoice in. And he's no ordinary babe, so any knowledge of his death won't matter."

"A mother still will lose her child, no matter the origins."

"That may be your vision, but it's not mine. So, please. Look adoring."

From the kitchen, across the corridor she could hear Tomaso screech. She suppressed a laugh. Tomaso was becoming cranky of late, escaping his leash and knocking over jars and sacks. Joanie had told the kitchen staff that he scared the rats and mice away, but Alys had no idea if that was true, or if the tom cat that scratched and chewed on the monkey as much as it chewed on him was the real reason. The two seemed to have come to a tacit agreement lately.

The baby blew bubbles, her legs waggling in the air. Alys looked at her and the baby smiled back.

"Joanie, I think her clout needs to be changed."

Joanie gave a little grunt. "Not at all. She had clean on just before I laid her on your lap."

Alys sighed and looked away for a moment, until, remembering, she pressed her mouth into an adoring smile. How long would she be able to endure this, she wondered? Alessandra had provided no objections at all to the project, with the proviso that the painting to be done here, at Alessandra's small palazzo. They had settled on an upstairs room with sufficient light that faced the canal so that the canvas and all the materials could be left without any interference and Alessandra could come and inspect it at will. This meant that Alys's hopes of painting were confined to a small board that could be stored away at a moment's notice, brushes abandoned and Alys taking her seat and pose should Alessandra's footfall be heard in the corridor.

She tried to think of her painting now as the baby wriggled and gurgled on her lap. She'd decided to paint Judith, just her figure grasping the hair of Holiphernes's head as it dangled bleeding and bodiless. It suited her mood. Even now, she could see Judith's arms, strong and sinewy for it needed such strength to cut off Holiphernes's head, she reasoned. She would study the anatomy of her own arm as it grasped something.

A soft slap against her hands caught her attention. Eleanor's hand reached out and latched on to Alys's finger. She felt the strength in the small hand, clinging so tight she couldn't loosen it. Eleanor gave a small cry. Alys felt something pull within her. The cry came again as a little wail. Alys looked across at Joanie. Underneath the sumptuous blue gown she could feel her bindings soaked through with the milk that had spilled from her breasts.

CHAPTER SIXTEEN
VENICE, LATE SUMMER 1447
ALYS

Alys unwrapped the bindings on her chest carefully and stared down at her breasts. They were smaller in size than they'd been a few weeks earlier, when Eleanor had been born and her milk had come in, but they were fuller than she'd been before she was pregnant. For a moment she imagined what it would be like to hold Eleanor there, to have her suckle with the same fierce strength as she had used to clench Alys's finger a few days ago.

Without thinking, she drew on a loose wrap and tied the ribbons closed, careful not to disturb Bitty who lay sleeping on the bed. The hour was late and most would be abed now. She made her way upstairs, along the corridor and opened the door without making a sound. She paused at the threshold, listening. She could hear short little breaths and then a soft sigh. She moved to the wooden cradle that stood in the middle of the room, careful not to disturb the wet nurse who snored in the narrow cot against the wall. Cautiously, she lifted the child into her arms and made soft soothing sounds. The wet nurse stirred in her sleep. Alys froze. After a moment, she moved again and quietly left, baby in her arms, and went back down to her room.

Once inside, she sat down on the bed, still cradling the child. By the light of the candles she could see the tiny blue veins of the baby's lids and on impulse leaned down and kissed them.

"Eleanor," she whispered. She shoved aside the cloth that covered her breast and pressed the baby's mouth close to it. Instinctively, the child opened her mouth and latched on. Alys felt a slight pain and pull, and a moment later a feeling she couldn't describe washed over her. She'd no idea if there was any milk there to feed Eleanor, but she didn't care. The child suckled peacefully.

∾

She could hear excited voices coming from the *sala*. She tugged impatiently at her gown, wondering what would have Alessandra in such a state.

"Leave this, Joanie, and go see what the commotion is about. The last time there was this much excitement the monkey had got loose in the *sala*. We can't have that again."

"Let me just finish lacing you up," said Joanie. "I'm sure it's nothing."

"No, it's fine. I can manage the rest. Just go."

Joanie left without further word and Alys considered the tight gown. Her breasts had enlarged again since she'd taken to the clandestine night feeds. She gave herself no time to reflect on it, she just did it, stealing away to Eleanor's room after everyone had gone to bed and bringing her back to her own for an hour or so to cuddle and nurse. The wet nurse suspected nothing as she snored through the night and praised Eleanor's sweet nature the next morning.

Joanie had given her a few sideways glances but had uttered no word about it, and though Alys knew her dear friend was no fool and probably knew the truth, she preferred to pretend she didn't. In the past days, though, her pose adoring the child on her lap, struck at the sittings for the painting, had become real and she came to miss the time when she was able to have Eleanor on her lap or at her breast.

Joanie burst through the door. "Oh Alys," she said in English. "You must come."

Alys turned to her. "What is it?"

Joanie kneaded her skirt. "It's Barnabas."

"Barnabas? He's here?"

"No, no. There's a messenger come. A man. Some friend of Barnabas's. 'e says Barnabas is in trouble."

"Trouble? What sort of trouble? What do you mean?" asked Alys sharply. "I thought he was in Africa?"

"'e was. 'e is. Only someone's gone and taken 'im from 'is trading caravan and are holding 'im captive."

Alys felt a pain, sharp as any knife, deep in her belly. "Who is holding him captive, Joanie?"

"You best get it from the man who came. 'e brought a letter written by Barnabas. Only written as 'e calls 'imself, Giacomo. Or so that's what I gather."

Alys made her way to the door, Joanie attempting to stop her to tie her hair back with a ribbon. She waved Joanie's efforts away and walked quickly across the corridor to the *sala*.

Once inside, Alessandra greeted her. "Oh, good," she said. "Perhaps you can make more sense of this. Apparently, Giacomo is held captive somewhere and he needs our help. How, I'm not so sure, and neither is

Captain Flores. And the letter he brings makes it no clearer. Either my Latin is poorer than I thought, or something else is going on."

Alys turned to face the man. "Captain Flores?" Though his dark hair and beard were unkempt and his face darkly tanned, he swept her an elegant bow. She didn't recall meeting him, but something about his name stirred a memory within her. "You are a friend of some longstanding of Signor Bonavillagio?"

"I am, madonna," he said. "We were first acquainted in England."

"Ah, I see. So you know him well enough."

Something flickered in his eyes. "*Si*, well enough."

He'd answered her question with that flicker and brief remark. He was most certainly the captain that had befriended the young Barnabas after he'd saved the captain's life. She remembered Barnabas telling her about him and his companion, the African man. The one who went off with Barnabas as a friend and mentor. And the one who was no longer a mentor, for reasons she was uncertain about.

She narrowed her eyes. "You have news of Signor Bonavillagio?" she asked.

"I do, madonna. I was telling Madonna Alessandra of the unfortunate events that overtook us when we were in the trade caravan." Flores explained the kidnapping by the Nubian Copts in the northern lands of the Ethiopes.

"And you were captured as well? How is it you escaped?" asked Alessandra.

"No, I wasn't captured. I remained with the caravan, but they insisted on confiscating the cargo and the money Giacomo had, in exchange for joining a caravan that was returning to Cairo. I had no choice but to do as they arranged. I waited there, hoping for some news and finally went to Alexandria to try to get back here to get help. It was there, after a few inquiries, that I found Hal and the Nubians."

"Do you know why Signor Bonavillagio was taken?" asked Alys.

"They thought he had a holy text belonging to them."

"Presumably Signor Bonavillagio didn't have this holy text?"

Flores gave a wry smile and shook his head. "He'd said something about one back in Cairo to our guide to ensure the guide's cooperation, but there was nothing to it. I presume the Nubians heard about it and took him to get possession of it."

Alys sighed inwardly. It sounded too much like Barnabas to doubt its truth. "What had he told them when they discovered he didn't have this text?"

Flores sighed. "I'm sorry. I only know what his companion, Hal, told me. According to him, Giacomo said that, though he didn't have the text, he knew where it was and could arrange for someone to buy it." He pointed to the letter Alessandra held in her hand. "I believe that's what the letter is about. Hal asked me to come here and deliver the message while he waits back in Alexandria with the Nubian escorts. They expect that I will return with the manuscript after making arrangements to buy it from the Grand Vizier. It's in his library."

"I see," said Alys and she frowned. "What does the letter say exactly?"

Flores shrugged. "It's in Latin.

Alessandra handed her the letter. Alys scanned the letter and bit her lip. The Latin she'd learned under the Duchess's tutelage was rusty, but she could read enough of it to understand that, somehow, they needed to produce a convincing manuscript if Barnabas was to be freed. And something more was there. She looked again and saw the letter was addressed to A. Regina Gregis. Who was that? Queen of the Port? Or wait, did he really mean docks? The thought made her stop. Queenhithe? Alys of Queenhithe? Was he addressing the letter to her really? Her chest tightened and she read the letter through, slower this time. It was only now that she questioned her immediate reaction, this burning desire to go to Barnabas's aid. All the hurt, the anger welled up in her at once and it caught her breath.

"The letter makes more sense now, but I don't know what we can do to help your friend, Signor Bonavillagio," Alessandra was saying to Flores. "I'm afraid that when he ventured into Africa he risked not only his life and money, but my money as well. And now he has lost it. I have no funds left to provide any kind of assistance. In fact, to state it plainly, your friend has caused me ruin."

"Surely not ruin," said Alys lightly.

Alessandra turned to face Alys. "Well, I will admit that I cannot lay the cause of my ruin entirely at his door. There is also you to consider, *cara mia*. You have a share in the blame."

"But surely I have a share in the cause of your imminent recovery? The painting progresses very well, in fact it's almost finished. And when it is, there's a fortune to be made from it and the other one."

"Bah, promises only. I cannot live on promises. Nor can you."

Alys remained silent, knowing that to say anything more at this point would only add fuel to the fire.

"Has he no money left behind that can help?" asked Alys. "And a manuscript? It mentions a text or manuscript. And he mentions a box. Has he any others we can use?"

"There's little money," said Alessandra after a pause. "Most of his funds were used to support this disastrous enterprise. And a locked box. I haven't the key, though."

Alys turned to Flores. "Are you certain there is nothing left that can support some kind of rescue?"

Flores reddened under her gaze. "I- I did manage to save a sack of pepper. One that Giacomo had hidden. And the other manuscripts. The two he had with him. But they're not holy texts. At least I don't think so. They're in Arabic."

"The pepper, can you not sell the pepper and use that? Will it be enough?"

Flores shrugged. "I don't know. It's not much. Just one sack. And I don't know if I can find a buyer. I'm no merchant. Giacomo and Hal dealt with those things."

Something shifted in Alys's mind. "Who is Hal? And how does he know Signor Bonavillagio?"

Flores gave her an indifferent look. "I believe they became acquainted during Giacomo's travels on the Sea of Marmara. He was a seaman of some sort."

"And he's called Hal?" said Alys. "Is he English?"

Flores nodded. "Though I don't know where he's from, or how long he's been away."

Alys grew tense. "What does he look like?"

Flores described him briefly and Alys's breath caught as the familiar description unfolded. If she put several years on her own memory image there could be little doubt. But it seemed impossible. Nevertheless, her mind was made up.

"What is it, Maria?" asked Alessandra. "You know this man, Hal?"

Alys turned to face Alessandra. "We'll arrange to sell the pepper to fund the trip. I will take those texts and go with Signor Flores to Alexandria to arrange for Signor Bonavillagio's release."

"But that is impossible. Why should you concern yourself personally?" said Alessandra.

"Because I intend to meet Signor Bonavillagio's friend."

"What could be the reason for that? What do you know of this man that makes you behave so rashly?" asked Alessandra.

"Because I'm certain that the man is my brother, someone I thought was long dead."

"But you must stay here, await his return," said Alessandra. "You have obligations, foremost of all to me. I will not let you go."

Alys gave her a direct look. "I have more than earned the amount you invested in me, Alessandra and I will give you more, if you insist, but I won't be diverted from my purpose. I'm going." She turned to Flores. "And you, signore, I hope you will escort me."

Flores glanced at Alessandra and then bowed. "Of course, madonna. It will be my pleasure."

∾

Alys stared at the small painting in front of her and gave a slight smile. There were only a few things she wanted to adjust and finish, but it would have to wait. Still, she was pleased, especially by the deep blue and gold of the dress which offset the flesh tones. The shape and strength of the arms that gripped the large knife and hair of Holophernes head were just what she'd envisioned. The power and energy they embodied rang of the anger she wanted to infer. Deep distress and anger, mirrored so well in Judith's face.

Across from her was the larger painting propped on the easel. It was nearly finished, too, and though many of the brush strokes were her own, she had little doubt that Carlo would complete it without any problem. She gazed at the image of the small child. Eleanor had been restless in the last sitting a few days earlier, as if she knew it would be the final time Alys could hold her, without any judging eyes. Alys bit her lip and blinked away the unwelcome tears that suddenly sprang up. She wouldn't think about Eleanor. She couldn't think about her if she was going to go through with her plan.

Alys turned her gaze back to her own painting and, on impulse, picked up a brush and dipped it into a daub of paint still wet on the palette. She hovered over the lower right-hand corner a moment before setting the brush to the canvas. When she'd done she set the brush down and laughed softly. *A. Regina Banchina.* Let them make of it what they would.

A short while later she left the room and paused at the stairs. She turned and made her way along to another room, one at the end of corridor. She listened outside before she slipped in. Eleanor lay in her cradle, the wet nurse in a chair, sewing by the small window. Alys smiled at the wet nurse and went over to the cradle, leaning in. Eleanor's eyes were closed and her small chest rose and fell in a deep sleep. Alys took one of Eleanor's hands with her finger and rubbed it. The baby stirred and sighed. Alys felt a small tug. She forced herself to quickly kiss the child's cheek and withdraw, before she lost her resolve. She left the room and closed the door behind her.

Back at the head of the stairs, she saw Carlo ascending purposefully. He looked up and frowned at her.

"So, you are deserting me," he said a bitter edge to his tone.

"It's not desertion," she said. "I'll return, I assure you. Besides, you have no need for me now. The world will see from your latest painting that you are a man of talent."

His face softened a moment and he reached for her hand, searching her eyes. "I had great need of you, once. But you had no interest, not really."

She gave him a pained look. "Oh, Carlo. I did care for you, you know that. And if things had been different...."

He withdrew his hand and drew himself up. "I have talent, yes. Great talent, I think not. But it will be enough. And that's all I ask." He bowed to her briefly. "And now I must wish you a good journey."

She squeezed his hand. "Thank you, Carlo," she whispered.

❧

Alys stood in the small cabin dressed in her plainest gown, cloak and shoes, a dark veil covering her face. It was hard to believe the journey was about to begin. Her mind fled to Eleanor, the moment before she kissed her cheek and her chest tightened at the thought of it. Eleanor was in good hands. Though Alessandra had professed disinterest, Alys knew the truth. Since the scene in Alessandra's bedroom, Alys had witnessed many other little stolen moments—a brief touch of the head, a caress on the cheek with a finger and countless other gestures that told a different story to the one Alessandra spoke. She had no fear that Eleanor would be banished to a remote place out of Alys's reach.

Joanie entered the cabin and placed a square cloth-wrapped bundle on the narrow box bed built into the side of the cabin. The two of them would sleep there and though it might not be the comfort to which she was recently accustomed, Alys knew she should be grateful.

Kristin Gleeson

That Flores had managed to secure passage on this merchant ship not just for him, but for two women as well, was no small miracle. And she mustn't forget the monkey. She glanced in the corner where Tomaso sat chittering in his little cage, his face peering angrily out at her. She'd insisted on bringing the monkey. It seemed right that it should go back to Barnabas, back to his real master. And she knew that without her presence, Alessandra would have wasted no time in poisoning the animal and making up some sad story about his death.

"Captain Flores bade me give you that," said Joanie, pointing to the bundle.

She was red-faced and sweating in her own gown and cloak, for the weather had grown muggy in the past few days. Summer was truly upon them. Alys looked at the square bundle and realised immediately what it must be. She picked it up and unwrapped it carefully. Inside, were the two texts. Neither one was very long and they were both in a script she didn't recognise, but she could see it was a fair match for the texts she'd found in the locked box. It had taken only a few sharp blows to open it.

Was the script Arabic? She'd no idea. Flores had only said he believed one of the texts described the route they took. She could only hope that it would suffice to secure Barnabas's release. And the copies would possibly serve. Surely they would value something so obviously ancient about their homeland. Perhaps in Alexandria they could find someone who would be able to read it. Or Hal might know more. She bit her lip. It seemed hard to believe that after all these years she would see her brother. Would she even recognise him? And what would he make of her? Well, she must face up to it, whatever he thought and said. She had chosen to come because of him, she told herself. She fingered the manuscript, her brow creased as

168

she bit her lip. She was a fool. That much she knew. A fool to keep chasing a dream of a person who had long ago died in spirit, if not in body. She made a snort of disgust.

CHAPTER SEVENTEEN
ROHA, THE ETHIOPES, SUMMER 1447
BARNABAS

I pulled the chain that secured me to the wall. As before, there was little give. I dropped my arm to my side and leaned back against the stone. How many days had I been down here? I could hardly trust the scratches on the wall I'd made each time the door had opened and someone had brought me a bowl of thin gruel and a goatskin of water. That had been my best guess of a day passing. Surely it was more than eight days?

I'd seen no one else since that first brief meeting with al Qali. Shortly after, I'd been bundled to this cell, left to here to rot. There was only pale shaft of light from a narrow slit in the wooden door, it was weak and provided little light. I did know that I was underground somewhere, because I had descended steps when I'd first been brought here.

I scratched my beard, aware of the small life that seemed to have taken up permanent residence there and elsewhere on my body. The manacle around my wrist chafed my skin. I couldn't understand many things about my imprisonment, the first being why I was still alive. Al Qali obviously wanted something from me, but I'd yet to figure out what it was. Or possibly al Qali wanted to torture me in as many ways as he could think of before killing me. Because one thing was clear, if I ever escaped from al Qali there was no question I would go after him until one of us was dead.

The door opened and a figure stood there, the light behind him casting him in shadow. I squinted, trying to see who it was. The figure seemed to be the same one who always brought my meals. He placed a bowl and a pitcher on the floor near me.

"What day is it?" I asked in Arabic.

The man came over and squatted beside me. I tried a few words of the Tuareg language I'd learned, but the man didn't bother to even look at me. He leaned over and, key in hand, unlocked the manacle around my wrist.

"You will wash first and then come with me," he said in broken Arabic.

I rose carefully, my legs stiff and unyielding from the little exercise of the past few days. I took a few steps and stumbled, my balance off. The man gripped my arm and steadied me. Carefully, I knelt beside the bowl and pitcher. The man poured the water in and handed me a cloth to dry myself. I set it down and proceeded to sluice off the dregs of my imprisonment the best I could in the situation.

When I'd finished he drew me up and led me forward while I tried to keep up. We went through the door and climbed up a few steps and turned right, entering a small corridor. We went along the corridor and came to a thick wooden door. The door opened on to a stone building that rose tall above me. Light streamed from a window above. Gradually my eyes adjusted and I realised I was standing in a church. A church hewn out of rock that rose tall and majestically around me. I stared in amazement.

"Here he is, lord," the man said.

Two men sat at a table to one side of the altar. One, white-haired and elderly, his face deeply lined, hunched in his simple white robe of linen that displayed a darker tunic beneath. Around his neck he wore an elaborate gold cross. Though I didn't know him there was something that was familiar. It was when I saw al Qali by his side that I realised what it was. There was no doubting the relationship between the two. It wasn't just the colour of the skin and the shape of the nose, but the eyes. They were the same. The same, except for the glittering hatred that shone out of al Qali's eyes.

"So, Father," said al Qali in Arabic. "This is the person I spoke to you about."

I bowed first to al Qali's father and then to him and forced an ironic smile on my face. "You'll forgive my state, I haven't been able to address my appearance sufficiently since my arrival."

"He speaks Arabic quite well," said al Qali's father.

Al Qali gave a brief bow of his head. "I thank you. He was an attentive student, but I was a strict master."

I directed my gaze at the older man. "Many apologies, sir, but I haven't had the benefit of an introduction,"

Al Qali gave me a dark look. "You will remain silent until you're spoken to."

Al Qali's father frowned at his son. "You may call me Hawqal."

"No!" said al Qali. "Tell him who you really are. Tell him that you're Jan Yekuno Amlek, named for the last king of the Aqau people from whom you're descended. And tell him also that you have the blood of the Gebre

Mesquel Lalibela running in your veins and that you named me Lalibela after that sainted man."

"All of that means nothing to this young man, I'm certain," said Hawqal calmly.

"Alas," I said, keeping my tone even. "I'm afraid that you're correct. But still, I would like to learn." I gave al Qali a polite smile. "As your son knows I always like to learn. He has already taught me so much. So very much."

Al Qali gave me a stern look and spoke in English. "Some things you failed to grasp. But know this, Giacomo, or should I say Barnabas, you will do as I bid this last time."

"But I have always done as you bid me, al Qali, and haven't always been pleased with the results."

Al Qali brushed aside my remark. "Enough of that. I hear you took a manuscript from Halil Pasha's library."

I raised my brow, unable to hide my surprise. "You heard that? Interesting."

"This manuscript. Where is it?"

I shrugged my shoulders. "How can I know? You certainly must admit that I don't have it on my person." I pulled at my ragged pantaloons and tunic. "Your men would have told you."

"Don't play the fool with me. My father has travelled a long way so that I can show him this manuscript."

"Which manuscript?"

Al Qali pursed his lips. "Don't provoke me, Barnabas. You can have no idea what my anger can do."

"Probably not, but you must concede that I have a full understanding of what your avarice can provoke you to."

Anger flashed through al Qali's eyes and when he spoke there was a dark edge to it. "There was no avarice involved with my dealings with Halil Pasha. That was an exchange. An exchange that left me cheated and now I will rectify that."

"You think I stole the manuscript you were promised from Halil Pasha's library?" My mind was racing, trying to make the connection to the manuscript and al Qali.

"I know you did, so there's no use in telling me otherwise."

"And which manuscript is that?"

Al Qali rose and slapped me across the face. "I have warned you once already."

Hawqal laid a restraining hand on al Qali's arm. "Calm yourself, son," he said in Arabic. "This is no way to behave."

Al Qali made a visible effort to compose himself. He sat down again.

"I apologise if I upset you," I said in Arabic. "You see, I took two manuscripts and I wasn't sure which one you meant."

Al Qali's face showed surprise. "Two? What two?"

"I have a manuscript that describes the various salt routes into the heart of Africa. It seemed an interesting and perhaps profitable bit of text."

"The other manuscript is the one that concerns me," said al Qali.

"But I can't conceive how it would," I said. "That's the cause of my confusion and what you perceived as dissembling. It is text that merely recounts some old French man's travel memories."

"But you know it's more than that, for you wouldn't have bothered with it, otherwise."

I shrugged. "Perhaps I thought it might be useful in my own travels. I do trade now in the many places he mentions."

"Yes, exactly. He mentions one area in particular and one person, or so I thought when I scanned the document before it was so rudely slipped out of my baggage."

"But how are you connected to Prester John?" I asked.

I'd realised that he was after the description of Prester John, but I could think of no reason beyond it, despite the delaying remarks I'd made. I would have to wait and hope that my admission about the manuscript wouldn't be to any great disadvantage.

"I am descended from him that you call Prester John. Such incorrect translation is a common fault among your people."

"My people?" I said.

"You people from the across the Mediterranean Sea who call yourselves Christian, but you don't know the word for 'Prester' means 'priest' and 'Jan' or 'John,' as you call him, is our word for 'king'."

"He was a priest king? Then there is no name for him?"

"Lalibela is his name. And my father should be his lawful heir. That manuscript contains proof that will allow me to challenge the usurpers, the Akara who sit on the throne and blasphemously claim descendance from Solomon."

I stared at al Qali. My first reaction was to laugh at such a mad claim, but I could see he was deadly serious and, if what he said was true, there seemed some plausibility to the whole claim. I looked over at Hawqal. He nodded slowly.

"What you say may be true, but I can't recall any particular point in the manuscript that would help substantiate your claim," I said carefully. "The writer talks of his meeting with a person who'd been to Prester John's kingdom and describes it in great detail, but I don't remember much beyond that."

"But he recounts the history, I am certain of it. I have searched years for this manuscript, since I first heard of its existence in Alexandria. I followed the rumours, the false trails, looking at every possibility in all the libraries across Christendom, until I discovered that it was most likely in Halil Pasha's library."

"And you used me to get it," I said coldly.

"Ah but Barnabas, you had so much talent. In so many ways. I couldn't fail to put such talent to the most important purpose of all. And you must admit, I have helped you in many ways. Raising you up from the gutter, enabling you to move in circles and achieve things you have never dreamed of as a child."

"Raising me up to be used as a sodomite, yearning for opium and coerced to commit murder," I said, my voice rising in anger. I fought to control it. It would do me no good to have him see how much his actions had affected me. "But," I said, striving for calm, "I concede that you have given me many advantages. I was able to read that manuscript with little problem. And I tell you there was nothing in there that could prove your claim."

"Is this true?" asked Hawqal.

Al Qali gave a small laugh. "You mustn't believe him, Father. He says it only to make us believe it's not worth retrieving."

I sighed audibly. "As I said. I haven't got it with me. As you recall you abducted me quite suddenly in the middle of the night. I was hardly sleeping with the manuscript tied to my waist." I searched his face but there was nothing there that indicated if I should tell him the rest. I swallowed. "The Nubians who held me, you might also know, took me from the Tuareg people I was travelling with. That's where you'll find the manuscript. It was packed among my things. And I have no idea where my things are now. With the Tuareg traders? With Flores? Perhaps neither. I'm afraid your quest continues, al Qali, or do you prefer Lalibela?"

Al Qali gave me a flat smile. "I realised that you didn't have the manuscript with you, of course. You shouldn't take me for a fool. And as no fool, I know you will have secured the manuscript in some manner, if only by making a copy and leaving it somewhere. And remember, it was I who taught you and know your capabilities. Shall I contrive a showstone? Or provide you with other means so that you can see where the manuscript is located?"

I stiffened. "You can't force me to see when there's nothing to see. You know that."

Hawqal gave his son a stern look. "What is this 'seeing' you talk about? What do you mean, showstone?"

Al Qali hesitated, then spoke. "It's nothing, Father. I merely meant to persuade this man to tell what I'm certain he knows."

"Mustapha, you know I will tolerate no sorcery. It's against God's law."

"It's nothing, Father, I assure you." Al Qali turned to me. "Think on what I've said." He added in English, "We'll speak further on this later."

Back in my cell I sat on the floor, contemplating the encounter with al Qali. The story he had told seemed more fantastical than anything else I would have imagined. Initially, I thought a desire for learning as much as possible drove him to find a particular manuscript, with, eventually, greed added, and finally revenge of some sort. But never this desire to prove himself an heir to a crown lost so long ago no one remembered. I tried to recall the words of the manuscript. I was certain there was nothing in them to prove what al Qali wanted.

I pushed aside the speculation. It did no good to dwell on the story. Al Qali had made it clear that I must somehow produce the manuscript, or at least tell him where it was. If it was as I believed, the copy might be on its way to Alexandria. But how to get it here? And could I rely on Alys? I knew better than to rely on Alessandra and only hoped that Alys would see the letter and take action. Even that was doubtful and I could hardly blame her. She could only view my treatment of her as abominable. She wouldn't have known how much it cost me to behave in that manner, how often I tried not to care for her, allow myself to love her, with the opium coursing through my body and the path of revenge I was set on.

And now that I'd rid my body of the opium and the path of my revenge seemed ludicrous in the face of al Qali's own madness, there was no hope for anything. It was clear that too much was left to chance. And at this point I had no faith in chance.

CHAPTER EIGHTEEN
ALEXANDRIA, EGYPT, SUMMER 1447
ALYS

Alys stared at the door nervously. She could feel Joanie's comforting hand on her arm. It would be any moment now. In the corner, in his little wooden cage Tomaso screeched. Calm enough on the voyage, the monkey and she had become friends of a sort, she giving him comfits and morsels through his little cage and he taking them with bared teeth, as if they both knew there was a role to play. Now, it seemed even he knew some things can only be left to chance.

During the journey he'd been a comfort, and still was, a companion to distract her from the loss of Eleanor. Her breast milk had long ago dried up with the help of Joanie's ministrations, and the physical pain of her once full breasts was gone, but the pain in her heart remained.

Arriving here in Alexandria had served as an additional distraction as one of the decisive moments in her journey approached. A bustling port, Alexandria held many cultures and races, as far as she could see, that teemed in markets and down alleys of stone and mud buildings, some crumbling and once great, others of a more temporary nature. Colourful canopies covered brightly arrayed stalls and shop entrances and the goods they contained gave off aromas that mixed spices, herbs, oils and perfumes. It had almost been a relief when Flores had installed her, Joanie and Tomaso in this sparse room.

"It will be fine, sweeting, you'll see," said Joanie.

"It's been years, Joanie," she whispered. "We're different people now."

She heard footsteps outside the door, rose and braced herself. Flores entered, his dark hair and beard, so familiar from the days of their voyage, trimmed and freshly combed. Behind him stood a man, less well groomed, but broader in chest and fair-haired. Her heart sank for a moment, for there was little that was familiar to her, that is until his inquiring gaze met hers and she saw his eyes.

"Sister?" Hal said.

"Hal?" she whispered. "Is it you?"

She moved forward tentatively and held out her hand. He took it, pulled her closer to him and clutched her face between his hands to examine her carefully.

"I can 'ardly believe, 'alfling," he said. "I never thought to see you again."

She put her arms around him and gave him a shy hug. "It's me, Hal. Your sister."

He drew her away from him and studied her. "But look at you. I can 'ardly call you 'alfling, now, can I? You're a woman." His face darkened. "In more ways than I'd like."

Alys looked away and Joanie came up behind her. "She's a good soul, and I'll 'ear no one say different."

Alys put her arm around Joanie. "This is my friend Joanie. We served together at the Duke of Gloucester's household."

Hal raised a brow and gave her a dubious look. "Worked for a duke, you say? And 'ow did that come about? Is that where you came into your pretty way of speaking?"

Alys grimaced. "There's much in both our pasts that we would want to acquaint ourselves with." She turned to Flores. "But we have our friend Captain Flores here," she said switching to Italian. "And we mustn't be rude. Besides, I would offer you some refreshment so we can exchange news with ease."

She gestured to the chairs provided in the small rooms that Flores had secured for her during her stay in Alexandria. In the next room were two cots that served her and Joanie. There were a few woven rugs on the stone floor and on the table to lend splashes of colour. It was not luxurious by any means, but it served its purpose.

On the table was some local fare: a dish of hummus, bread, olives, figs, and falafel. A flagon of wine and some stoneware cups were also provided. She poured the wine, taking great care to steady her hands, and gave a filled cup to each of them. They took it from her and the silence stretched. Tomaso gave a long screech and all eyes turned to him.

"Jacko's monkey," said Hal and gave her a puzzled look. "You brought Tomaso?"

"I thought he belonged with his owner," said Alys.

Hal glanced at Flores. "I thought he gave the monkey to some whore he'd bedded, as company for her dog."

Alys felt a twinge at the thought of Bitty. She'd left him behind for more than practical reasons. Somehow she felt the dog would guard Eleanor. A foolish thought, but one that strangely gave her comfort.

Hal was staring at her. "It was you."

She blinked at him and gave a small nod. "A courtesan, not a whore, Hal. There's a world of difference, you know."

"You mean you pay more for a courtesan," said Hal in a dark tone. "It wasn't what I would want for my sister, no matter how much she's paid."

"But you weren't there, were you?" Alys snapped in English. "You were who knows where. For I had no word of your whereabouts, and I was left alone when Mother died."

"Mother is dead?" asked Hal.

"What did you think? That I would desert her as you did?"

Hal looked ashamed. "I'm sorry. My tongue ran away with me." He turned to Flores and spoke in Italian. "You must accept my apologies, Flores. Old hurts over things that are now in the past."

Flores shrugged and gave a slow smile. "There is much between a brother and a sister that no else can appreciate. I own to two sisters and they do very little of what I tell them, even though they are younger than me."

"I'm glad you understand," said Hal.

"Si, of course. I too would be angry if I knew my sister had led such a life and born a child to add to the shame."

Alys stood up on impulse and threw her wine at Flores. "How dare you, signore. You interfere in affairs that don't concern you."

Flores raised a brow and wiped his face with a cloth he pulled from his sleeve. "Not the best wine, at least. So there is no wastage."

Hal grabbed Alys's arm as she placed the cup on the table. "Is this true? You've borne a child?"

Alys gave him a level look and shrugged off his hand. "As I've said, there's bound to be much in both our pasts. And you know nothing of mine in the years since you've gone, so it's not your place to judge."

"A child? Whose is it? Do you even know?" Hal said.

"We're not here to talk about my past," said Alys. "We must focus on the matter at hand. Have you any news of Signor Bonavillagio?"

Hal remained silent for a moment, visibly trying to control himself before answering. "There's been no word, as yet. Flores says you have a manuscript. Is it the text they want? Jacko said it was in some library belonging to a Grand Vizier. How did you come by it?"

"I have a copy," said Alys. She glanced at Flores. "A copy and the original that Flores had among…Signor Bonavillagio's things." She'd paused a moment, unsure how to address Barnabas, but she opted for caution in the end.

Hal gave Flores a puzzled look. "You had some of Jacko's things?"

Flores looked blandly at Hal. "Merely a sack of pepper and the texts he'd left behind. I sold the pepper and we're using it to pay for our efforts here."

Hal frowned and nodded. "Only one sack? But there were more."

"Gone," said Flores with no elaboration.

"The text is in Arabic, I think," said Alys. "It might pass for the manuscript they seek."

"It's a holy text," Jacko said. "Does it look like a holy text?"

"I'm not sure," said Alys. She decided not to tell him that she doubted greatly there was anything holy about the text. "But we can hope that it will suffice. At least until we can free Signor Bonavillagio."

"We?" said Flores. "You and your maidservant will return on the next ship."

Alys straightened. "No, I will accompany you." Joanie gave her a firm kick under the table, her disapproval clear.

"You will not," said Hal. "It's no place for a woman. These men may be Christian, but they're from parts that have no respect for woman and their virtue."

"But my dear brother," said Alys. "You've already pointed out that I'm no virtuous woman, so it matters not. I assure you I will be properly veiled and keep away from them."

"But why would you want to go?" asked Hal.

"But don't you remember, I'm the woman who has roused enough affection in Signor Bonavillagio that he gave me his prized monkey. Such affection cannot go unrewarded. I must do what I can to help him. I speak and read many languages." She looked at Flores and then Hal. "Can either of you boast the same? Do you speak Latin, Captain Flores?"

"I can speak Latin to some degree," he said carefully.

"And do you read it? I think not."

He shrugged and shook his head.

"There, you see? You do need me. I can communicate with these Christian Nubian men. I alone will be able to reason with them and try to convince them this text is something they want so we can secure Signor Bonavillagio's release."

"You speak some truth," said Flores.

"No," said Hal. "No, I won't let you."

Flores put a hand on his shoulder. "You've no choice, amico. She's right. She's Giacomo's best chance."

Alys allowed herself a brief moment of satisfaction. She'd won this point over Flores and her brother, she only hoped she could do the same over the Nubian men she would have to deal with.

∽

She stared at the three Nubian men with all the regal hauteur she could muster, the image of the Duchess looming large in her mind. The claustrophobia she felt in this small private courtyard of the inn where they arranged to meet was not entirely due to the badly plastered high walls and the presence of a fountain, or even the presence of Hal, Flores, Joanie and the three Nubians. It was the tense atmosphere that threatened to close in on her.

The manuscript lay wrapped tightly in cloth on her lap, her hands placed protectively over it. Her thick veil was drawn back from her face. Beside her, even under her thick veil, Alys could feel Joanie's disapproval strongly. They all sat on stools at a scarred wooden table, Hal on her other side and Flores at Joanie's side, each man wearing a long dagger in his belt.

"Of course, I am the person to whom the letter was directed," she said in Latin. "I have a long acquaintance with Signor Bonavillagio and we've frequently done business together."

The three men exchanged glances. They were all dark skinned, darker than any she'd seen, bar one. The tall, bearded one, dressed in a white linen tunic belted in the middle with a mantle draped across it of a brilliant blue, had introduced himself as "Kephale" in barely understandable Latin. It took some time for her to realise that "Kephale" was his title and not his name. He seemed to be in charge and he now nodded slightly. He'd spoken in halting Greek, at first, and then some Arabic, but she'd only shaken her head. The Duchess had taught her only French and passable Latin.

"You have holy book?" asked the Kephale.

She concentrated on his words, trying to understand. She nodded. "You may examine it, but I will keep it with me until we have Signor Bonavillagio safely in our company."

"He is not here. We will take book and let him go when we are home."

"Then I will have to come with you," said Alys. "Because I'm not giving up this book until I see Signor Bonavillagio."

The Kephale's face darkened. "No. You cannot come. Too dangerous for women."

She straightened and lifted her chin a fraction higher. "You have no choice, sir."

"What are they saying?" said Hal insistently behind her in English.

"I'll explain later," she said.

She watched the three men consult. The shorter, younger one seemed to be opposed to the points the other two were making. His eyes flashed and his mouth tightened. He glanced over at Alys and she forced a calm look in return.

The discussion continued. The Kephale eventually put an end to it by grasping the younger man's arm and speaking a few words in a firm manner. The matter concluded, the Kephale turned to Alys.

"We are not happy, but we will let you come with us," he said. "But we see holy book first."

"Of course," said Alys.

She looked down at the bundle and wet her lips. It was the moment of truth, now. Or at least one of them. Would they be able to read the Arabic in the text? She unwrapped the bundle and lifted the text out and placed it on the table close to the Kephale. He drew it close to him and the two other Nubian men crowded near. The Kephale scanned the covering page and then opened it carefully, almost reverently to the next page. The old parchment curled a little at the edges, a consequence of the time it had spent rolled up. The script was faded in places, but still decipherable. The Kephale frowned, studying the text. He placed a finger on a word and muttered something to himself. The younger man questioned him and he turned and spoke an answer. Their companion bit his lip when the Kephale put a question to him and shook his head.

Joanie gripped Alys's hand under the table. Alys could see Hal's hand edging toward his dagger and Flores leaned forward. The Nubian men looked up and the Kephale regarded Alys gravely and gave a great sigh.

"It is not clear to us if this is what we seek," he said. "But we will take you with us to our home. There our priest Paulos will tell us if this is the holy text. He reads this language."

Alys felt some of the tension leak out of her body. "Very good. My men will leave with you as soon as possible."

They nodded reluctantly and discussed the arrangements. It was only later, back in her rooms with only Joanie for company, that she allowed herself a smile. But the smile was fleeting. She was only over the first hurdle. She had to make the journey and then, when she got to this Nubian community, find a way to secure Barnabas's release before they discovered this text she had wasn't the holy book they wanted.

CHAPTER NINETEEN
THE NILE RIVER, SUMMER 1447
ALYS

Alys sat silently, watching the landscape drift by. The boat on which they travelled, a *felluca*, powered by oar and sail when the wind favoured them, moved slowly up the Nile, past countless trees, open grassland, and occasionally groups of people crowded along its banks. From the shade of her covered canopy on deck she would on occasion lean forward, startled by some strange animal or other unusual sight. The long lizard-like animals that swam in the river in particular had caught her attention earlier, and when she questioned one of the three Nubian men, they'd warned her of its danger. Looking at it, she'd had no doubt that they spoke the truth as it snapped its large jaws open and shut. She'd given thanks that she was safely aboard and out of its way.

They'd been making their way up the Nile River for some days now, fighting treacherous currents at times, and violent downpours. Alys had grown used to the shouts and general hum that issued from the traffic on the river and along the banks. The heat was what she'd found most difficult, in between the drenching rain, and she was glad that she had insisted both she and Joanie purchase clothes in Alexandria that were more suitable to the climate. She now wore a tunic and cloak of lightweight linen of the palest blue edged in a border of a darker blue. Covering her hair and, when necessary her face, was a matching veil. Joanie wore a similar garb, only hers was a darker colour. Alys's legs were bare of all hose, and the shoes on her feet were open at the toes and the back. It felt strange to have the air on them in this manner. The last time she'd had her feet bare like this outside was when she was a child, running around in Queenhithe.

Alys was glad of the enveloping veil, for it protected her from curious eyes that peered out at her as they encountered various craft on the river, inhabited by traders, travellers and other people journeying to their destinations. For the most part they remained on the boat at night, her Nubian escorts taking turns overseeing the helmsman's progress, while the others slept, or at least tried to sleep in the confines of the *felucca*.

She looked at the Nubian men now, trying to detect any sense of urgency or suspicion. She'd guarded the manuscript well since they'd left Cairo weeks ago. The Kephale had continued in his barely polite manner towards her and towards Hal and Flores. It had been a difficult relationship in such close quarters, sharing the ad hoc meals the boatmen had secured for them.

She glanced at Tomaso, secure in his little wooden cage. She gave a smile and leaned over and opened it, removing the monkey carefully. He chittered at her, baring his teeth angrily. She made some soothing noises and stroked his head. He bared his teeth again. She picked up a date from the bowl beside her and made to hand it to him. He tried to snatch it from her, but she pulled it away. She shushed him and he sat there silently, eyeing the date. She nodded and murmured praise, handing him the date. He took it greedily and made short shrift of it.

They continued in that manner for a while, he taking the date, nut, piece of bread or whatever morsel she decided, politely and she praising afterwards and petting him. Eventually, when it seemed his belly was full, she settled him in her arms after a little coaxing. A few moments later his eyes closed, his tail curling up under him. She smiled.

Hal ducked under the canopy and took a seat beside her on the wooden couch.

"When do we get to Dongola?" he asked softly in Italian. "Have they said? We seemed to go far the last few days with the strong wind."

Dongola was the place where they would disembark and take up their journey by camel. It was also a place where they could at last, she hoped, have a wash and a change of clothes. She'd no real hope of better fare than the plates of olives, dates and goat cheese they'd been having the past several weeks.

"Soon, I think," said Alys. "They didn't say exactly, but I shouldn't think it would be too long."

She gave him a faint smile. He'd spoken little to her directly in the days since their departure and made no real effort to address her privately. But now Joanie was at the stern of the *felucca* talking to Flores and Hal, it seemed, had taken this opportunity to seek her out.

Hal nodded at her answer absentmindedly. Clearly their arrival in Dongola wasn't paramount in his mind.

"Exactly 'ow long 'ave you known Jacko?" he asked her in English.

Alys eyed him carefully. "A good while," she said eventually.

"Years?"

She nodded.

"What is it between you two? You aren't just friends. It's more than that. It's got to be. Why else would you do this for 'im? Even 'is friend, one time lover and business partner didn't want to do this much."

Lover? Alys momentarily focused on that thought. Of course, Barnabas and Alessandra had been lovers. Though she'd been rumoured to have no attachment for the men she entertained in her glory days, the story surrounding Alessandra's final client was that he was the exception. Was Barnabas this person? She'd not pursued the stories too much, giving the excuse that Alessandra's past was no concern of hers, but she had wondered.

"I-I was helped once by your friend, Jacko," she said. She could think of nothing else to tell him.

"Alys," he said, his tone kind and sympathetic. "What was it that brought you to Venice in the first place? You didn't travel across Christendom on a notion. Was it Jacko?"

She looked at him and tears welled up in her eyes.

Hal gripped her arm. "Why?"

Alys stifled an hysterical urge to laugh. She took a deep breath. "I served in the Duchess of Gloucester's household," she said. "She took a liking to me and I became her personal servant. She was kind to me and when she fell from favour I went with her into exile. There, she taught me much. When I was forced to leave she provided me with funds. As did her husband, the Duke." She looked up at him. "So you see I had the funds and manner to be able to travel and I chose to come to Venice."

"As a whore?" he said, an edge in his voice.

"Of course not," said Alys abruptly. "I didn't choose to be a courtesan. We were attacked on the road and all my money and goods were stolen."

Hal gave a disapproving snort. "You should never 'ave left England."

"Well hindsight can give you great wisdom, but it's a little late for those thoughts."

"Is that why you limp?" he asked. "The attack?"

She grimaced. She'd taken great pains to ensure her limp was no longer noticeable, especially around Hal, but on a boat and on uneven ground, it wasn't always possible.

"Yes," she said simply.

"And the child? Is it Jacko's? Or does it belong to one of the other men you've bedded." He glanced at the monkey, still curled in her arms. "It is Jacko's isn't it."

She tried not to wince at his tone. She knew underneath it all he was angrier at himself than her, knowing as she did he felt things would have been different if he hadn't gone away. But of course he would never say that to her. She could see that.

"It's not what you think. It was a difficult situation. And yes, I've had men, but not the many you might think." She placed a hand on his arm and looked into his eyes. "It doesn't change who I am, Hal. Nor does it change the love I have for you. It's done."

"What of the child?"

"Eleanor is safe with Alessandra for the time being," she said calmly.

She felt the familiar pang that had plagued her on waking every day since she'd left Venice. Was Eleanor safe and well cared for, really? She pushed aside her concern. She must just assure herself that all her arrangements for Eleanor were for the best and see her task here to its completion.

"But when you return to Venice? What will you do with this child then? Leave her to be raised as a whore, or courtesan as you call it, like you are?"

She suppressed the remark that rose to her mind. It was no one's business but hers what she intended. She wouldn't succumb to Joanie's pressings on the matter, why should she to Hal? Yes, he was her brother, but she hadn't seen him since she was a child. He held no claim on her. Only he did, she admitted. He did.

"You're her uncle," she said softly. "And no, I would not have her raised as a courtesan. I want much more for her."

"Well, what then?"

She took a deep breath. "I have some money put by. And I have means of earning my keep that don't involve entertaining men. And when I have enough money, I shall return to England, with Joanie and Eleanor."

"And Jacko? What of 'im? Does he know about...Eleanor?"

"How would Jacko know?" she said in an ascerbic tone. "The two of you were long gone on some hare-brained scheme by the time I knew I was to have a child."

Hal looked away, shamefaced. "That's true. Sorry."

"Oh, Hal. Let's not argue about this. Tell me instead of your own experiences. Have you been at sea all this time?"

Hal shifted uncomfortably and looked out into the distance, his face darkening. "There's not much to tell, really. I went to sea. First on the trade ships that crossed back and forth to Bruges and the like. Then I caught ship to Calais and then other ports and eventually ended up in the Sea of Marmara. It weren't a pleasant time, there, on that ship. And the ones just before it."

He paused a moment, visibly fighting to control his feelings. Alys squeezed his arm and he glanced at her.

"It was there I met Jacko. On the Sea of Marmara. He was a passenger, of sorts. Not a willing passenger, if you get my meaning. Being attached to that Grand Vizier in a special way."

She studied his face and the untold words that he spoke with his eyes. Realisation dawned on her. "You mean he used Jacko in an…" she searched for the phrase, "an unnatural way?"

Hal nodded. "Not that I ain't seen that often enough at sea, mind you, there's many a man who would fill his urges in that way after months at sea with no sight of a woman. No, it was a mean, terrible way he 'ad a grip on Jacko. Kept 'im tethered by making 'im crave the opium drink. Got so Jacko couldn't do anything without that drink and 'e could only get that from the Vizier."

Alys blinked, trying to make sense of all that Hal had just told her. Was that the cause of Barnabas's cruel and volatile behaviour the last time she'd seen him? She recalled his words, searching for a new meaning in his determined statements that denied any future for the two of them. She thought it was his need and desire for revenge that had driven him and made him break any connection they had. Could she have been wrong?

"That's partly why I ask you if he's the father," said Hal. "You don't want him around your daughter. Not really. When a man is taken by this kind of need, there's nothing that can get in the way. That's not the kind of person you want around 'er."

She gave a wry smile. "I thought you were his friend."

"I am. But I tell you true, sister."

"Can't he quit himself of this addiction?"

Hal shook his head sorrowfully. "He can try, but few do. The last time I talked to 'im, 'e said he had. But I don't know how true that is."

Joanie came over, leaving Flores to brood at the side of the *felucca*. "You're looking very peaked. Is it the sun? Shall I pull the cloth down on the side of the canopy?"

"No, Joanie. I'm fine, really," said Alys. She glanced at Hal who had flushed a deep shade of red, his eyes suddenly on his feet. "I think my brother is suffering from the heat more than I am."

Joanie gave Hal a sideways look. "Would you like a cool drink, Hal?"

Hal shook his head and muttered a refusal. He shuffled his feet and finally beat a hasty retreat to Flores.

"Now what's the matter with 'im?" Joanie said.

Alys gave a soft laugh. "Nothing serious, I think. He's progressed though. He managed a few moments and a shake of the head. Give him a bit of time and he'll be able to string a whole sentence together in your presence."

Joanie gave her a thoughtful look and glanced over at Hal again. A moment later she gave large snort that became a giggle. She slapped her hand over her mouth and pulled her veil to hide it. Her eyes, though, still danced merrily.

⁓

Alys blinked hard, glad for the veil's protection on the rest of her face against the biting sand that blew across their path as they made their way along the street. Half the buildings were in ruin, wet sand heaped up against them, but she could find traces of their former glory. Granite pillars topped with carved elaborate cornices and capitals stood alone, holding up nothing, or lay on their sides, asleep, as it seemed was most of the city. The Egyptian Mamelukes had overrun this city that once held Nubian Christians and it was clear that the glory suggested by these impressive ruins was a thing of the past.

The Nubian men led her and the others to an inn of sorts, discussing the particulars in a language Alys had never heard before. It seemed that they came to some arrangement and she could eventually find relief in a sparsely furnished room with a pallet and cot, a cedarwood stand that contained a brightly painted bowl, and a threadbare woven rug covering the dirt packed floor. In a small window, a carved wooden grille filled the opening. Through it she could see the street, where several men with weather lined faces walked in both directions wearing robes and turbans for the most part, some darker skinned than others. In the distance she thought she spied a woman, dark eyes showing, carrying water in a jug on her shoulder.

Behind her, Joanie placed Tomaso's wooden cage on the floor. He chittered and gave one long screech.

"I agree Tomaso," she muttered. "This place does give me the creeps. 'Tis worse than being on that boat with all gawping at you as they pass by."

"Well, we won't be here long," said Alys.

Hal came in the room, carrying her small chest. She smiled at him and gave her thanks after he placed it next to the wooden cage.

"We're next door," he told her. "Should you need us." He knelt down and spoke a few words to the monkey and glanced at Joanie. Alys suppressed a smile.

"Let Tomaso out, will you?" she said. "He's been cramped up in that cage for so long."

Hal turned the wooden peg that held the door fastened and carefully withdrew Tomaso. The monkey looked eagerly around, chittering even more. Alys went to her chest and withdrew the monkey's harness she'd fashioned some days before and put it around his chest. At her word Hal placed Tomaso on the floor and she allowed him to roam the small room. There was little enough to get him into trouble and it would do no harm for a while.

The three of them watched the monkey, deriving some amusement from his antics as he climbed the bed, lifted the small cushions and pillows, pulled at the covers and then scampered off under it. Moments later he emerged, dust motes clinging to his nose and ears. Hal gave a hearty laugh, glanced at Joanie and then Alys in embarrassment, reddening visibly.

"I best be off," he said. He nodded to his sister and Joanie and left.

Joanie turned nonchalantly to the chest and unpacked a few things they would need for the night. A while later a tap came at the door and Hal handed Joanie a cloth-wrapped bundle and a flagon that served as their evening meal. After a few words of thanks from Joanie, delivered in a teasing manner, he beat a hasty retreat and left them to their meal.

Alys and Joanie sat on the bed, dividing the meal between them. Tomaso came over and inspected the food. She bade him sit, and he gave her an indignant look. She held up a morsel of food, taking it away when he tried to snatch it, as she'd done in past times, and eventually he gave in. She allowed him to take the food from her hand and he chomped on it noisily.

Eventually, after they'd finished their meal and Tomaso was safe back in his cage, Joanie's yawns proved too much for her and she declared herself ready for her bed. Alys followed suit and the two of them were tucked up and the flame from the small oil lamp blown out. Alys could hear Tomaso's breathing and Joanie's soon after in rhythms that assured her they were asleep. Her own mind was restless with worry and she knew it would be some time before her body's desperate need for rest would overcome her mind and allow her sleep.

After some time of busy thoughts, she eventually got up and made her way to the chest. She removed the small key from around her neck and placed it in the lock that held the chest secure. Inside, on top, was the manuscript. She drew it out and removed the cloth that covered it. It was still intact, unharmed. That it might be otherwise seemed doubtful, but Alys had to be sure. So much depended on it.

Alys removed the manuscript and on impulse, she took it with her to the bed and placed it under one of the pillows at her head. She wouldn't trust the Nubians not to steal into the room in the night and try to take it. She eased herself under the covers once again. In his cage Tomaso gave an inquiring chitter. She shushed him and he quietened. She relaxed back onto her pillow and tried for sleep once again. A few moments later she felt something crawling on her. She opened her eyes and stared into Tomaso's face. She smiled at him and he burrowed into the small of her neck, his head on the pillow next to hers.

Her body, bone tired after what seemed like endless nights cramped on a pallet on board the boat, relaxed. With Tomaso curled up next to her, she somehow felt reassured. Outside, the sounds of activity slowly died out and some distant music drifted in. It lulled her and she could feel herself settling into sleep.

It was a deep sleep, so badly needed, which made the brutal awakening that much worse. A hand shook her, then covered her mouth. She opened her eyes and a figure loomed over her, holding a knife to her neck. He wasn't one of the Nubian men, she was certain. He leaned down and spoke softly with menace into her ear. She shook her head not understanding the language. He tried again, this time in Latin.

"Where is the manuscript?"

She stared at the man, his face and head completely swathed in a dark cloth, so that only his glittering eyes revealed his serious intent. Beside her Joanie stirred and wakened, rising up. With one fierce movement the man hit her with his fist, knocking Joanie back on her pillow. Tomaso jumped up and screeched indignantly. He leaned over and tried to bite the man's hand, but the man withdrew it just in time, cursing loudly.

"Tell your servant that if she screams or tries in any way to raise the alarm, I will kill you. Understand? And make that animal behave."

Alys nodded and he released his hand from her mouth. She clutched Tomaso to her and told Joanie what he'd said, unable to control the shake in her voice. When she'd finished he dragged her out of bed still holding Tomaso, dislodging the pillows that had covered the manuscript. He continued holding the knife to her and leaned down to pick up the manuscript. He'd got what he came for and there was nothing she could do to stop him.

But he didn't release her. He dragged her towards the door, stopping only to open it quietly, pulling her through it. She briefly thought to raise the alarm, but the knife pressed tightly against her throat. He dragged her along the short corridor to the entrance, Tomaso's arms wrapped around her neck and she heard a door open quietly. Another figure came up behind her. She could smell the strong odour of his body. She strained to see who it was, but the knife prevented her.

Out in the street, she was shoved into a small lane where two other men waited, dressed in dark colours and headcoverings like the others. A donkey with a cart strapped to it stood behind them. The man holding the knife spoke softly and one of the other men came up and bound her hands, taking Tomaso from her and throwing him into the street. Another bound her feet. Those tasks complete, they bundled her into the cart and covered her with a rug.

Alys tried to sit up, but she found it impossible with the bone rattling bouncing of the cart's progress along the streets of Dongola. A short while after the cart had rattled forward, the rug lifted slightly and Tomaso slipped in beside her. Eventually, after what seemed like hours, the cart stopped and the rug was thrown back. She blinked her eyes against the dust and looked around, craning her neck to see over the cart. Though it was still dark, she could make out the dark robed men dismounting from donkeys. Beyond them, another man, equally dark clad, waited with several camels crouching, ready for mounting. Words were exchanged and nods. One of the men came over to her, unbound her and dragged her to the awaiting camels, Tomaso clinging to her neck.

Three of the men climbed on the camels and the man holding her surrendered her to the lead camel. The man mounted, and she was set before him, her legs forced to straddle the camel. Tomaso clambered up beside her and sat in her lap.

The man removed the gag and spoke in her ear. By his voice she could tell it was the one who had held a knife to her throat.

"Get rid of the monkey," he said.

She shook her head. "The monkey stays with me." Her voice was hoarse with fear and dryness.

"You will behave, do you understand?" he said. "Or my knife will find its way to your throat once more."

"I will behave if you allow me to have my monkey."

The man held the knife closer to her skin so that its sharp edge pricked her. A moment later he released it.

"Very well. But one false move or word and you and the monkey are both dead. Agreed?"

"Agreed," she said. "Can I ask where you're taking me?"

"You will see," he said.

At his order the camel rose, as did the other camels around her. They all moved forward, slowly at first, and then picking up the pace. One of the camels moved ahead, taking the lead and looking out, while the other two kept pace beside her. She glanced across at the rider on her left. He wore a dark turban and cloth wrapped around him like the others, but there was something familiar about him. He looked at her, noticing her glance and there was no mistaking his amused eyes. It was Flores.

CHAPTER TWENTY
ROHA, ETHIOPIA, SUMMER 1447
BARNABAS

I carefully wiped myself dry. I took as much time at it as possible, savouring this opportunity to remove the traces of my close confinement. In the past few weeks it had become a weekly ritual I'd been allowed. An opportunity to wash and then, afterwards, combing my beard. Today they had even trimmed it. They hadn't let me shave, possibly because of the risk of having a knife in my vicinity.

Once I was groomed and ready, the two men led me down the corridor and into the church, as they had previously. There, al Qali and his father sat in two different chairs, with a vacant one for me. I rubbed my wrist where the manacle had been fastened not long before. This whole semblance of a friendly exchange of views and ideas seemed a farce, but in my current position I had little choice in the matter. I could participate or, refusing to speak, be led away to be punished later. I chose to face him, and in doing so try to conquer the demon in me that still quailed at his voice and felt compelled to do his bidding as I'd been forced to do so many times.

Was this the point of the exercise? To try to make me aware of the power he still held over me? I had yet to discover anything. All I knew was that each week we sat and talked about different topics which ranged from philosophy and mathematical theories, to history and culture while I kept my hatred close to the surface. Usually, we spoke in Greek or Latin, but today was different. We spoke in Arabic.

"You are well, my friend?" asked al Qali in a pleasant tone.

"The meat was a little underdone yesterday. You might want to consider hiring a different cook," I said.

"Ah, that humour of yours," said al Qali. "I can imagine Halil Pasha appreciated it very much."

My mouth tightened. This was the first time he'd mentioned Halil Pasha. "Not as much as you might hope."

"But you must have provided him with interesting conversation. All that I taught you wouldn't have gone to waste."

"Oh, he wasn't particularly interested in my competency in mathematics, or my knowledge of obscure French poems. Well, perhaps the poems."

"Do you write poetry yourself?" asked Hawqal.

I pulled out my grin. "Not that you would notice. There are some poets I admire."

We discussed a few for a little while. I noticed his Arabic wasn't as fluent as his son's, so there wasn't much to be said.

"Did you find any in Halil Pasha's library?" al Qali said, interrupting impatiently.

"No," I said. "I wasn't looking for poetry."

"What were you looking for?" asked al Qali.

I gave al Qali an innocent look. "I was merely assisting there. And working with my teacher."

"Your teacher?" al Qali's voice had an edge.

I nodded. "I had many teachers of one sort or another. You'd be amazed at all the opportunities to learn that I had."

"Ah, but surely nothing of great value. I taught you well."

I shrugged. "What you value may be very different to what others value."

"Anything of note?" said al Qali. "Intellectually speaking, of course. I know your little play with words and meanings that you find so amusing, but I've no time for games."

I gave him a direct look. "The palace is a great centre of learning. It's a pity you didn't get an opportunity to look through the collection thoroughly. Scholars would find it rich in resources."

Al Qali's face darkened. "We have what we need from there. Or we will."

"But even if it is the manuscript you need, what do you hope to do with it?" I asked.

Al Qali glanced at his father and lifted his chin. "We will show our people. Raise an army and take back the throne, invoking the name of Lalibela."

I gave him a puzzled look. "I seem to remember reading in Halil Pasha's library about the Zagwe dynasty. Wasn't it the case that they took the throne from the people who are there now, restored to their heritage? Doesn't that dilute some of your claim, in view of that fact?"

"The Zagwe took it with the approval of the Pope. Through marriage," said al Qali. "Those usurpers took the throne back by more devious means."

"But it still poses the question of the Zagwe having any more right to the throne than those who rule now."

"No!" said al Qali. "This is my birthright."

"Son," said Hawqal. "Enough. This man has said what you will not hear. It is done. I am interested to see the document you told me about, but it will not change what cannot be changed. Too much time has passed. Who cares for Lalibela now?"

"You're wrong, Father," said al Qali sharply.

His father sighed. "There is no interest, now. Not with the Mameluks pressing us from the north and non-believers from the south."

"You would return to Alexandria to beg and scrape a living?" asked al Qali bitterly.

"Your mother's people are from there," said Hawqal in Greek. "I will not have you talk about Alexandria, or her people, with such disdain. It was there you were able to educate yourself to the extent you have."

"With my lineage, I was entitled to such an education."

"The world cares not," said Hawqal said carefully. "You must learn to accept that."

Al Qali closed his mouth in a stubborn line. "You'll see. I'll show you and all the others."

I'd watched this exchange with growing interest and some degree of alarm at al Qali's emotional extreme. Though he might be verging on madness, it would do no good to underestimate him.

Al Qali turned to me, suddenly recalling himself. "You too will see," he said continuing in Greek.

"It's possible you will see the evidence in the text that I didn't," I said carefully. "You know much more of the situation and the possible statements that would support it than I would, after all."

Al Qali gave a slow smile. "Yes."

"But how will you locate it? I don't have it in my possession any longer."

A light glimmered in his eyes. "Oh, there is no need to worry about that. The manuscript is on its way as we speak."

Stunned, I said nothing for a moment. "You found it?"

"In a manner of speaking, it was never lost. Our friend Captain Flores looked after it."

"Flores? But how do you know that? And how do you know the manuscript is coming here?"

Al Qali gave me an amused smile. "Come, come, Giacomo," he said, switching to Italian. "I gave you credit for more intelligence than that."

"Flores is in your pay," I said flatly, responding in Italian. Perhaps because I didn't want to acknowledge such a truth and its consequences, but I hadn't thought of Flores betraying me in this manner until that moment.

"Very good."

"From the very first?" I asked.

"Well, it depends on what you mean by that. Flores is a practical man at heart. After your initial contact with him, he chose to send me word of your plans and mentioned the manuscript that was in your possession. I knew at once it could only be the manuscript I sought. He accepted my offer of payment in return for sending me word of your location."

"My son gave his word you would not be harmed," said Hawqal in Greek. "It was merely that we would retrieve the text."

I raised my brow a fraction at this comment. Clearly Hawqal either couldn't follow the conversation in Italian or knew little of his son, if he thought that was the truth. "But the Nubian Christians who abducted us—that wasn't part of your plan, was it?" I said in Greek.

Al Qali's face darkened. "I had nothing to do with that. No, the intent was to retrieve the manuscript, as my father said. It was by great fortune that Flores was able to discover where you were taken."

"I would say it had nothing to do with fortune." I said. I knew by now that it was Ezekiel who betrayed us to the Nubians. And when we'd been taken, Flores got Ezekiel to tell him where we were. Had he followed Hal and the men to Alexandria? Most likely.

"Well you can't tell me that your sole purpose was to retrieve the manuscript. Flores could have brought that to you directly. No, it's clear you want me here for some purpose."

I glanced at his father, who looked at al Qali with some puzzlement. I'd talked in Greek, so it would be clear to his father and I watched the growing concern form in his face.

"Perhaps I wanted to question you in depth about Halil Pasha's library. To know what else you might have seen in the library."

"But you've done little of that."

Al Qali gave a grim smile. "There is time enough. I know you share my curiosity about learning. You can at least acknowledge that I fed that curiosity and helped you become what you are."

"Oh, I know the debt I owe you," I said. "I've forgotten nothing of what you taught me. So how long must I remain here for you to be sufficiently satisfied?"

"Be certain you will greet them when they arrive with the manuscript."

I tensed, fearing what I would hear. "They? Is Hal coming as well?"

Al Qali gave a slow smile. "Hal and that woman you care so much about. The courtesan."

"Alessandra? But she's merely a business partner. Why is she coming?"

"No, not her. The other one. The one who I believe was your sweetheart in London. The one who knows you as Barnabas."

Fear stirred inside me. Fear, not for myself, but for Alys. I tried to calm my breathing. "What is it that you want with her?"

"Why Barnabas, she has taken it upon herself to come to you with the manuscript. It has nothing to do with me. But I confess, I do find it all very interesting. This devotion, this obvious care for you that has taken her so far from her home." He glanced at his father. "But you mustn't worry. She'll be an honoured guest."

"Like I'm an honoured guest?"

Al Qali forced a smile. "You are a special guest. And now, though my father and I have enjoyed these little visits, I'm afraid I must call a halt to this one. We have other pressing matters we must attend to."

I sat in the dark, going over my conversation with al Qali again. I'd done it countless times and I always came to conclusions that gave me no comfort at all. It might be true that Alys had made the journey of her own accord, though I could hardly understand why, given our last meeting. But I could see no other explanation. There was nothing that would force her to come to Roha, or at least nothing that I could discern. Why would she come to help me? And most importantly what use had al Qali for her? Because there was no doubt in my mind, Al Qali was glad of her imminent arrival.

I forced myself to set that question aside and consider the real issue. Now that al Qali knew she was coming, what would he do with her? Would he allow her to return home? I turned over the idea in my mind and tried to be as objective as possible. Al Qali would do what served him best. I had no illusions about his regard for me. Underneath the façade of using me as a guarantor for the delivery of the manuscript there operated another reason for my presence. I had become some kind of figure in his mind from whom he needed approval. But I also knew I represented a threat because the text didn't hold the proof he needed to gain his throne. Who would challenge him? His people, the people among whom he would raise support, would have no access to the text. And if they did, it was unlikely they could read Arabic. It was clear his father couldn't, so it was safe to say that the common people would take his word, or enough of his word to foment rebellion.

No, it was clear al Qali would wish me out of the way. Once the manuscript was safely in his hands I would be killed quietly in my prison here so I'd no longer be a threat. And he could tell his father that he'd sent me home, or some such convincing story.

But what purpose would Alys hold in this narrative? Was there a purpose? Other than al Qali knew I cared for her. Was it just that? To simply dangle her fate in front of me as some kind of torture? Did al Qali hate me that much? I could provide no other service for him that I could discover.

I sat a while, reviewing what I knew of al Qali and his relationship with me and stopped, groaning at my stupidity. It could only be one thing. He wanted me to act as his seer. Knowing my reluctance to use the showstone for him in the past, especially since its use led me into Halil Pasha's captive hands, he knew he would need something to compel me to do it for him again. That something was Alys.

CHAPTER TWENTY-ONE
ROHA, THE ETHIOPES, LATE SUMMER,
1447
ALYS

Alys gazed at the impressive stone building hewn out of the mountainous area with such determination. It rose high with carved arches. Beyond that, she could see another wall with windows that were even more distinctly shaped in an Arabian style, with keyhole arches.

Around her, within a stone's throw were other, equally impressive stone buildings carved out of this volcanic rocky homeland of the Ahara region. One, she'd noted as she looked down at it when she passed it on her donkey with Tomaso, was in the shape of a cross, so she could only imagine it was a kind of church. She confessed herself surprised. And to some degree it gave her hope. Could she appeal to some Christian for assistance? She glanced at Flores, who sat upright on his donkey in distinct discomfort, and decided it was a foolish hope.

She thought of Hal and Joanie back in Cairo and prayed that the Nubian men hadn't harmed them.

Since their journey here had begun, Flores had grown increasingly surly as the heat seemed to give him the most terrible rashes, and the donkey gave him the most searing saddle ache. If her own situation hadn't been so dire she might have been amused, but as it was, she only suggested to him that he ask his companions for advice on relief since they would be more accustomed to the climate and its problems. That he refused to do so out of some sense of manly pride did give her satisfaction. Let him suffer, she thought, for such is his treachery he would do well to suffer more.

They halted the donkeys and Alys dismounted with the assistance of one of her captors. He gestured her to follow, another man giving her a little shove from behind to assure her compliance. She walked the path that led across a small bridge to the entrance of the building, limping badly. The various events on the journey had done nothing but make her leg worse and she could feel a searing pain with every step.

She shifted Tomaso in her arms, trying for an easier gait. The monkey had found the journey difficult enough, forced to perch in front of her on a camel that he soon was at odds with. When they transferred to donkeys, he was able to at least spend some time running along beside them on a makeshift tether of woven reeds. She'd managed to find enough food and some water for him, but the men who'd accompanied her had threatened more than once to kill him on the spot. That he'd increasingly sustained her just by his needs and his antics was enough reason for her to continue to insist on his importance and his survival.

Now, as she entered the building, she clutched the monkey to her chest, deriving some courage and comfort from him. Once inside the building, she felt the cooling effect of the stone walls immediately. Light filtered in through the windows, high enough to cast light, but little heat. Brightly coloured woven cloths hung on the walls, but they couldn't disguise the clear evidence of neglect that revealed itself in the cracks and chips in the exterior and interior.

At the far end of the hall was an altar, and upon it, a cross. Alys gave it a puzzled look. Was this a church or a residence? The placing of the carved cedarwood chairs, cushions and a small cedarwood table led her to believe it was the latter. Perhaps it was a priestly residence.

"Welcome to Roha, my friends," came a voice in Italian.

Alys turned and saw a figure emerging from an entrance to her left. She stared at him a moment as it all fell into place. Flores's old companion. She remembered Barnabas's description. "You are Signor al Qali, I presume."

Al Qali bowed to her and smiled. "Mustapha al Qali," he said. "And here, I am Lalibela. At your service, madonna." He gestured to one of the chairs. "Please, take a seat. And you, dear Captain Flores, please rest yourself, too."

Alys took the seat but Flores gave a curt nod. "Greetings, Mustapha. If it's all the same to you, I will stand. Nothing personal."

Alys allowed herself a private smile before focusing on al Qali. He wore a white tunic edged with gold thread embroidery, a stole draped across one shoulder. A long dagger was belted at the waist, sheathed in a gem-encrusted scabbard. A choice of clothing clearly meant to impress. With a few words he dismissed their escort, leaving only Flores, Tomaso and Alys.

"I understood you to be a scholar and Signor Bonavillagio's tutor," said Alys. She gestured around her. "I had no idea you were more. Are you a priest here? But then you're not a Christian, or least that was what I understood. Perhaps you are a guest of the priest who lives here?"

Al Qali gave a humourless laugh. "You take the offensive tactic, I see. Perhaps to put me off my guard? But I will gladly tell you who I am and what I do here. I am Lalibela, descendant of the great Lalibela and true heir to the throne of this kingdom. What you see around you is the palace, perhaps a little faded in its glory, but nonetheless still sacred and awaiting father and I, the last of the Christian priest kings, the Prester Jans or Johns, as you so quaintly call them, to reclaim it and the kingdom."

Alys blinked and looked around at his palace. This and the other stone buildings, though impressive, spoke of another time. The grass huts and the tents she'd seen dotted below and around the buildings as they made their way here, all spoke of the present.

"I thought you were one of those of the Muslim faith."

His face darkened. "While I might know well the tenets of that faith and have been compelled at times to be seen to observe some of its practises, it was not willingly done."

"I had no idea," she said. "But how does the manuscript fit into all of this?"

Al Qali held up his hand. "All in good time. For now, it is fitting that I offer you refreshment. It must not be said that I don't provide adequate hospitality for my guests."

He clapped his hands and a man, equally dark skinned and dressed in a long white tunic, came out and bowed to al Qali. They exchanged a few sentences in a language incomprehensible to Alys and the man nodded and withdrew. A short while later the refreshments were brought and handed round first to Flores, then Alys and finally al Qali.

"Please, Flores, would several cushions strategically placed help you in your discomfort?"

Flores gave a grim smile and conceded with a nod. He put the cushions on the vacant chair and sat down gingerly. Alys, meanwhile, fed a few bits of food to Tomaso, who thankfully had remained silent for most of the exchange, content to stay on her lap, rather than explore the new surroundings. Could it be that he too felt the underlying menace that emanated from al Qali?

"That creature you have there," said al Qali, as if her thought had directed his attention to Tomaso. "Why is he with you? I can see no purpose for him, except as a nuisance."

"He is a friend," said Alys.

"A friend," said al Qali carefully.

"He was Barnabas's," said Flores. "He picked it up on his travels. She dotes on it now, won't let it out of her sight."

Al Qali gave Alys an interested look. "Truly? How fascinating."

"H-he is clever," said Alys lamely.

"Like his master?" said al Qali. "Does he speak Italian and Arabic and see the future?"

"Of course not," said Alys curtly. "But he has learned to do things for me. He'll take food from me. And recently he escaped from his cage by turning the peg. He'd learned that by watching others release him."

Al Qali gave a mirthless laugh. "Ah, perhaps he could teach his master something, then."

"So you have imprisoned Signor Bonavillagio?"

Al Qali waved a hand. "Please, let us dispense with this Signor Bonavillagio nonsense. I know you and he have been long acquainted, as much as you might pretend otherwise. His name, we all know, is Barnabas."

She gave a small nod. She straightened and took a breath. "I have the manuscript. Will you let him go?"

"I think you mean I have the manuscript," al Qali said smoothly. "My servants are securing it now."

Her mouth formed a stubborn frown. "But I still insist on seeing him."

"I think it's my turn first," said Flores darkly. "I only require my payment and then I'll be off."

"No, no, Flores, what is the haste? You must be my guest for a while, I insist."

Flores gave a grim smile. "Ah, but no, al Qali. I fear I have had enough of this climate and wish to be quit of it as soon as possible."

"But Flores, amico mio, you will find the climate different inside these walls and the other buildings we have here. I would like to show them to you, show their wonder and skill. You will appreciate it and the other fine things that are here." He gave a small grin. "There are some very enticing feminine attractions that are exactly to your taste, if I recall correctly."

Flores paused and then gave a reluctant nod. "Very well. Just a short while."

"Of course, of course," said al Qali. "But you may discover that the attractions are just too difficult to resist and find your stay lengthening." He turned to Alys. "Now, you require some proof that Barnabas is indeed here?"

"If you please," she said stiffly.

He cocked his head. "Oh, and it pleases me, madonna. It pleases me very much."

~

When Barnabas appeared an hour later with a servant carrying the cloth-wrapped manuscript Alys hardly recognised him under the beard, dark tan and strange clothes. It was when he turned his achingly familiar eyes on her that she felt her heart contract and she tightened her hold on Tomaso. He gave a little squeal, glared at her and gnashed his teeth briefly. She made some soft soothing sounds and he quietened.

Barnabas gave her a brief bow. "Madonna," he said in a light tone in Italian. "I see you have looked after my little friend well." He turned to Flores. "My captain. You are here as escort, I think. I would say what it a happy reunion it is to have you and my former mentor, together once more, but I fear I'm past my childish admiration and dreams."

"Ah, Barnabas, amico mio," said Flores with a wry grin. "You must not take it to heart so. You know it is all about profit and good times. We've had the good times and now it's time for the profit."

"Were they such good times?" said Barnabas, coolly. "I seemed to remember you were stabbed badly by some cutthroat. Or had he a good reason? I can well believe that. Perhaps you betrayed him as well."

Flores forced a laugh. "You were always a person who liked to twist words. Such a clever tongue. Isn't that what drew you to him, al Qali? Showed real promise?"

"It was indeed," said al Qali. "I thought it was a good indication of his aptitude. And when I discovered his most remarkable talent, there was no question I would take him under my protection."

"And you protected me so well," said Barnabas. He flashed a smile.

Al Qali laughed this time. "I did, as you well know. Didn't I give you sanctuary when all of London's nobility were calling for an end to your life?"

"It wasn't quite that. They wanted to question me."

"They wanted to torture you, make you confess everything they put to you and then hang you."

"So you said. But that passed soon enough and I became your tool."

"No, you were more than a tool. You were vital to my plan," said al Qali. "As you are now."

"You want me to act as seer for you again."

"Of course," said al Qali. "You are matchless in that talent."

"Let this woman go, then," said Barnabas. "She's brought you your manuscript, you can have no further use for her."

"No, Barnabas, no!" said Alys. "He will kill you once he has what he wants."

Barnabas looked at her, his eyes searching hers, a hint of pleading in his. He gave her a tired smile. "Ah madonna, he will always need me, but you, he has no use for you."

"Oh, but I do," said al Qali. "You know that your love for her guarantees that. You may try and hide behind this pretence of 'madonna' this, and 'madonna' that, but I know who she is —your own dear Alys. The one who you mentioned when first you confided all to me. The one you kept vigil for all those years afterwards, when your trust of me disappeared, despite all your attempts to disguise that from me. Did you think I would use her to force you into compliance? If it had suited me at the time,

I would have, but it proved unnecessary in the end. Until now."

"No force is required," said Barnabas darkly. "You'll let her go. I've said that I will act as seer for you."

"But no," said al Qali. "I'm afraid it's not your decision. I have the upper hand and I will release her when I'm ready."

"We'll do it now," said Barnabas. "Bring a bowl of water and I'll try. There are no guarantees, though. I can only see what is there, if you remember."

"Oh, I remember," said al Qali. "But that will be for later. Now, I await my father. Together you and I will show him the manuscript and read the pertinent section to him."

Barnabas gave him a hard look and a sharp nod. He looked over at Alys again and she tried to read his unspoken words, but could see only a reassurance she didn't feel. Under her grip Tomaso shifted uneasily, strangely silent amid the tension. She stroked his fur, but her hands shook so she stopped.

Flores reached over and poured himself some more wine and tossed it back in a gulp. Barnabas, who'd remained standing, shifted his weight and edged closer to al Qali. Eventually, a servant entered leading an elderly dark-skinned man that Alys could only conclude was al Qali's father. Al Qali made the introductions and Hawqal bowed and regarded Alys intently.

"My son," he said in Greek to al Qali. "What has this woman to do with this?"

"She carried the manuscript, here, Father. That is all."

"You have given her refreshment?"

"Of course," said al Qali sharply.

"But she must be tired after her journey. She should be taken away to rest."

"She will, Father, she will," his voice filled with impatience. He drew up a chair beside his and ushered his father into it. "Let me show you what she brought, first."

Al Qali picked up the manuscript from where it had been placed on the small cedarwood table earlier and unwrapped it carefully. He turned the pages, one by one, skimming the contents, his eyes alight with anticipation. Alys watched him with growing nervousness and glanced at Barnabas. He was frowning.

"It's the manuscript you seek?" asked Alys in English.

Al Qali looked up at her blankly for a moment. "Yes, of course."

Alys opened her mouth to speak again and glanced at Barnabas. He gave her a warning look so she shut her mouth firmly.

"Here," said al Qali. "This is the passage, Father. Let me read it to you."

Al Qali proceeded to read slowly, translating into Greek and enunciating each word as though it were in a tongue he wasn't used to reading. Alys concentrated hard, trying to understand his words. She managed to make out that someone had met a group of men, men from a place in the Ahara region who told the men their story. They explained they belonged to the true rulers of the kingdom of Prester John, of the Zagwe. They were the priest kings who had their palace in Roha, the home of Lalibela, the great priest king who built the twelve churches out of rock. These men were his descendants and were forced to leave their land, to go to other kingdoms and live like common men, instead of the noble priest kings they were.

Barnabas raised his brow at the conclusion of al Qali's reading. Hawqal put a hand on his son's arm and narrowed his eyes. He spoke rapidly and forcefully in a language that Alys realised was the same that al Qali had spoken to the servant.

"Barnabas," said al Qali in rapid Italian. "Tell my father that what I said is what is written here. He feels that there is some doubt because of the dating. It explained that the dates of these manuscripts are only approximate."

Barnabas bowed and moved over to al Qali and his father. Al Qali pointed to the passage.

"You might interpret it that way," said Barnabas.

"Now is not the time for games, Barnabas," said al Qali, an edge in his voice.

"Oh, I know this is not a game," said Barnabas. He flashed al Qali a smile. "Let me look at it closer. Sometimes I have trouble with these Arabic words."

Al Qali gave him a suspicious glance, but allowed Barnabas to lean closer. Alys watched Barnabas's hand move towards al Qali's dagger. She held her breath, willing Barnabas's actions to succeed. He clutched the dagger and started to withdraw it. Al Qali grabbed his hand, but Barnabas resisted, pulling hard on the dagger's handle. The dagger slipped out of its scabbard and the two wrestled for possession.

Hawqal stood, barking an order to his son, but al Qali ignored him. Al Qali pulled harder and wrested the dagger from Barnabas and lunged at him.

Alys stood, Tomaso falling from her lap. "Barnabas, no!" she screamed. "Be careful."

Barnabas stepped quickly away and avoided the dagger's thrust. Al Qali came at him again, striking him hard against his arm, slicing deep. Blood burst forth, flowing freely.

"Must I take off your hand?" al Qali said, his eyes flashing. He thrust his dagger again, this time aiming for Barnabas's heart.

Alys ran forward, but Flores caught her and held her tightly. She watched Barnabas dodge and struggle against al Qali's attack, knowing it couldn't end well. Tears formed. She mouthed Barnabas's name and pleaded to God for his protection.

But it wasn't to be God that answered her call. Tomaso, incensed by the shouts and his mistress's distress, darted towards the scuffling legs and bit down hard on al Qali's exposed ankle. Al Qali shouted in surprise and pain, and Barnabas, seeing al Qali's guard drop, snatched the dagger from him and headed towards Hawqal. He grabbed the startled Hawqal from behind and held the dagger to his throat. He shouted brief instructions to Alys in English.

Flores dropped his hold on Alys to go to al Qali's aid. Alys caught up with him and grabbed the small sword at Flores's side with both hands and brandished it.

"Now," said Barnabas calmly in English. "I believe I have the upper hand."

"Not for long," said al Qali angrily. "I will see you killed."

"You may try," said Barnabas. Blood coursed down his arm, but he kept his grip tight. "But if you want to see your father unharmed, you will provide donkeys and sufficient food for us to return to Dongola. Your father will come with us until then. Once there, I will release him and he can make his way back here, or to Alexandria if he wishes. Isn't that where his home is?" Hawqal said something to al Qali. Al Qali shook his head and responded. He frowned. "Very well, it is done."

CHAPTER TWENTY-TWO
ROHA, THE ETHIOPES, LATE SUMMER, 1447
BARNABAS

The small group was silent. I adjusted my grip on Hawqal, to ease the tension and pain. He'd moved little since I first seized him and had made no attempt to wriggle or manoeuvre himself to a more favourable position for escape. It was as if he could sense my fierce and sweating grip might slip at any moment from the pain of the injury and do unintended harm.

I could feel the blood flowing freely again, despite the makeshift bandage. Alys had tied it on, standing with me, well away from the others, the sword gripped under her arm and the monkey squatting on the ground beside her. Now she brandished the sword afresh, covering my back like some brave woman warrior of myth, her copper hair flying wild and catching the light. Tomaso squatted beside her, his tether attached to her wrist and he eyed Alys's opponents with a fierce glare.

We made our way to the three saddled donkeys, walking carefully, facing al Qali and Flores who stood watching and waiting for any opportunity to foil our escape. It was risky, this makeshift plan, and most likely going to fail, but it was the best I could fashion, given the time and the circumstances.

"Shall I mount first?" Alys asked in English, in a low voice.

"No, wait until Hawqal and I have mounted. I'll have him ride in front of me until we are well clear of this place. You can pull the other donkey behind."

Hawqal called across to his son and said a few words in their own language.

"Barnabas," said al Qali in Italian. "Please, let me at least bid my father farewell. I promise I won't try anything."

I glanced at Hawqal. The man gave me a pleading glance. "Please," he said. "I am old. This could be the last time I will see him. I pose no threat, feeble as I am. And I promise, my son will do you no harm. I give you my word."

"It's not your word, I hold in distrust," I said. "It's your son's." I paused, sized up al Qali's expression and gave a quick nod. "You may come close, but you may not touch, I'm afraid."

Al Qali approached slowly, his empty hands held out. When he was an arm's length away I told him to halt.

"My son," said Hawqal in Greek. His face was hard and there was an edge to his voice. "We must make our farewells. I must tell you now that I am sorry I have failed you as a father and as a priest."

"What do you mean?" said al Qali. "Get rid of these wastrels and return. I promise you we will have all the honour that is due to us, soon. Or do you reject your heritage? Must I do everything myself? Have you not the courage to take your rightful place? Is that it? Is that why you say you are sorry?"

Hawqal sagged against me, suddenly a dead weight. I looked down, saw that his eyes were closed and for a brief moment thought that he was gone. His eye flew open. In an instant, he grabbed my dagger from me and lunged forward to thrust it into his son's chest. He turned it hard and upwards. Al Qali fell against it hard with the blow, emitting a gasp. Hawqal released the blade, tossed it aside and al Qali fell to the ground.

Hawqal knelt beside him, tears coursing down his face. "My son, my son," he wailed in Greek. "What was it that I said or did that led you to this path? That made you become such a person that can only bring shame to his family?"

I knelt beside him and put my hand on his shoulder in comfort. Al Qali's chest rose and fell, his eyes flickering.

"You aren't to blame for what he became," I said. "It was in part the way the world treated him. Instead of respect for his great learning and abilities they could only mock him and his origins, not realising that he had far more knowledge and ability than they could ever imagine for themselves."

"He was proud," muttered Hawqal. "Always proud. Too proud, I'd tell him. You must learn to accept what God decrees. But he would challenge God, question His reasoning and actions."

"He's not alone in that," I said.

Hawqal sighed and took al Qali's hand in his. "Mustapha al Qali," he said in a formal tone. "Your sins are before you and before God. Do you confess and repent of them?"

Al Qali's lips moved silently. Hawqal leaned closer, putting his ear to al Qali's mouth. I could hear nothing, but eventually Hawqal sat up. "I hear your confession and repentance and hereby absolve you of them and commit your soul to God in his name." He gestured over al Qali, pressing his fingers to his mouth and head and chest. Al Qali's breathing became ragged. A rattle sounded deep within his chest. I bowed my head and moments later, Mustapha al Qali breathed his last.

We remained unmoving for some time, each of us lost in our own thoughts. I could hardly make sense of what had just occurred and laboured hard to clear my head and act. It was only when Hawqal made to stand that I came to myself and helped him up.

"We'll remain and help see him buried," I said.

Hawqal shook his head. "There is no need. You are ready, you must go. This is for me and my son only. I have the servants to arrange things."

I nodded. I didn't want to intrude on his grief, one that could only be filled with complex feelings of his son and his own actions against his son. "I offer you my deepest thanks for helping me."

Hawqal turned pained eyes toward me. "It wasn't to help you that I did what I did."

"I know," I said simply. "You have my thanks, nonetheless."

Hawqal glanced behind me. "Please take your other companion with you, too."

"You mean Flores?"

Hawqal nodded. "And the manuscript. I have no need for it. I can only hope it might benefit you in some way. It has brought nothing but evil to me and mine."

I weighed the benefits of Flores's skill with a sword in what would be a dangerous return journey against his potential for treachery and concluded my need for him was greater. I put out a hand. He hesitated then gripped it hard. "I will take Flores and the manuscript then," I said. "And may its removal from your company bring you some peace. You will remain here?"

Hawqal sighed. "For a time. I have not the stomach to return to Alexandria just yet."

I nodded. I knew in my heart that Hawqal would never return to Alexandria. I would be surprised if he lasted more than a month or two in this remote place. It was clear his heart was broken and he had nothing to live for.

We journeyed slowly, speaking little, too stunned by the day's events to do anything more than stay on our donkeys and follow our escort. Hawqal had been kind enough to grant us a guide who would see us to Dongola, since we had little idea of the way through endless scrub and then desert. The guide was taciturn too, whether by nature, or the shock of the events that he'd heard about.

My injured arm throbbed, and the pain kept me present and focused on our course, instead of drifting off into numbness as was clearly the situation for Alys. I dared say little to her, noting her pallid complexion under the sweat that gathered at her brow and the glassy eyed stare she directed towards the horizon, Tomaso perched in front of her. She'd held and guarded him well since his heroic dash to bite al Qali, murmuring unending endearments and assurances for the first part of the journey.

Flores was lost in his own thoughts, muttering under his breath, his eyes alight with anger and frustration. He'd demanded some form of payment for all his troubles from Hawqal initially, until the old man's quelling look made him cease and turn away. It hadn't stopped him from trying to take the scabbard from al Qali's side and protest to me when I gripped his hand hard and pulled him away from it. He'd relented in the end and forced a laugh. Having some pity for him, I promised him a small fee if he would arrange our sailing back to Venice. That at least would ensure his cooperation and allegiance while we journeyed from Dongola.

When dusk approached, the guide halted us to make camp for the night. I dismounted gratefully and helped Alys, taking Tomaso and then assisting her. She looked into my eyes and I could see the fatigue there, but beyond that was something more. A question. I hoped I knew the question and that I had the answer she wanted to hear. I gave her a reassuring smile and set her on the ground.

"Your arm," she said. She touched it gently. "It's still bleeding. I'll wash and rebind it."

"Later. We'll set up our camp and eat, first. Give you time to rest. You're exhausted."

Alys frowned. "We shouldn't put it off too long."

Flores came over, looked at my arm and shook his head. "He cut you deep."

I forced a smile. "It's a clean cut, though, so it shouldn't be a problem."

He gave a sceptical snort. "I think you need to have it sewn." He looked at Alys. "Have you any means to do it?"

Alys bit her lip. "No. You recall I was rudely abducted?" she said in acerbic tone. "My sewing things are back with Joanie. I'll just have to bind it tightly and hope that holds it."

She touched the bandage tentatively. It was soaked through with blood and at her touch I could feel more oozing forth. I winced at the stab of pain that rose above the dull throb that had accompanied me on our journey.

She gave me a worried look and I kept the smile plastered on my face. "It'll be fine," I said.

At my insistence, after the camp was established, our bedrolls in place, we shared sparingly the provisions we'd brought. I had little appetite, but made myself eat, not only to fortify myself against the arduous journey that remained, but also because I knew I was fighting against time and circumstances that meant it likely my arm might prove troublesome. I could only hope we could reach Dongola, or somewhere it might be properly tended, before that happened.

When our meal was finished Alys came to my side immediately with a cloth and one of the flasks of water we'd brought with us. Carefully, she unwound the bandage and cleaned what she could of the wound and started to wrap it up firmly in a clean strip of cloth she tore from her scarf edge. It was a painful process for me, but I knew it had to be done.

"It's still bleeding," she said quietly in English. "But at least it bleeds any foreign substances free of it."

"You have learned healing skills?" I asked her.

"I have learned many unexpected things over the years," she said with a wry smile. Underneath I could detect slight nervousness. "But yes, I learned something of the skill when I injured my leg. Joanie is more skilled than I, though."

"Joanie is your servant?"

"Joanie is my friend," she said firmly. "A true and loyal friend who has stood by me since London."

I was quiet for a moment, not certain how to begin. "I am sorry."

She raised her eyes to mine, pausing in her action. "Sorry for what?" she said carefully.

I placed my free hand on hers. "For everything. For what I dragged you through during the years of our separation."

She shrugged and avoided my eyes. "I was a foolish girl. You didn't ask me to follow you."

"Don't shift the blame. You suffered and I was at fault. I only wish it could have brought you to a better fate."

"Are you saying I dislike my choices?"

"I'm saying that you've suffered because of me." I nodded to her leg. "Physically and in other ways, too. I wasn't worth it, especially after I treated you so badly when we met again in Venice. I can only apologise and make the feeble explanation that I did it for what I thought was the best."

"What you thought was best?" There was a hint of bitterness in her tone. "And it did not occur to you that I might be consulted in this matter? Would it have harmed you to have told me the reasons for the manner in which you behaved that night and your choice to leave without a word afterwards?"

"I'm sorry," I said softly. "I know it was wrong of me, but I was in no position to form any relationship with anyone."

"The opiate addiction? Or do you mean your hell-bent desire to seek out al Qali and wreak some kind of revenge for what he did to you?"

I frowned at her. "What do you know of that?" I said darkly.

"Hal told me."

"Hal? Why would Hal tell you?"

She cocked her head slightly. "Oh, but you wouldn't know, would you? Hal is my brother."

"Your brother?" I could only parrot her words in surprise. "But how can that be?"

"I'm certain I told you I had a brother who went to sea when I was young. Well that was Hal. That he should turn up in your company is one of life's tricks," she added in a tired manner.

I squeezed her hand. "You have been fortunate in that, at least. To have been reunited with your brother."

"Yes," she said tightly. "And with God's grace we will be reunited again."

"And what else would you have in the future, by God's grace? Is there some hope that I might feature in it?"

Alys looked at me fully for the first time and her eyes, full of sadness and other more complex emotions, welled with tears. "I don't know, Barnabas. So much has changed."

"Have you any amount of feeling left for me?" I asked, afraid of the answer. "I have no right to expect anything, but can I have some hope that we might build upon a little amount?"

She bit her lip. "There is much to overcome before we can turn our minds to the future," she said. "I can promise nothing."

"You understood what I meant in the letter. You even travelled here, all this way to bring the manuscript. You must have felt something to have undertaken such a journey." I tried to keep the note of pleading out of my voice. "I'm sorry," I added. "You're right. I mustn't press you."

Alys took a deep breath. "Meeting my brother drew me to Alexandria. And perhaps the fact that your dear *amore* Alessandra wasn't willing to help you. Also, I wasn't certain I could trust Flores." She glanced in Flores's direction. "It seems that was a good instinct. But whatever instinct it was, besides that one, that led me onward in the journey I cannot say, nor can I say if it still is present." She gave me a kindly look. "I am no longer a young girl with her head turned by the first person to pay her a modicum of attention. My life is complicated. And for now, it's not my own. I have obligations and other connections that I must consider. I'm not sure how you have a place in my life and if I would wish you to."

"Do you mean Alessandra?" I asked. "I can fix that. I'll work something out with Alessandra, you've no need to worry on that score." A thought struck me and I tried to keep my tone light and neutral. "Unless you have formed an attachment with someone else? One of the people you've…entertained?"

She gave a slight smile that didn't reach her eyes. "Alessandra does figure into the complications, yes. But there is no need for you to 'fix' it for me. I assure you, I have my own plans in that direction. No, my connections are elsewhere. I have a brother, for one. Discovered after many years of separation. I would spend some time with him if I can."

"But I am happy for you. Hal is a good man and I would never think of interfering with that."

She gave me a level look. "And I also have my painting. I've been an apprentice since I came to Venice. I couldn't think of abandoning that now." She drew herself up. "I am quite good."

I stared at her, trying to make sense of this woman before me. What she was feeling, what was driving her? A painter. If I'd given it any thought it wouldn't have surprised me, but I hadn't and it shamed me. I lowered my head, conscious of the trickles of sweat running down my face and my back.

"I'm glad for you. I always thought you were talented."

She sighed. "No, you thought it was charming at best. Something to amuse."

I lifted my eyes. "I was a boy, Alys. Young, stupid and thinking with my lower half instead of here." I pointed to my heart. "But I did feel for you here, that I'm sure about."

"And you speak in past tense now," she said with a laugh that held a hint of bitterness. "Oh, Barnabas, you're still a child in some ways. But a child who has lost its light-hearted joy in the world."

"Perhaps. You always possessed more sense than I did." I squeezed her arm. "I'm better, now, Alys. I promise. It's over. The opiates, the need for revenge."

"Well, it's certain that your desire for revenge against al Qali is over. You've achieved that."

I grimaced and wiped my brow of sweat for the third time. "Believe me when I say al Qali's death brought me no satisfaction." The moment I said the words I knew they were true. "I achieved nothing but hardship and near death for too many people. And I'll have to live with that for the rest of my life."

She studied me a few moments and gave a little nod. "Perhaps you're not as much a child as I thought," she said softly. "Now, you must get some rest." She looked at me carefully, put a hand to my face and frowned with concern. "You're flushed."

I shook my head. "I'm fine. It's merely the heat. After all this time, I'm still not accustomed to it."

"No, there is no heat, the evening is cool. You're feverish. Let me get you to bed."

Kristin Gleeson

I rose and opened my mouth to say something boyishly comic and the view spun around me. A moment later I collapsed.

CHAPTER TWENTY-THREE
ROHA, THE ETHIOPES, EARLY AUTUMN, 1447
ALYS

Alys pressed the cool cloth along Barnabas's temples and cheeks. They were still burning hot. He stirred and muttered a few words. She knew the fever still raged and the danger loomed as large as ever. It was the third day and still he sweated, tossed and turned. The precious water she used to give him to drink and to bathe him was running out. They had no choice but to move to a place where there was water, and less likely, a physician of some sort.

She knew his wound was festering and the poison was racing around his body. The longer it was left untreated the worse it would be. She'd tried to recall all she'd learned from Joanie and the physician who'd treated her leg. That had festered too. But there was little or next to nothing at hand in this remote place. No, there was nothing for it. They had to move. And the guide, who continued to cast impatient eyes at her and Barnabas, was clearly getting restless. She couldn't guarantee that he would remain with them. After all, what kept him here but a request from an old man who really had no authority? He could easily return now and say that he'd done as the old man had asked. No one would be the wiser.

Flores watched her carefully from where he leaned against an old ruined wall that made up part of the small, deserted settlement where they'd made camp. She knew he was sizing up the situation, too. Better to have the guide take them to a settlement with people where she could at least hire someone if need be. She still had the manuscript and a small gold ring that Fabriano had given her. Those would fetch some money, surely? She glanced at Tomaso, squatting in his wooden cage. No, she couldn't bring herself to sell Tomaso. She would find a way.

"Alys! No. Please don't leave," said Barnabas. His eyes opened, unseeing and he thrashed his arms around as if trying to fight off a foe.

"Sssshhh," she said. "It's all right. I'm here. Alys is here."

She took his hand in hers and that seemed to calm him a little.

"Alys," he whispered, squeezing her hand hard. "You must listen. The danger is ahead. I'm sorry, so sorry. The woman is evil and I have put you in her hands."

"I understand," she said. "Calm yourself. I'm here, by your side. There is no woman." She glanced at Flores. Had he planned some extra treachery? No, it was probably just the fever speaking. Barnabas didn't suspect anything, really. He'd been speaking out of his delirium since he'd fallen ill.

After a while he calmed enough to fall into a troubled, restless sleep. She used that opportunity to speak to their guide. It was a difficult task, given that his Greek was poor and she had nothing of his own language, but eventually she managed to convey that they would journey on today. They would either create a makeshift litter for Barnabas if they could find sturdy enough branches, or if that failed, they would strap him to his donkey. The guide had told her if they headed towards the Atbara River which fed into the Nile, they could reach it that night. There were settlements along the river. They would surely find some kind of assistance in one of them.

Later, when she could smell the water amid the blowing dust that came from the parched ground, she wondered if her decision had been the right one. Flores had seemed to agree with her, but that meant nothing. And Barnabas was beyond consultation. In the end, they hadn't found branches large enough or sturdy enough to support Barnabas's weight, so Flores and the guide had strapped him to the donkey. That had meant their progress was slow to ensure that Barnabas didn't struggle and fall off. It was dusk now, and the seemingly endless journey had done nothing to help Barnabas's situation. In fact, for the past hour or so, the restlessness had ceased and he was deathly still. She couldn't bear to think what that might mean. Instead, she willed the journey to finish.

When they came up over the rise and looked down the bank to the river in the growing dusk, Alys could only just make out the outline of huts. As her eyes adjusted, so her hope increased. She glanced over at Barnabas lying strapped astride the donkey. His head sagged to one side like a man with a broken neck. Was it too late? She held Tomaso a little tighter. He was her talisman.

"Barnabas," she said in an encouraging voice. "Please hold on, help is at hand."

There was no answering stir or any other sign that she might have been heard. She urged her donkey onwards to a quick trot and the others followed.

⌇

Alys insisted they stop as soon as they entered the settlement. She dismounted her donkey and hurried to Barnabas to check for his breath. It was faint, but still present. She sighed in relief and then with some hasty words and gestures conveyed to the guide that he must find them somewhere to stay at once. She tried not to make it seem like an order, for she knew that they relied on his kindness and charity, rather than any authority she had, but the insistence in her voice was still present. After a moment, she pulled the small gold ring from her finger and handed it to him, bidding him to use it if he must to obtain a place and someone to attend Barnabas.

He paused, raised his brows and cast a glance at Barnabas. He pulled a face and gave a nod.

"He is like me," said Flores coming up beside her. "He thinks we put ourselves at unnecessary risk for a man who is sure to die."

"He will not die," said Alys firmly. "He's strong and has survived much. He will survive this."

Flores shrugged but said no more. What more was there to be said? Alys knew the chances were that Flores spoke the truth; there was no need to harp on it.

The guide found them a small hut in which to stay. It was clear from the small pile of possessions stacked in a corner that some poor family had been displaced for the night. She chose not to think about how that had been arranged. Her first thought must be of Barnabas.

"Someone will come to attend him?" she asked the guide, indicating Barnabas.

The guide nodded. "An old woman."

She looked at him, hoping for further information, but he turned away and left the hut. She followed him and they began to unstrap Barnabas. Flores came to help. Carefully, under her intense supervision, they brought Barnabas inside to lie on the pallet that she'd prepared. Once settled, she knelt beside him and put a hand to his face. She could see a light flutter around his eye. He was still alive, at least. His face was pale, and when she leaned down to listen for his breath it was still barely perceptible.

The woman came, old but majestic in her draped cloths of startling colours, now faded by time, and scars marking her face in an odd pattern. Slung across her shoulder was a large bag. Someone of consequence. Alys drew some hope from that. To achieve consequence, surely she must have some skill.

She nodded to Alys and then swept her out of the way before she knelt beside Barnabas. She opened each of his eyes and peered into them, then his mouth. She looked at his hands, squeezed his fingers and prodded the wound. She felt his stomach, first one side and then the other, all the while grunting and frowning. She raised her head up, closed her eyes and spoke some words in a mesmerising rhythm.

When she'd finished speaking she remained silent for a moment, her eyes still shut. Alys stood completely still, watching her. The woman opened her eyes and said some phrases. Alys shook her head, unable to make sense of them. The woman tried again, this time in a different language. Alys still didn't understand and shook her head again. Alys held up her hand and went outside to retrieve the guide from where he'd been sitting, munching on some fruit with Flores. She gestured to him to follow and he got up and went inside with her.

The woman, seeing the guide, spoke rapidly to him. He nodded and then turned to Alys.

"She says that the devil spirit is in him. It will be hard to get it out."

"The devil spirit?" Alys said incredulously.

The guide shrugged. "She say demon, but same thing."

"What of his wound?"

"She cannot help that if demon inside. She must get demon out first."

"Can she do that?"

The guide shrugged again. "She will try."

Alys bit her lip. "How will she do that?"

"I do not know her ways. They are not God's ways."

The woman wasn't a Christian. Should she let her near Barnabas? But Alys put the question aside, because the answer was already clear. Barnabas had no chance without this woman's help. With it, he might actually live. She couldn't lessen his chances.

Alys watched helplessly as the woman settled herself by Barnabas and began to unpack her bag. Smaller pouches, tied firmly, were lined up in front of her, along with feathers and a wooden rattle. She spoke to the guide and he disappeared, only to return with a jug of water and a bowl.

The woman untied one of the pouches and poured some of its contents into the bowl, along with a few drops of water and began to make a paste with a small pestle that was in her bag. Alys could only surmise it was some kind of herb. She watched the woman add contents, some of it granular, from other pouches. She used the pestle to mix them together. When she was finished she put the bowl aside and rose, the feathers and rattle in her hand. She lifted her head up and chanted, waving the feathers over Barnabas's body in one hand, and shaking the rattle in the other hand.

At first Alys wanted to laugh which quickly shifted an urge to snatch the rattle and feathers from the woman's hand. It was blasphemous after all. But something about the chant, its rhythm, or the sound of the words as they slipped off the woman's tongue, halted her. Was it just the same as a prayer in this woman's faith? Was it any different from the incense and chanting of any priest? She closed her eyes a moment and offered up her own prayer. She'd prayed enough on the journey, but that had seemed to yield little assistance. Or none that she could see, except if she counted it as God's blessing that Barnabas had survived this long.

She felt a hand on her shoulder. The woman motioned her to stand. Alys did as she was told. The woman passed her one of the feathers and spoke to the guide.

"She says you must help chase this demon away. It is making his spirit sick. She says only you can do it. You must do it with love in your heart. Love for your man."

Alys stared at the guide and then the woman, her thoughts frozen. The woman nodded at her and moved Alys's hand that held the feather back and forth over Barnabas's body. The woman let go of Alys's hands after a while and Alys continued on, waving the feather, thinking of nothing but how her hand seemed heavy.

She looked down at Barnabas, his pale and drawn face and saw traces of the boy she once knew. The impish, charming young boy who could make her laugh and whose naughty antics seemed all the more engaging for the manner in which they were delivered. And the boy, whose earnest attempts to steer a true course through the mire that others had drawn him into, tugged at her heart until she had succumbed wholeheartedly. So wholeheartedly that she had travelled half of Christendom to find him. And if she was to be honest, travelled even further afield, into the heart of worse dangers than she had ever imagined. Had it been worth it? She thought of Eleanor and tears came to her eyes. She wouldn't give up Eleanor, not now. Eleanor was worth everything she'd gone through. She was the child of Alys's heart. And she was Barnabas's child. She hadn't told him about Eleanor, not yet. Not until she was certain what Barnabas wanted. Not until she was certain what she wanted.

Alys dropped her hand a moment. She looked down at Barnabas, bit her lip and then knelt.

"Barnabas," she whispered in his ear insistently. "You must get better. Fight this. Fight it for me and for our child, Eleanor. We have a child Barnabas, we have a child."

She searched his face for any sign that he might have heard, but he remained still. She leaned down, kissed his lips full and hard, willing him to feel what her kiss was trying to convey.

The woman placed a hand on her shoulder and lifted her up. Alys still clutched the feather in her hand and on the woman's nod began to wave it back and forth again. The woman resumed her chanting while Alys watched Barnabas and waved her feather.

It may have been hours or it might have been less, but the woman eventually ceased her chanting and motioned Alys to stop. She collected the feather from Alys and knelt back down beside Barnabas. He remained as he'd been since they'd first arrived, pale and still.

The woman unwound the makeshift bandage from around Barnabas's arm and prodded the wound a little. It oozed blood and the flesh around it was angry and puckered. Yellow pus gathered in one corner. The woman dabbed away the pus and then plastered the wound with the paste she had prepared. When she was finished, Alys offered a fresh bandage, torn from her own veil which was now half its original size. The woman wrapped the fabric tightly around Barnabas's arm and gave a grunt.

She rose with effort and spoke to the guide. The guide looked at Alys when she was finished. "She says she can do no more. Now it is waiting."

"Is the demon gone?" Alys asked.

The guide relayed the question. The woman shrugged and said a few words. "Time will tell," the guide translated.

Alys sighed and nodded. She went over to the woman, took her hand and squeezed it. Alys looked into the woman's eyes and tried to convey her gratitude. The woman gave her a little pat on the shoulder and smiled compassionately. A moment later she had gathered up her things and swept out of the hut as majestically as she'd arrived.

Alys turned and looked at Barnabas. Exactly how much time must they wait before they would know if the demon had gone?

∽

She refused to move from his bedside. Even when Flores entered the hut and told her he would keep watch so that she might get some air and clear her head, with the guide escorting her, she refused. He'd insisted she eat something at least and brought her a small plate of food, but she found she couldn't manage much.

Despite her vigil, there was no change in Barnabas. His breath was still shallow and faint, but at least it hadn't ceased altogether. She'd clutched his hand and whispered to him words of love and encouragement often since the woman had left. Now, she wiped a hand across her brow wearily and wondered what more she could do.

She reached for a flagon beside her, noting that Flores had at least filled it since she'd last drunk from it. To be honest he'd been good enough, bringing her food, drink and filling the water pitcher that she'd used to bathe Barnabas. Flores spent most of his time elsewhere, coming inside only to sleep and not every night. She could only imagine how he kept himself amused, and assumed several women had found their beds warmed by him.

She leaned for a moment against the wall and closed her eyes. Her back was stiff and her whole body ached with a tension that had enveloped it since Barnabas had fallen ill. She'd slept in snatches, like this. Her head leaning against the wall, or stretched out beside Barnabas, in case there should be a change.

Now, she thought to get the woman healer back here again, to ask her what it meant that Barnabas stayed in this state of limbo, getting neither better nor worse, as if he was trying to make up his mind whether he wanted to live or die. She'd done all she could to convince him. Tried to show and speak of her love for him.

She opened her eyes and looked at him again. "Live, you bastard," she said in a low voice. "Don't you dare die on me after all I did for you."

He remained unmoved by her anger or her words. She gave a disgusted sigh and closed her eyes again.

"I'm a bastard, am I?" came a weak voice. "Well, you're probably right, though I never knew who my parents were."

For a moment Alys thought it was a ghost speaking. Her eyes flew open and she leaned over Barnabas. His eyes were open and he gave her a faint smile.

Alys stared at him and then broke into a joyful smile. "Barnabas!" She took his hand and kissed it. "You're awake. How glad I am to hear you speak."

"So you're not offended by my parentage?"

She laughed. "After everything else I've put up with from you, how would that offend me?"

CHAPTER TWENTY-FOUR
THE ETHIOPES, EARLY AUTUMN 1447
ALYS

It was two days before Barnabas was well enough to be moved. Flores used the time as he had in the days past, namely finding his own amusement and returning only to bring them food and water. Alys tended Barnabas, but not with the intensity she had since their arrival. She allowed herself short periods outside, the guide escorting her as she walked the small settlement and viewed the river.

She'd spoken little of consequence to Barnabas, not wanting to tire him, and also because she had no desire to discuss anything important with him while he was in such a weakened state. And he had little energy for it. There was time enough for that. She felt some measure of contentment, as much as could be found in this remote place away from the usual comforts and with the dangers that still lay ahead.

She stared along the bank, watching the river's flow and the few small boats and barges that floated upon it.

They were sturdy enough craft, carrying a mixture of dark-skinned people with flowing robes or scantily clad with beads and feathers and other ornaments. Some were Arabs too, their lighter skin and eye colour marking them out to some degree. Soon they would join those boats, making their own journey downriver, hopefully to join the Nile and make their way to Dongola. Would Joanie and Hal still be there waiting for her in hope? She could only pray that they were, or there was word of them, because there was no other alternative she could think of.

She took a deep breath and turned away to make her way back to the hut, wrapping her threadbare head covering closer around her. When she arrived back at the hut Barnabas was sitting up, his colour improved. His eyes lit up when he saw her and she gave him a generous smile.

"You're looking much better," said Alys.

"I feel like a weakling," said Barnabas. "It was all I could do to sit up."

"You *are* a weakling. You shouldn't try to do much, yet. Give your body time to recover."

She moved over to him and knelt down, reaching for the bandage around his arm. "I'll just check this. The healer woman said to leave it on until you could move your arm on your own."

"Healer woman?"

She nodded. She hadn't told him about the healer. All she'd thought about since he'd wakened was to get him to eat and to rest. Another thing she hadn't talked to him about.

"She came at the guide's bidding. A local woman who seemed to be trained in healing, though her approach was a little unorthodox." She smiled, recalling the treatment.

"She had me waving a feather over your body while she chanted and shook a rattle."

"I would have loved to have seen that," said Barnabas.

"It was strange at first, but after a while it felt right." She shrugged. "In any case, whatever it was she did, she seems to have cured you."

Barnabas wrinkled his nose at the odour emitting from his arm when Alys uncovered the wound. "I'd say it was kill or cure, if that paste is anything to go by."

Alys laughed. "Cure, I would say. The wound on your arm is looking a good deal healthier." The paste had dried to a crust, but through the cracks she could see the angry colour had faded and there was no sign of the pus.

"You were very ill," she said becoming serious. Did he remember anything of the ritual, or what she'd said? "You were close to death. Delirious and raving. Do you recall anything?"

Barnabas looked thoughtful. "I remember dreams. Vivid dreams." He looked up at her. "You were there, I think."

He stared at her, his eyes going glassy. For a moment, she thought the fever had returned. She took his hand and placed her other hand on his brow. His eyes cleared and he smiled grimly.

"Sorry, I was trying to remember what I saw. It-it was something about you, I know. Some sort of danger." He gave her an unconvincing smile. "Never mind. It will come to me. And if it, doesn't it's probably not important."

"You did cry out a warning to me at one point, was it that you're thinking of?"

"What did I say?"

She could see he was concerned and she searched her mind for his exact words. "Something about a woman.

You warned me about her and you were sorry that you put me in her hands." Could he have meant the healer? Though it was more like Alys put him in the healer's hands, rather than the other way around.

"Was that all?" Barnabas said. "Did I say anything about what kind of danger?"

Alys shook her head. "Not really, why?"

He frowned. "Because I think it's important. I think you're right. My vivid dream. I remember a bit, now. There was a woman. A woman wearing a veil, standing in the shadows. She was holding something." He looked up at her. "But why did I associate the danger with you?"

"Perhaps it was something to do with al Qali. Or our journey? There are plenty of women wearing veils."

He slowly shook his head. "No, there's something else about the figure." He paused a moment, looking thoughtful. "She wasn't wearing an Arabic veil."

"One of the tribal women? Was she dark-skinned?"

"I don't know," said Barnabas. He shook his head again and sighed. "It's not clear."

She forced herself to put on a reassuring smile. "Never mind. It will come to you, if it's important."

She could see he didn't believe her. She didn't believe herself. The unspoken thought hung between them. Was it a danger closer to home? And which home? Venice, or even back in London? They'd been through enough to know anything was possible.

As if reading the direction of her mind, he leaned over and squeezed her hand. "There are two of us now," he said softly. His eyes contained a hint of a plea.

She bit her lip and took a deep breath. "Barnabas, I mentioned before that it was more complicated for me than you supposed. It's not just Hal. There's someone else."

"Someone else?" he said abruptly. Pain filled his eyes. "I should have expected that. Of course, it's natural and I'm a fool to think you might still have some feelings for me."

"Barnabas, listen, please. It's not what you're thinking. It's only that... I'm not sure how you will like this—"

Flores burst in. "You must come and see. This you won't believe. Madonna, I can hardly believe it myself."

"What is it?" asked Barnabas sharply.

Flores gave a broad grin. "No, I won't spoil the surprise. You must come see for yourself."

"I've had enough of your surprises," said Barnabas curtly. With great effort, he swung his legs to the side of the bed.

Alys laid a hand on his arm. "No. You need to conserve your strength. I'll go and see what it is. I promise I'll return immediately."

He nodded reluctantly. She cast a curious glance at Flores, trying to read from his face what the surprise might be, but all she could see was amusement. What would amuse him and amuse her might be entirely different things. With resignation, she followed him silently out of the door.

He led her to the edge of the settlement and pointed. In the distance she could see several riders astride donkeys. One was unmistakeably a woman. But there was something familiar about her manner and figure, even from this distance. She looked at the rider next to the woman and laughed. There was no mistaking it now. Joanie and Hal were approaching, accompanied, as far as she could tell, by the Nubian men who'd escorted them to Dongola.

∽

She couldn't stop hugging Joanie tightly. Her eyes flowed tears that had refused to be shed during the many dreadful days since she'd left Joanie, and even then couldn't remember when she'd last cried. It was as if all the burdens of the years had come undone with Joanie's compassionate embrace and murmured endearments.

Eventually, Alys forced herself to pull back and look at her dear friend, but words wouldn't come. Joanie felt no inhibitions.

"Look at the state of you!" she cried. "Brown as that ass I've sat on these many days and more." She pinched her cheek lightly. "Skin and bones you are, too. And what are these shadows beneath your eyes, hmm, sweeting?"

"Oh, Joanie," Alys said and sniffed. "I can't tell you how good it is to hear your scoldings."

As soon as Alys had recognised Joanie and Hal in the distance she'd rushed back to Barnabas to tell him the good news. His face had lit up with a joy she hadn't seen on him for a long time. At his encouragement, she had returned to Flores to greet them as they entered the settlement. They had hardly had time to dismount their donkeys when Alys was hugging first her brother and then Joanie unashamedly, dignity forgotten and veil discarded in a heap at her feet.

"You haven't managed to lose our good friends," said Flores now to Hal.

"And good thing, too," said Hal. "It was down to them, wasn't it, that we found you. They wouldn't rest and neither would we." He eyed Flores dubiously. "And you, where do you fit into this?"

"Ah, we'll save that story for later," said Alys. "You must come see Barnabas. He's waiting for you."

"Barnabas?" said Hal.

"Jacko," said Alys.

Joanie frowned at Hal and gave him a shove. "You know who he is. No need for innocence." She looked at Alys. "I told him the lot. So you needn't worry now. He understands."

Alys cast a glance at Hal and then Joanie. Exactly how much of "the lot" did Joanie mean? Well, in truth, it made no difference now. It was done. He must make of it what he would.

Hal came over to her and gave her a tight squeeze on her shoulder. "You've no cause to worry, 'alfling. You'll always be my sister."

Alys gave him a smile and wondered if she should thank him or slap him. Her life and choices were what they were. She would make her own choices, as she'd always done.

The Nubian leader stepped forward and put a restraining hand on her arm.

"We would speak with you," he said in halting Greek. "About the manuscript."

She nodded to him. "I must tell you that the manuscript is not mine to dispose of. Its owner is here, though, and I'm certain he will be happy to discuss it with you."

"We have come a long way. We'll find quarters and come to you later, if you will give me your direction."

Once she'd given him the simple instructions he nodded and led the other two men away, each leading their donkeys. Their well-worn robes were sweat-stained and covered in dust and grime from the road but they walked with considered dignity. She could only admire the unswerving faith and determination that had kept them focused on their objective for so long. She would talk to Barnabas. Perhaps the manuscript would help them in some manner. Or maybe he could help them in some other way. But that was for later.

Flores led them to the hut that had served as Alys's home for what, in some lights, seemed like a lifetime. Joanie chattered a little about their journey, but Alys took little of it in. She just basked in Joanie's presence and kept casting considering looks at Hal who strode ahead beside Flores. She hadn't missed the hands that had lingered around Joanie's waist as Hal had helped her to dismount the donkey, or Joanie's coquettish look in return. It seemed much had happened on their journey as well.

When they arrived at the hut, Alys found Barnabas leaning against the door frame. Unable to wait any longer, he had struggled from his bed and made it that far. After hefty embraces Alys managed to persuade him to return to his bed, but it took great effort.

"I'm not an invalid," he said.

"You are an invalid," said Alys firmly.

"What 'appened?" asked Hal. "You didn't say that Jacko was injured. Was it al Qali?"

"We all have tales to tell," said Barnabas.

He sighed and leaned back against the cushions. It was clear his recent efforts had taken their toll. In the corner, Tomaso started to make a fuss, disturbed by the excitement around him. Alys went over and released the monkey, taking him in her arms.

"All in good time," Alys said. "For now, you must rest. Flores will talk to the guide and see what can be done about extra accommodation for Hal and Joanie."

"Nonsense," said Barnabas. "They can sleep here. I'll sleep on the floor with Hal and you and Joanie can have this bed."

"Don't be foolish," Alys said. "You're not well enough."

"I am improving all the time," he said firmly. "And tomorrow or the next day, as soon as passage can be arranged, we'll travel onwards."

She saw the stubborn set to his face and knew he wouldn't be moved. She shook her head.

Joanie nodded to Tomaso. "I see our friend is none the worse for wear. And he's reunited with his proper master, now."

"Oh, I'd say that it's Alys who is his proper master," said Barnabas.

Alys frowned at the change of subject, but she knew the matter was lost. "Well, Joanie and Hal must be famished, so we'll all go off in search of food, and leave you to get some rest if you're going to resume the journey so soon."

Barnabas only frowned his objections. The look on her face was warning enough. The four of them made to go and Alys bade them to continue on ahead without her for a moment. When they'd left she looked at Barnabas.

"The Nubian men are here," she said quietly. "They were the ones who helped Joanie and Hal to find us. I'm not sure how, but I can guess why."

"The manuscript," said Barnabas. He frowned. "What did you tell them?"

"Nothing. Except that you are its owner and that it's to you they must speak."

He sighed and nodded. "And they'll come here?"

"Yes, after they have found somewhere to stay."

"Soon, then. Good. It's best that we speak without the others."

"What will you say to them? Will you give them the manuscript?"

He gave her a wry smile. "It would do them little good. No, I'll be honest with them. It's the least I can do. Better than to raise their hopes any longer."

"Are you certain you want to meet with them alone? They may not like what you tell them."

"I'm certain. I don't think they would do me any harm. And I intend to promise that I will do my best to search for the manuscript they seek and send it on to them."

She smiled at him. "Good. I think that's a worthy gesture."

He shrugged. "It might end up being an empty gesture. I can give no guarantee that I will be able to obtain anything."

"No, but I'm glad you thought to try."

He smiled, and on that she left him.

❧

By the time the group had returned, laden with what food and drink they could obtain in a small trading community, Barnabas was sitting on the edge of the bed, fully clothed, stowing away a small bundle. He gave Alys a brief smile and then demanded that they lay out their wares and tell him the full tale while they ate.

It was clear, though they never said, Joanie and Hal had used every pressure to convince the Nubian men to take them with them in their search for Alys and Barnabas.

"There was no choice. We would 'ave never found you otherwise," said Hal with a shrug. "As it was, they lost the trail a few times and by sheer luck we were able to pick it up from people in settlements or villages who'd seen you."

"Very good fortune," said Alys.

Joanie waved her hand in dismissal and pressed Alys for her tale. It was a tale that Alys suddenly found herself reluctant to tell, so she gave only a summary that omitted any part that Flores had played in her capture. Barnabas added nothing, either. It would save for later. Perhaps it was too fresh, or just too deep in her emotions that she couldn't think about it any more. She looked at Barnabas. Was that what it was like for him and his time with the Turks? She had asked him only once and he had dismissed her question with a change of subject and she had left it at that. Now, she thought she understood better why he wouldn't want to tell even her.

Later, when the others were talking among themselves, Alys took the moment to talk with Barnabas privately. "They came?" she said softly.

He nodded.

"How did they take it?"

"Well enough. They are patient men." He took her hand and kissed it. "And you are a patient woman."

CHAPTER TWENTY-FIVE
THE NILE RIVER, AUTUMN, 1447
BARNABAS

I lay back, resting on the small hammock that was slung in the space below deck, my mind too restless to sleep. It had been two days since we'd secured passage on a *felucca,* a lateen-rigged trading ship, and boarded her. They were common enough on the Nile, as well as the Mediterranean, but since the dry season was on us and the waters had begun to recede, making the journey difficult for any large ship, we were fortunate indeed. She'd brought a large shipment of goods, the last until the rains started to fill the banks once again. The owner was happy enough to carry us, in the light of the few goods he had as cargo on his return journey. Though he frowned at Joanie and Alys, I'd made certain they were well covered and promised him half of the remaining gold that Joanie and Hal still carried immediately, and the other half when we arrived. I would sell the manuscript in Cairo and use those funds to pay for the remainder of the journey.

Though I had recovered some of my strength, I was privately glad that I wasn't facing the journey on the back of a donkey and could safely remain seated while we sailed north. The winds were favourable, so I calculated that we should be in Cairo in perhaps ten days. And from there it was a short journey to Alexandria. It was critical to make it as quickly as possible in order to avoid the winter storms. The storm season meant fewer ships travelling to Venice. From there it would be another week or so before we reached port and home. In less than a month we could get on with our lives.

But what lives would they be? Alys hadn't promised me anything in words, but I took hope from her manner and actions. Since Hal and Joanie had arrived it had been difficult to find moments alone, so there had been no real opportunities to discuss any plans in more depth than we had already done.

I was determined to convince her that we would make a life together, no matter what the complications. I would get Alessandra to release her and together we would go somewhere. Perhaps Genoa, where I could start afresh. Would I be bold enough to go to the place that my fake self was born? Bruges might be better. I still had my connections there. I smiled. Would I dare to set up in London? Giacomo Bonavillagio, Italian merchant, a man without an English past.

I heard a noise and saw Alys descending the few steps to the sleeping quarters. The light caught her hair as she unwrapped her veil. She made her way to Tomaso's cage. He'd been forced to remain inside at the insistence of the ship's captain. Alys had reluctantly complied and spent an hour or so every day with him on her lap as she fed him nuts, dates and other tidbits she managed to scrounge. Now, the moment she released the rope that held the cage shut, he opened the door and scrambled into her arms.

I closed my eyes, knowing that she would walk over to check on me, to ensure I was sleeping, as she had instructed. I had walked the perimeter of the ship several times today until she'd called a halt and sent me below. I heard her soft footsteps come towards me and stop by my side. I resisted the urge to move. She gave a satisfied sigh and walked away.

I opened my eyes cautiously and watched as she took a seat on one of the benches that were at the small rough table. Tomaso sat on her lap and she talked softly to him, withdrawing her store of treats from the folds of her gown and offering them to the monkey. She sat there, murmuring her endearments and stroking Tomaso as he gobbled his treats in perfect contentment, until a noise above made her pause. A moment later Joanie came below.

Joanie spent much of her time in Hal's company, the two easy companions and something more, I could see. They had the look of new lovers, needing to touch whenever possible, exchanging smiles and looks whenever any excuse allowed them. I was glad and thought the pair fortunate to have such an uncomplicated relationship. My relationship with Alys was never so, but perhaps it might be one day.

"There you are," said Joanie.

"Sshhh," said Alys softly. "Barnabas is asleep."

"Aye," she said in a lower voice. "And well 'e should be. I thought 'e would wear a hole in the deck before 'e stopped."

"He's determined to get his strength back."

"It seems to me 'e's going the wrong way about it. Rest is what will do it."

"He'll do it his own way, you know that."

"I do, I suppose," said Joanie. "Look at you. You spoil that animal, you do."

"He deserves it. He was a great help with al Qali."

"I know, I know. But you treat him like he was your child."

"No. Don't think I'm confusing the two."

"I don't, I just know you miss her." There was a pause. "Have you told Barnabas about the baby?"

"N-no. I haven't had the chance."

"Don't you think you should tell 'im? Soon?"

"Yes. Don't worry. I just need to find the right time."

Joanie sighed. "You should do it now, before it's too late. Before 'e gets wind of it and gets the wrong idea."

"Hal won't tell him, will he?"

"No. 'e knows not to say a word. I told 'im it was up to you to do the telling."

"Thank you, Joanie. You are the dearest friend in the world. And I'm only too glad that Hal has found you. I couldn't think of a better match."

Joanie gave a small laugh. "Well I'm glad that it's got your blessing, and all. We're contented to be together, for the moment. There's plenty to get through before we decide what might be permanent."

"Well, if any two deserve to have everything turn out well for them, it's you two. I pray that it may be so."

"And I pray that it may be so for you," said Joanie. "Now come, let's go up on deck. There will be plenty of dank old corners in Venice."

I listened to Tomaso being replaced in his cage and the two of them retreating up the steps. I suppressed the urge to call out. To demand Alys tell me what she'd meant by the conversation with Joanie. What child? But I wanted to give myself time to think. Time to dissect every word I'd heard. But all I could think of was that Alys had a child. I shouldn't be surprised. It happened on occasion with a courtesan. Usually, if it did happen, they would be quietly and effectively eliminated at the first sign of pregnancy. But this wasn't one of those times. Whose child was it? The words echoed in my mind and I opened my eyes and made to get up.

Alys stood in front of me. "You heard," she said. "Somehow, I knew it. Somehow I could sense you were awake."

"I was awake," I said in an even tone. It took great effort to maintain a neutral quality. "You have a child." I made it a statement. After all, there was nothing to dispute.

Alys drew herself up. "A daughter. Eleanor," she said.

"And is she as fair as you?"

"Fairer. She will be a beauty."

"Like her mother."

Alys shook her head. "No, she has a good amount of her father in her."

"You mean she is dark-haired."

Alys cocked her head and gave a half smile. "No, as I said, she is fair. She has her father's blonde hair and his large blue eyes. At least for now. I'm told eye colour can change in a baby."

"The father is fair-haired," I repeated dumbly. I tried to recall the fair-haired nobles and well born men in Venice.

"Yes," she said. "My only hope is that she doesn't inherit her father's tendency to mischief. A little imp, he was. Bold as brass."

I stared at her, trying to confirm the meaning of her words. I could tell nothing from her expression. I reached over and took her hand. "The child is mine?" I asked softly. "But how is that possible?"

She raised her brow. "You mean I have to explain? You seemed to need little instruction that night, if I remember."

I kissed her hand and then drew her to me. "Why didn't you say before?"

"You mean you're glad?"

"Of course I'm glad." I pulled her head down and kissed her deeply. "More glad than I can ever tell you. Alys, it is you I love, and no one else. I can only hope that you could love me in return."

She pulled back. "You trust me when I tell you that it's yours?"

He looked at her. "Should I doubt you?"

She shook her head. "No, there's nothing to doubt. You're the father. And if there was any doubt you have only to look at her to know she is yours."

"She is called Eleanor?" I wrinkled my nose. "Really?"

Alys gave me a light slap on my arm. "Of course. Who else would I choose? You shouldn't quibble. After all, it was through the Duchess that I first came to know you."

I laughed again, too full of joy to dispute any of what she said. "Well my daughter is certainly a duchess in my eyes, if not the rest of the world."

"Wait until you see her," said Alys shyly. "You will fall in love with her in an instant."

"I don't have to wait, I love her already." I said. I pulled her on top of me and the hammock swung perilously. "And I love her mother equally."

As I had hoped, we made swift progress downriver to Cairo. The currents and wind were with us and so we were able to find ourselves in Alexandria within the space of a fortnight. I'd sold the manuscript to a very willing merchant who peddled texts, bound and unbound, in a stall in one of the main markets. It was enough to see us home. There, I could retrieve my money from Alessandra, purchase Alys's contract and secure a future for the three of us.

It didn't take me long to grow used to the idea I was a father. Alys teased me with a few words when no one was around or shaded comments in the company of others. My strength grew, and with it my desire to be quit of the ship and find a more comfortable bed fit for the two of us. It wasn't until Alexandria that I was granted this wish.

It was Joanie who laughingly shut Alys and I together in the small room that was our temporary chamber in the middle of the day. Finally alone with Alys, I approached her and caressed her face, staring into her eyes.

In the face of our first encounter since that fateful night in Venice, she grew suddenly shy and cast her eyes downward. I lifted the veil from her head and let it drop to the floor. With my right hand I cupped her chin and kissed her slowly, parting her lips. Slowly, I moved to her throat and neck, sliding my hand along her breastbone and under her robe. I loosed the ties that held it shut and pushed it from her shoulders, the thin fabric fluttering in a puff to the floor. I untied my own robe and pulled the tunic over my head and drew her against my bare skin. We embraced, taking time to feel our skins connect and the arousal to form with a lasting strength.

I led her to the bed, conscious all the while that this was a passion fuelled by more than the desire that had taken me in Venice which had been fed on alcohol, drugs and tangled emotions that were knotted to a cruel extreme. Now, it was as if our lovemaking was washed of all its past impurities and allowed to begin anew. As she stirred and rose to meet each caress and joining with equal fervour, I could only look with hope and joy at the future. Something I had never been able to do before. It was with that lingering thought I fell asleep, spent and content with my arms around Alys.

I awoke sometime later with a start. Alys hovered above me, her hair a waterfall around her and her face a mixture of fear and concern.

"What is it?" I asked.

"You called out in your sleep. That woman. The veiled woman."

I blinked, trying to recall. The veiled woman in the shadows. I could see her now. Not in Arab dress. I was right about that. It wasn't tribal dress either. No, she was wearing black. And the dress was Venetian.

"Alessandra," I muttered.

"Alessandra? The woman was Alessandra?" Alys clutched my arm. "What else did you see?"

I frowned. Eventually I shook my head. "That's all. Just that. Alessandra, standing in the shadows."

"What was she doing?" There was hint of desperation in her voice.

"Just standing. Nothing more." I put a reassuring hand over hers. "I'm sure it's nothing. Just me thinking over our next meeting, I'm sure."

Alys shook her head. "No, you said before it was a warning. You told me I must be careful."

I looked at her and saw the fear fully present now. "Not this time, though. I'm sure it's fine."

"Can you not see more?" she asked in a small voice. "I know you said you would never act the seer again, but could you look in a bowl of water? Just this once?"

I tried to put all the conviction I could in my voice. "I don't think there's any need. I'm sure there's nothing to see, Alys. It was only my desire to get Alessandra to release you from your contract making itself felt."

She searched my face and eventually nodded. I pulled her into my arms again and we lay back against the pillows. I could feel her mind working actively, but she said nothing. I gave an inward sigh. All the early contentment had gone. Though I might have allayed some of Alys's fears I had done nothing to allay my own.

CHAPTER TWENTY-SIX
VENICE, LATE AUTUMN 1447
BARNABAS

The favourable wind and weather held for us and my prediction of a return to Venice before the end of the month had proved true. Despite our speed, it still seemed interminable for me and also Alys. We'd spoken little about her worries, but I knew they were still foremost in her mind. She hadn't voiced exactly what kind of threat she imagined was present in Alessandra, but I could well imagine. All the funds I had left would be gone, secreted somewhere and a new business partner acquired to act as her protector. Left penniless, I would have no recourse against her. I still had other funds, not as much as I had in our business and kept with her, but a small nest egg that wouldn't see me destitute. Still, it wouldn't be enough to purchase Alys's contract and set myself up afresh. But there was no doubt which I would choose. I would find other ways to make my money. Alys and I would build some kind of future with our daughter, even if it wasn't the one I hoped for.

I tried to allay her fears with my assurances for the rest of the journey and to some degree she accepted them. But it was still with some level of trepidation that we stepped off the ship in Venice's dock area and made our way to secure a gondola to take us, Tomaso and our baggage to Alessandra's palazzo.

Overhead, the sky was the dull grey of approaching winter and a chill fog moved along the lagoon in wispy tendrils. Alys drew her shawl around her. She'd purchased it from a stall in Alexandria and its bright colours made her skin seem pale and ghostly in the Venetian light. Alys wore Venetian clothes now, her light cottons and linens traded long ago for the heavier fabrics of Venice and Christendom. The Arab clothes had given her a sensuous, willowy grace which, combined with her recent motherhood, made her all the more desirable. Now, she appeared more the marble Madonna sculpture—smooth and perfect, but distant.

She sat tensely against me, gripping my hand hard. Joanie cast worried looks at her, her hand through Hal's arm. Flores was the only one who seemed unconcerned. He'd been pleasant enough on the journey home and I continued to wonder exactly what he wanted from me. There was no reason to remain in our company now that we had returned to Venice. When I'd asked him his plans he had only shrugged and said that he was without a ship for the present and would kick his heels until he had a better opportunity present itself.

The gondola made its way along the canal, moving into the lagoon and then along past the Doge's palace, the two columns topped at the landing of San Marco and then the bell tower, which rose up above the mist and fog, like an unearthly presence that floated over the city. We travelled onward, into the Grand Canal, passing houses, villas and palazzos that lined the main canal, their windows and doors pulled closed in this increasingly drenching mist and fog. Various craft drifted by, evident only by the faint light from their lantern, the noise of their oars which carried through the fog, along with a few shouts, some laughter and snatches of conversations. As we journeyed through this ghostly city, we spoke little, too aware of what might lay ahead.

The canal snaked its way up into the heart of the city and we passed under the Rialto Bridge and eventually heaved off, down the small canal near Rio Marin on which Alessandra's palazzo was perched. The gondola halted by the nearest steps and the gondoliers helped us unload the baggage. The two small chests containing Alys's things and some of Joanie's, now scarred and edges worn with the effects of the journey, were joined by the bedraggled Tomaso in his cage and some other small bundles acquired in Alexandria. My own belongings and Hal's, as far as I knew, were scattered to the winds.

Above us, the windows and doors, like most places, were shut against the damp misty fog, though it was only midday. Joanie climbed the steps quickly ahead of us and tugged the large bell pull hard. I could hear the bell peal its signal faintly. We waited, but there was no clattering indication of a door opening. Joanie frowned and pulled the bell pull again. The peal echoed once more. Eventually, we heard the sound of the door starting to open and Joanie's face relaxed. A woman appeared, a servant by the looks of her, but one I'd never seen at Alessandra's. Had she acquired new staff?

"You can tell the Madonna Alessandra that Madonna Maria and her servant have returned," said Joanie in Italian. "And if you would be so good as to prepare a bath for my mistress in her room. And ask Madonna

Alessandra if she would receive her friend, Signor Giacomo and his companion."

The woman gave her a puzzled frown. "I am sorry signora, but I don't know who you mean. There is no Madonna Alessandra here."

Joanie stared at the woman, too stunned to speak.

"There must be some mistake," said Alys, clutching my arm.

I leapt up the steps. "What do you mean? Who lives here now?"

"Why Signor Grimani and his family," said the woman.

"And how long have they lived here?" I said.

"These past three months, signore."

"And do you know anything about the previous inhabitants? The Madonna Alessandra?"

The woman shook her head. "Nothing, signore."

"Would anyone in the household know? Your master perhaps?"

"I shouldn't think so, signore."

I nodded and thanked her for her time. She closed the door in haste, a clear desire to shut out the unpleasantness we brought. I turned to Alys and saw the alarm and distress on her face.

"Don't worry," I said. "We'll find them. They simply moved house. I'm sure they left news of their location with someone." I turned to Joanie. "Do you know any of the servants who work hereabouts?"

Joanie pointed to the house a few doors down. "There are a few women I was friendly with in that household. I'll go and ask."

She climbed down the steps and paused by Alys and laid a comforting hand on her shoulder. "We'll find her sweeting, never you fear."

I watched Joanie make her way to the house, knowing all the time that the "her" Joanie had spoken of to Alys wasn't Alessandra, but Eleanor. And with all my heart I hoped she was right.

We stood there, impatiently waiting for Joanie's return. I took Alys's hand and held it. Hal moved closer to us, standing silently while we all turned our eyes in the direction where Joanie had gone. Mercifully it wasn't long, but still too long for two parents who awaited what would assuredly be dreadful news, but still maintained the hope that it wouldn't be. One sign of Joanie's face told me my worst fears were confirmed.

"They're gone," said Joanie. "About three months back, they packed up and left."

"We know that, Joanie," said Alys impatiently. "Do we know where they've gone?"

Joanie cast a worried look at Alys. "No one knows anything, except that the servants were all dismissed."

"All of them?" asked Alys. Her eyes filled with tears. "Then she's gone somewhere else," she wailed. "And she's taken my daughter with her."

Alys's body drooped. She went over to the villa steps and collapsed onto them, putting her head in her hands.

I moved over to her and put my arm around her shoulders. "We'll find her, I promise you."

Alys looked up, her face tearstained and she buried her head in my shoulder. "Please, Barnabas. Please do all you can to help find her."

"You know I'll do everything in my power," I said. I kissed the top of her head. "Now, who among her friends might know where she's gone? You would know her current companions more than I would."

Alys thought, looked over at Joanie and bit her lip. "Crivelli," she said softly. "He might know."

"Crivelli?" I asked. "Who's he?"

"A painter. He often did commissions for Alessandra. They would sell the paintings on and split the profit." She rose quickly, dashing the tears from her cheeks. "We should go there. He's certain to have some idea where she's gone."

"She might have had a fall in fortune," said Hal, a false note of optimism in his voice. "And moved to small place."

Alys looked at him and gave a weak smile. "Perhaps. Crivelli should know if that's the case. Joanie and I will go and ask him."

I took her hand. "We'll all go. And if he doesn't know, we'll go to someone else until we find a person who does know where she is."

Hal and I secured another gondola and gave the directions. The tension during this journey was even greater than before and no words at all were spoken. We finally arrived at the steps by St. Simeon's, disembarked and threaded our way through the small alleys to his quarters. The owner of the building clearly recognised Alys and Joanie and I made no comment on that fact. Now was not the time to query the past.

Joanie led the way up to the door to his rooms and gave it a hefty knock. It was only on the second attempt that the door was eventually opened and a dark-haired man stood there, his shirt hanging loose and his hose and porpoints hastily tied. He held a flagon of wine. He eyed Joanie and then Alys, his face a mixture of emotions when he spied her. It was only then that he noticed me.

"Well, it's the prodigal daughter," he said and forced a laugh. "Returned from your little adventures at last." He gestured behind him. "I would ask you in for a celebration, but you see I am otherwise engaged."

"Where's Alessandra?" Alys said sharply. "We returned to her palazzo to find her gone."

"Ah, yes. Alessandra. She's gone, *amore mia. Scomparso.*" He waved his hand. "Disappeared into thin air. Sold the paintings, packed her bags and left. Mind you, I got a handsome profit from them, even if it was less than she promised."

"She sold the paintings? Which paintings?"

"Why all of them. The ones of you, the perfect Madonna and the one by you. That dark one. Even that."

"You gave her my painting?" Alys said sharply. "You had no right to do that."

Crivelli laughed. "Oh, I think I have every right. After all was it not with my paints, my canvas and my instruction? You left with barely a word and no concern for me. And who knows if you would have returned? Oh no, my marble Madonna, I had every right."

I'd heard enough. I pushed forward and gripped his arm hard, squaring up to him. "We haven't come to hear your whining, we just want to know where Alessandra has gone."

He gave me a sour smile. "As I just told the signorina, I know nothing more than that she has packed up and left."

"Left Venice?" I asked.

He shrugged. "I presume so. She had enough money to do it. She said she wouldn't require my services any more. But that might be because she thought our dear little Maria wasn't returning."

"And you know nothing of the child?"

Crivelli glanced at Alys and shook his head. "No. Why would I? It is no concern of mine."

With great effort, I refrained from punching the man. I still needed more information. I could always deal with him later. "Do you know who Alessandra's sold the paintings to?"

Crivelli paused a moment considering. "Yes. Though I doubt he wants to make it public knowledge."

"Fabriano," said Alys flatly. "It was Fabriano, wasn't it?"

He gave her a wry smile. "No, as a matter of fact it was Antonio Nani, the Doge's nephew."

Alys paled. "Antonio Nani bought the paintings?" she whispered.

"Yes, though he asked me to make a few adjustments. Alessandra told him I was happy to oblige, the bastard. But still, the money was good, so I could hardly object. It would remain in his private collections."

"Do you know where Nani's quarters are?" Alys said in a strangled voice.

Crivelli shrugged. "His offices, only."

"Tell me," she said, her voice firmer now.

I waited impatiently in the large receiving room outside Nani's private office. Beside me, Alys, clearly nervous and anxious, clutched her hands tightly and kept licking her lips. Joanie and Hal stood to one side, acting the servant part, but anxious nonetheless. We'd been told it was our great fortune that Nani was in, though if he would receive us was yet to be determined. While we waited, men entered and exited the room, clearly acting on business that seemed official and other business that appeared a more private nature. I could see the man's taste leaned toward the carnal, both in his companions, men with dissipated complexions and manners, and in the room's décor of paintings of naked nymphs and gods engaged in various pleasurable activities.

I was grateful to see no evidence of Alys among them. Since Crivelli's disclosure earlier I had to keep my imagination in tight control and steered my thoughts to the important concern at hand.

The door opened and a man appeared. He was tall and slim, his dark hair curling to his shoulders. He gave a small bow to Alys.

"Ah, my little Venus. She has returned. And with a companion, I believe." He turned to me and gave a smile that didn't reach his eyes.

I bowed. "Signor Giacomo Bonavillagio, at your service."

"You are not a Venetian," he said.

"No, signore, I am from Genoa."

He nodded. "Ah, that explains it."

"We've come to request a moment of your time," said Alys. "Just to ask you for information, nothing more."

"Information?" said Nani, raising his brows. "Now that can be worth much gold for some."

"If you would accept our gold, I will gladly give it," I said.

He shrugged. "What information do you seek?"

"We understand that you bought paintings by Carlo Crivelli from Madonna Alessandra," I said.

Nani nodded, an amused look on his face. He glanced at Alys. "And you want them back?"

"No, no," said Alys hastily. "We only wondered that in the course of the transaction she might have said to you that she was leaving Venice."

Nani cocked his head, looking at me and then Alys. "I see. Well, *mi dispiace*, she said nothing to me about her plans." He paused a moment, a clear dramatist. "I have heard since, however, that she has left Venice."

"Do you know where she's gone?" Alys said hastily.

"No. I know nothing of where she's gone, only that she left three months ago with that friend of hers, Tomaso."

"Tomaso?" I said sharply. "Tomaso Cortini?"

"Yes," he said.

I froze and tried to focus on Nani's words. Tomaso Cortini, who had found every reason to despise me, the man who I had humiliated in cards and countless other little things, had my daughter.

"You know Tomaso?" Alys whispered.

"Yes," I said, my voice hardened. "I know the man." I looked over at Nani and nodded to him. "We're indebted to you for your help."

He nodded back. It was then that I caught a glimpse inside his office. There on the wall was a painting of Alys, her breasts bare, a child on her lap. My child. I glanced at Nani again and he gave me an amused look. I nodded curtly again, forced a smile and took Alys's arm steering her away before she caught sight of the painting. Hal, giving me a look, ushered Joanie out with equal haste.

Once outside, Alys turned to me. "What do you know of Tomaso?"

"I know that he has no liking for me. And like the monkey he's named for he can bite if you're not careful. Does he know you?"

She looked down at the monkey, huddling in his cage, his fur soaked with mist, nodded and bit her lip. "He desired to be...one of my companions, but Alessandra put him off. She felt he wasn't suitable." She looked out to the canal. "It's not good, is it? Alessandra has gone off with our child in the company of a man who has no liking for you and was thwarted in his pursuit of me."

I took her in my arms. "Does Alessandra know that I'm Eleanor's father?"

Alys paused and shook her head. "No, no she doesn't. She thinks Fabriano is the father. At least that's what I told her. And I don't think she would harm Eleanor. She'd come to care for her, though she tried to hide it." She closed her eyes a moment and then looked up at me. "Oh God. That's it. She's taken Eleanor away from me. She wants her for herself."

I cupped her face and hushed her. "We can't be certain about that. And if that's the case we do know that Eleanor won't come to any harm."

"But she'll do her best to hide, to go somewhere and lose herself so that there's no trace."

I took her hand and held it tightly. "I promise you that I'll find her. No matter where she's gone, whatever it takes, I'll track her down. I swear it on our love and everything else I hold dear."

She looked at me and nodded. I kissed her hand and held her tight again, hoping that I could make good on my words.

Watch out for the next novel in the series, available in 2018. You can learn more by signing up for my newsletter at www.kristingleeson.com

CHARACTERS

Venice

Barnabas/Giacomo/Jacko

Alys/Maria Barnabas's childhood sweetheart

Joanie-Alys's childhood friend, now servant

Hal

Alessandra- former courtesan, Alys's sponsor

Captain Flores-former companion to al Qali

Tomaso the monkey

Tomaso Cortini- gamester and poet, friend of Alessandra's

Carlo Crivelli- a painter, Alys's mentor and admirer

Cosimo Fabriano- prominent Venetian politician who has bought Alys's courtesan's contract

Antonio Nani- nephew to the Doge

Portugal

Prince Henry the Navigator

Polo Bellini –Italian seeking Prince Henry's support to capture slaves in Guinea

Nuño Tristam - friend of Prince Henry, killed in Guinea 1446

Antam Gonsalvez - noble in Prince Henry's household

Africa

Mustapha al Qali – Barnabas's former mentor who sold him to Grand Vizier in return for a manuscript.

Hawqal- al Qali's father

Ezekiel- Barnabas's guide in Africa

Mousa ag Amastan- Tuareg leader

Paulos- Coptic priest who tends Barnabas.

HISTORICAL NOTE

The legend of Prester John obsessed many people over the centuries, most particularly from the 12th century onwards after reports of his existence came from a German chronicler, Otto of Freising who recounted in his *Chronicon* of 1145 that the previous year he had met Hugh, Bishop of Jabala in Syria at the court of Pope Eugene III in Viterbo. Prince Raymond of Antioch had sent Hugh to seek aid against the Saracens and request a second crusade. Hugh reportedly told Otto of Freising about a Nestorian Christian, Prester John, who was both priest and king and had regained Ecbatana in a battle and had set out for Jerusalem until floods on the Tigris halted him. He also claimed that Prester John was both wealthy and descended from the three Magi. In 1165, a letter purportedly written by Prester John to the Byzantine Emperor began circulating throughout Europe filled with the marvels and richness of his kingdom and it captured the imagination of Europeans. It also prompted Pope Alexander III to write a letter that he entrusted his physician, Master Philip of Venice in 1177 and Master Phillip wrote back to the Pope describing his journey. What became of him once he reached Ethiopia is not known.

Many legends arose about the exact location of Prester John's kingdom. Originally it was thought to be in India and other parts of Asia, but European ideas about those regions were very vague. Eventually, the speculative location was moved to Ethiopia, a once powerful Christian region, now obscure since the expansion of the Muslim faith. Explorers and missionaries from Portugal and other countries followed that theory until the 17th century. Prince Henry of Portugal, known as Prince

Henry the Navigator, was among those interested in locating Prester John's kingdom. He was intent on exploring Africa with the purpose of converting the people to Christianity. He set up a navigation school in Sagres and funded many voyages to Africa by explorers eager to exploit his desire to convert souls. Their interest was more focused on acquiring riches, either through the slave trade or other resources discovered there.

The identity of Prester John was another area for speculation. I chose to use one avenue that was pursued in the book, *The Prester Quest,* by Nicholas Jubber, published in 2006 which was part travelogue and historical narrative that explored the notion that Gebre Mesquel Lalibela was the true identity of Prester John. Lalibela was Emperor of Ethiopia during the Zagwe Dynasty, reigning from 1181-1221. The complex monolithic churches located in what was then Roha and now called Lalibela, are attributed to his reign, though some buildings could have earlier origins. The churches are rough-hewn out of rock and have become a UNESCO heritage site.

The painter, Carlo Crivelli, mentioned in this series, was a painter who lived and worked in Venice a little after this time period. I confess I took some liberties with his life story. In actual fact he was born around 1430, trained in the school of the Venetian Vivarini and then at Padua. He left Venice for Zara in 1459 under threat of penal sentence for living with a seaman's wife whom he kept secluded. In 1468 he moved to the Marches and remained until his death, painting commissions from wealthy families and ecclesiastical institutions. He painted one of his most famous works, *Madonna with Child* for the Duomo in Ascoli.

AUTHOR'S NOTE

I would like to thank profusely my Beta Girls: Karen, Jean, Claire, Babs and Jane. Without their help and input this novel would be so much less than it is now.

Originally from Philadelphia, Kristin Gleeson lives in Ireland, in the West Cork Gaeltacht, where she works as a librarian and runs a book club. She holds a Masters in Library Science and a Ph.D. in history and for a time was an administrator of a large archives, library and museum in America. She also served as a public librarian in America.

Kristin Gleeson has also published *The Celtic Knot Series* and *The Highland Ballad Series*. A free novelette prequel, *A Trick of Fate* is available free on Amazon and other retailers. In addition to her novels, she wrote a biography on a First Nations Canadian woman, *Anahareo, A Wilderness Spirit* that is also available.

If you have enjoyed this book please post a review. It helps so much towards getting the book noticed.

If you go to the author website and join the mailing list to receive news of forthcoming releases, special offers and events you'll receive *Along the Far Shores,* and *A Treasure Beyond Worth* a **FREE prequel novelette** to *Along the Far Shores.*

www.kristingleeson.com